*Praise for* Salmon Fishing in the Yemen

'This highly original novel blends satire with gentle humanity in a tale of what happens when idealism meets self-serving politics and bungling bureaucracy ... A stunning debut' *Daily Mail*

'This is a book of considerable charm, an echo-chamber of a dozen different voices adroitly ventriloquised ... [it is] a moral tale about the importance of believing in something and the comparative importance of everything else' *Independent*

'Paul Torday's debut novel is about an impossibility ... And the remarkable thing is that a book about so deeply serious a matter can make you laugh, all the way to a last twist that's as sudden and shocking as a barbed hook ... To write a novel lampooning the looking-glass world of Blairite government must have given Torday as much gruesome fun as he gives his readers ... *Salmon Fishing* is extraordinary indeed, and a triumph' *Guardian*

'[A] remarkable, unusual debut novel about political spin and unlikely dreams brought vividly to life ... [Torday has] a rare talent' *Herald*

'[A] tender-hearted book ... [a] thoroughly enjoyable debut' *Sunday Times*

'[A] wonderful first novel ... really funny ... a book you can't put down easily. Torday has an easy command of the gripping twists that play readers through the streams of a story, and at the same time he's a master of character ... a tour de force'

*Evening Herald*

'[A] delightfully funny debut ... It's funny, ambitious, multi-layered and quirkily imaginative, yet still – especially in the case of a sub-plot featuring a deniable British raid inside Iran – frighteningly relevant'

*Scotsman*

'Suffused with warmth; with magic and a fond quirkiness ... This is a clever book encompassing sport, political spin and scientific experimentation. Torday's ease with language is masterful; and he has a beautifully judged sense of place ... There's a clever sense of denouement, but ultimately it's the characters that make this page-turning tale shine' *Irish Examiner*

'An amusing satire on the tensions between the West and the Middle East, and a commentary on the value of belief to mankind ... The success of the book lies in the charm of Mr Torday's storyline – his love of salmon fishing shines through his text – and his skill at portraying the petty officialdom and manipulativeness of modern government. Adding breadth is a sharply drawn cast of characters' *Economist*

Paul Torday burst on to the literary scene in 2006 with his first novel, *Salmon Fishing in the Yemen*. It was an immediate international bestseller that has been sold in 25 countries and is now also a film starring Ewan McGregor, Kristen Scott Thomas and Emily Blunt. His subsequent novels have all been published to great critical acclaim. He is married with two sons by a previous marriage, has two stepsons and lives close to the River North Tyne.

*By Paul Torday*

Salmon Fishing in the Yemen
The Irresistible Inheritance of Wilberforce
The Girl on the Landing
The Hopeless Life of Charlie Summers
More Than You Can Say
The Legacy of Hartlepool Hall

# Salmon Fishing in the Yemen

PAUL TORDAY

PHOENIX

A PHOENIX PAPERBACK

First published in Great Britain in 2007
by Weidenfeld & Nicolson
This paperback edition published in 2012
by Phoenix,
an imprint of Orion Books Ltd,
Orion House, 5 Upper St Martin's Lane,
London WC2H 9EA

An Hachette UK company

1 3 5 7 9 10 8 6 4 2

Copyright © Paul Torday 2007

A CIP catalogue record for this book
is available from the British Library.

ISBN 978-8-7538-2906-6

Typeset by Input Data Services Ltd, Bridgwater, Somerset

Printed and bound in Great Britain by Clays Ltd, St Ives plc

The Orion Publishing Group's policy is to use papers that
are natural, renewable and recyclable products and made
from wood grown in sustainable forests. The logging
and manufacturing processes are expected to conform to
the environmental regulations of the country of origin.

www.orionbooks.co.uk

This book is dedicated to my wife Penelope,
who can catch salmon in bright sunlight and at low water,
to the friends I fish with on the Tyne and the Tay,
and to the men and women of the Environment Agency,
without whom there would be far fewer fish in our rivers.

# Contents

Extracts from a Return to an Address of the
Honourable House of Commons by the
Foreign Affairs Committee and a
Report into the Circumstances surrounding the
decision to introduce salmon into the Yemen
(Yemen Salmon Fishing Project),
and the subsequent events.

# I

## The origins of the Yemen Salmon Project

Fitzharris & Price<br>
Land Agents & Consultants<br>
St James's Street<br>
London

Dr Alfred Jones
National Centre for Fisheries Excellence
Department for Environment, Food and Rural Affairs
Smith Square
London

15 May

Dear Dr Jones

We have been referred to you by Peter Sullivan at the Foreign & Commonwealth Office (Directorate for Middle East and North Africa). We act on behalf of a client with access to very substantial funds, who has indicated his wish to sponsor a project to introduce salmon, and the sport of salmon fishing, into the Yemen.

We recognise the challenging nature of such a project, but we have been assured that the expertise exists within your organisation to research and project manage such work, which of course would bring international recognition and very ample compensation for any fisheries scientists who became involved. Without going into any further details at this time, we would like to seek a meeting with you to identify how such a project could be initiated and resourced, so that we may report back to our client and seek further instructions.

We wish to emphasise that this is regarded by our client, who is a very eminent Yemeni citizen, as a flagship project for his country. He has asked us to make clear that there will be no unreasonable financial constraints. The Foreign & Commonwealth Office supports this project as a symbol of Anglo-Yemeni cooperation.

Yours sincerely


*(Ms) Harriet Chetwode-Talbot*


National Centre for Fisheries Excellence
Department for Environment, Food and Rural Affairs
Smith Square
London

Ms Harriet Chetwode-Talbot
Fitzharris & Price
Land Agents & Consultants
St James's Street
London


Dear Ms Chetwode-Talbot

Dr Jones has asked me to thank you for your letter dated 15 May and reply as follows.

Migratory salmonids require cool, well-oxygenated water in which to spawn. In addition, in the early stages of the salmon life cycle, a good supply of fly life indigenous to

2

northern European rivers is necessary for the juvenile salmon parr to survive. Once the salmon parr evolves into its smolt form, it then heads downriver and enters saltwater. The salmon then makes its way to feeding grounds off Iceland, the Faroes or Greenland. Optimum sea temperatures for the salmon and its natural food sources are between 5 and 10 degrees Celsius.

We conclude that conditions in the Yemen and its geographical location relatively remote from the North Atlantic make the project your client has proposed unfeasible, on a number of fundamental grounds. We therefore regret we will be unable to help you any further in this matter.

Yours sincerely

*Ms Sally Thomas (Assistant to Dr Jones)*

**Office of the Director, National Centre for Fisheries Excellence**
*From: David Sugden*
*To: Dr Alfred Jones*
*Subject: Fitzharris & Price/Salmon/Yemen*
*Date: 3 June*

Alfred
I have just received a call from Herbert Berkshire, who is private secretary to the parliamentary under secretary of state at the Foreign and Commonwealth Office.

The FCO view is very clear that this project is to be given our fullest consideration. Notwithstanding the very real practical difficulties in the proposal from Fitzharris & Price, of which as your director I am fully aware, the FCO feel that we should seek to give what support we can to this project.

Given the recent reductions in grant-in-aid funding for NCFE, we should not be too hasty to decline work which apparently connects us to excellent private sector funding sources.

Yours
David

**Memo**
*From: Alfred Jones*
*To: Director, NCFE*
*Subject Salmon/Yemen*
*Date: 3 June*

David
I appreciate the points you have raised in your memo of today's date. Having given the matter my fullest consideration, I remain unable to see how we could help Fitzharris & Price and their client. The prospect of introducing salmon to the wadis of the Hadramawt seems to me, quite frankly, risible.

I am quite prepared to back this up with the relevant science, should anyone at the FCO require further information on our grounds for not proceeding.

Alfred

**Office of the Director, National Centre for Fisheries Excellence**
*From: David Sugden*
*To: Dr Alfred Jones*
*Subject: Salmon/Yemen*
*Date: 4 June*


Dr Jones

Please accept this memo as my formal instruction to proceed to the next stage of the Yemen salmon project with Fitzharris & Price. I would like you to meet Ms Harriet Chetwode-Talbot and receive a full briefing, following which you are to develop and cost an outline scope of work for this project for me to review and forward to the FCO.

I take full responsibility for this decision

David Sugden


From: <u>Fred.jones@ncfe.gov.uk</u>
Date: 4 June
To: <u>David.Sugden@ncfe.gov.uk</u>
Subject: Yemen Salmon Project


David

Can we talk about this? I'll pop round to your office after the departmental meeting.

Alfred

From: Fred.jones@ncfe.gov.uk
Date: 4 June
To: Mary.jones@interfinance.org
Subject: Job

Darling

I am being put under unreasonable pressure by David Sugden
to put my name to some totally insane project dreamed up
by the FCO to do with salmon being introduced into the
Yemen. There have been memos flying around on this for days
and I suppose I thought it was so bizarre I didn't even mention
it to you last time we spoke. I popped into David S's office
just now and said, 'Look, David, be reasonable. This project
is not only totally absurd and scientifically nonsensical, but
if we allow our name to be involved no one in the fisheries
world will ever take us seriously again.'

Sugden was totally stone-faced. He said (pompously), 'This
one is coming from higher up. It isn't just some minister at
the FCO with a bee in his bonnet. It goes all the way to the
top. You've had my instruction. Please get on with it.'

I have not been spoken to like that since I left school. I am
seriously considering handing in my resignation.

Love

Fred

PS When are you back from your management training
course?

From: Mary.jones@interfinance.org
Date: 4 June
To: Fred.jones@ncfe.gov.uk
Subject: Financial realities

Fred
My annual salary is £75,000 gross and yours is £45,561. Our combined net of tax monthly income is £7333 out of which our mortgage takes £3111, rates, food and other household expenses a further £1200, and that's before we think about car costs, holidays, and your fishing extravagances.
Resign your job? Don't be a prat.
Mary
PS I am home on Thursday but I have to leave on Sunday for New York for a conference on Sarbanes-Oxley.


**Memo**
*From: Andrew MacFadzean, principal private secretary to the secretary of state for foreign and commonwealth affairs*
*To: Herbert Berkshire, private secretary to the parliamentary under secretary of state, FCO*
*Subject: Salmon/Yemen Project*

Herbert
Our masters tell us this project should be pushed on a bit. The sponsor is not a UK citizen, but the project can be presented as a template for Anglo-Yemeni cooperation, which of course has wider implications for perceptions of UK involvement in the Middle East.

I think you could quietly drop a word in the ear of David Sugden, whom I believe is the director of the fisheries people at DEFRA, that a successful outcome to this project might attract the attention of the committee putting forward recommendations for the next New Year honours list. Equally it is only fair to point out that an unsuccessful outcome might make it difficult to defend NCFE against further cuts in grant funding in the next round of negotiations with the Treasury for the new financial year. This might help get the right messages across. We have, of course, talked at a senior level to the appropriate people in DEFRA.

Keep this off the record.

Lunch at the club at 1 p.m. tomorrow?

Yrs

Andy

**Memo**

*From: Director of communications, prime minister's office*
*To: Dr Mike Ferguson, director veterinary, food & aquatic sciences, Chief Scientists' Group*
*Subject: Yemen salmon project*

Mike

This is the sort of initiative that the prime minister really, really likes. We want some broad-brush comments on feasibility from you. We do not require anyone to say absolutely that it would work, only that there is no reason for not trying.

Peter

**Memo**

*From: Dr Michael Ferguson, director veterinary food &*
*    aquatic sciences, Chief Scientists' Group*
*To: Peter Maxwell, director of communications, prime*
*    minister's office*
*Subject: Yemen salmon project*


Dear Mr Maxwell

Monthly average rainfall in the western mountains of the Yemen is around 400 millimetres in each of the summer months, and mean temperatures at elevations above 2000 metres fall to a range of between 7 and 27 degrees Celsius. This is not uncharacteristic of British summer weather and therefore we conclude that for short periods of the year conditions exist, particularly in the western provinces of the Yemen, which are not necessarily inimical to migratory salmonids.

We therefore speculate that a model based on the artificial release and introduction of salmonids into the wadi systems for *short periods of the year*, linked to a programme of trapping the salmon and returning them to cooler, saline water during other periods of the year, would not be an inappropriate starting point for a modelling exercise to be carried out by the departments with the relevant expertise. I believe NCFE is the most appropriate organisation for this.

I hope this brief note is sufficient for your purposes at this stage?

Yrs

Michael Ferguson

PS Have we met?

**Memo**
*From: Director of communications, prime minister's office*
*To: Dr Mike Ferguson, director veterinary, food & aquatic*
    *sciences, Chief Scentists' Group*
*Subject: Yemen salmon project*

Mike
That's great. No, we haven't met, but I look forward to it some day soon.
 Peter


**Memo**
*From: Peter*
*To: Prime minister*
*Subject: Yemen salmon project*

PM
You will really like this. It presses a lot of different buttons:
- positive and innovative environmental messages
- sporting (cultural?) links to a Middle Eastern country not as yet closely aligned with UK interests
- secular Western technology bringing improvements to an Islamic state
- a big, positive news story that will take front-page space away from less constructive news items coming out of Iraq, Iran and Saudi
 A great photo opportunity: you standing in a wadi with a rod in one hand and a salmon in the other – what an image that would be!
 Peter

**Memo**
*From:    Prime minister*
*To: Director of communications*
*Subject:    Yemen salmon project*

Peter
I like it. The photo idea is great!

# 2

## Extracts from the diary of Dr Alfred Jones: his wedding anniversary

**7 June**

Until today, my diary has for the most part been used to record the times of meetings, appointments with the dentist, or other engagements. But for the last few months I have felt the need to set down some of the thoughts that come and go, the increasing sense of intellectual and emotional restlessness which has grown in me as I approach middle age. Today's date marks our wedding anniversary. Mary and I have been married now for over twenty years. It seems right, somehow, to start recording the pattern of my daily existence. Perhaps it will help me find a perspective from which I can appreciate and value my life more than I am able to just at present.

For Mary's anniversary present, I have bought her a subscription to *The Economist*, which I know she enjoys reading but begrudges the cost of buying for herself. She bought me a replacement brush for my electric toothbrush, which is most useful. I never think much about anniversaries. The years pass seamlessly. But for some reason tonight I feel I ought to reflect on what is now many years of marriage to Mary. We married not long after leaving Oxford. It was not a whirlwind romance, but I think ours has been a calm and settled relationship suitable for two rational and career-minded people such as ourselves.

We are both humanists, professionals and scientists. Mary's science is the analysis of risks inherent in the movement of cash and credit around the world's financial systems. She has written papers such as 'The role of SDRs (Special Deposit Reserves) in mitigating unusual flows of non-reserve currencies' which have attracted a great deal of attention and I enjoyed reading myself, although I could not follow some of the algorithms. Mary has now moved from the more academic wing of the bank into the managerial side. She is prospering, well paid and respected, and likely to go far. The only disadvantage is that we are tending to see a little less of each other as she has to travel a great deal these days.

I made my name with my study 'The effects of alkaline solutions on freshwater mussel populations', which introduced some groundbreaking new concepts concerning the mating of freshwater mussels. Since then, my career has developed too. I am not as well remunerated as Mary, but my work gives me satisfaction and I believe I am well thought of by my peers.

Mary and I have chosen not to have children. Our lives are therefore relatively unruffled. I am aware that a childless marriage is sometimes an excuse for selfishness and therefore we both make a conscious effort to engage with our community in the little spare time that we have. Mary gives lessons in economic theory at our local immigration centre to migrants from Chechnya and Kurdistan, who seem to end up in our area. I give lectures to the local humanist society from time to time. Last week I gave the third in a series of talks, 'Why God cannot exist', and I like to think that these talks in some way provoke the audience to question the superstitions of earlier eras which still linger on in the religious teachings that regrettably persist in some of our schools.

What else can I say about more than two decades of marriage? We both keep ourselves fit. I go running two or three times a week; Mary does Yoga when she can. We were vegetarians but now eat fish and white meat, and I allow myself alcohol from time to time although Mary does so rarely. We enjoy reading as long as the books are improving or informative, and occasionally go to the theatre or to art exhibitions.

And I fish, an unreconstructed activity of which Mary disapproves. She says fish feel pain whereas I, as a fishery scientist, know that they do not. It is perhaps the one subject on which we have to agree to disagree.

So there it is: another anniversary. This year has been much like the last year, and that year was very like the one before. If I occasionally wish for a little more excitement, a little more passion in our lives, I can usually put this down to neglecting to follow the dietary guideline that people of my blood group (Type A) should follow: not too much meat. Occasionally I fall prey to temptation and eat some beef, and so it is not surprising I then have irrational feelings of ... I am not sure what? Am I bored, perhaps? How could I be?

It only takes something like this Yemen salmon project to raise its head to remind me that I have a dislike of the irrational, the unpredictable and the unknown.

**8 June**
We had a departmental meeting today to consider the final draft of my paper 'Effects of increased water acidity on the caddis fly larva'. Everyone is being very complimentary, especially David Sugden. Is this a peace offering? He has not pressed me again about the Yemen salmon project and I, of

course, have done nothing. I have just kept my head down and am waiting for the whole issue to go away. Anyway, the director's public praise for the work on caddis flies was a pat on the back for my team. In fact, David went so far as to say that, following the publication of my article, there was probably nothing further worth saying about the caddis fly. Praise indeed. At such times I know that the money doesn't really matter. Mary sometimes complains that I am not paid enough, but there is much more to life than one's salary. I have moved forward the boundaries of human knowledge about a little brown insect that, insignificant as it may be in itself, is a vital indicator of the health of our rivers.

Both *Trout & Salmon* and *Atlantic Salmon Journal* want a press release.

Mary is in New York. She was home all of Friday and Saturday. Nevertheless, the fridge is empty. I have just been down the street to the late-night Indian takeaway, to buy a few things to eat, and I am sitting here writing up my diary and mopping balti chicken from my lap after some of it slipped off the plastic fork. I have just realised that I forgot to buy any coffee for tomorrow morning.

A last word of self-reproach after a day of professional triumph. How selfish I am, going on about my own success with my caddis fly research – I want to record my admiration for Mary, whose work, which I alluded to in yesterday's entry and although of a different nature to mine, has attracted comment and admiration at her bank, InterFinance S.A. She is on the fast track at InterFinance. I am a huge believer in women doing well, and to see it happen to one's own wife in the male-oriented world of finance is very rewarding. The female caddis fly also plays a profoundly important role in her social group.

15

## 9 June

My bowel movements this morning were somewhat affected by the takeway, perhaps not surprisingly. I did not go for my usual morning run as I felt rather unwell. There was no coffee left in the tin, and the single pint of long-life milk was well out of date. I arrived at the office feeling out of sorts and it took me a while to get into gear.

It is odd how quickly things can change in one's life. For the last two days I have been contemplating the tranquil and intellectually engaged nature of my life with Mary, and the intense reward I can still derive from a piece of scientific work well done. All that seems, for the moment, as nothing.

I now have to record one of the most unpleasant incidents of my professional career. At 10.00 a.m. I was sitting with Ray, selecting the most visually compelling photographs to accompany the caddis fly article, when Sally came in and told me David Sugden wanted to see me right away. I said I would go along to David's office in a few minutes, as soon as Ray and I had finished.

Sally gave me a strange look. I remember her exact words. She said, 'Alfred, the director means *right away*. He means *now*.'

I stood up and apologised to Ray, telling him I would be back in a few minutes. I walked along the corridor to David's office feeling a little angry. Ours is a consensual department. We are scientists rather than managers. Hierarchies mean little to us, being treated as human beings means everything. David has, on the whole, got the hang of this and although he is a career civil servant he has fitted in quite well. He has certainly been here long enough to know I do not like being bullied or pressurised.

When I entered David's office I forced myself to smile and

keep any sign of annoyance out of my voice. I said something like, 'What's the emergency?'

I think it is important to remind David that he is a manager and that I am a scientist. Without scientists, there would be no need for managers.

As usual David's desk was absolutely clear of paper. A flat-screen computer monitor and keyboard sat on it, otherwise it was several square feet of matt black metal, relieved only by two sheets of paper. He lifted one of them, without inviting me to sit down, as he usually does. He waved it in front of me. I could not see what it was. Then he told me it was my P45. He put it down on the desk and waited for me to say something. At first I did not take in his words, then my heart started hammering. I replied that I did not understand.

David looked at me without smiling. He said, 'I know you live somewhat in an ivory tower, Alfred, but even you must be aware what a P45 is? You need it for the Inland Revenue and social security people when your employment is terminated by your employer – in this case, us.'

I stared at him. David put down the first piece of paper and picked up the second. He explained that it was a letter, drafted in my name, to Fitzharris & Price. It was a request for a meeting to discuss the Yemen salmon project in the near future. The tone of the letter was apologetic and wheedling, explaining my delay in replying was due to pressure of work and expressing my hope that the opportunity to work together was still there. After I finished reading it I found I was trembling, but whether with annoyance or alarm, I was not sure.

David picked up the P45 again and took back the letter to Fitzharris & Price. He held them up in front of me and explained in a neutral tone of voice, 'Dr Jones, you can leave the office with your P45 or you can take away this letter and sign it and get it sent by messenger round to Fitzharris & Price. Personally, I am wholly indifferent which you choose to do, but I believe Fitzharris & Price has been told you are the man to talk to, otherwise I have to say I would not have given you the luxury of this choice.'

I looked around me for a chair. I saw one on my left and asked if I could sit down.

David looked at his watch and told me he had an appointment with the minister in half an hour. He said, 'The minister will be asking me for a progress report on this project. What am I going to be able to tell him?'

I swallowed several times. My legs were trembling. I pulled the chair across, sat in it and said, 'David, this is wholly unreasonable —'

He interrupted me. 'Which piece of paper are you going to leave this office with?'

I could not speak. This Nazi behaviour shocked me to the core. I pointed to the letter to Fitzharris & Price.

'Then sign it now.'

'May I have a moment to read it?' I asked.

'No.'

For a moment I almost lost control. I wanted to crumple the letter up and fling it in David Sugden's face, but instead I found myself reaching inside my jacket for my fountain pen, and then I pulled the hateful rectangle of paper towards me and signed it.

David immediately took it from me and told me he would send it by messenger himself. He said he had cancelled all my diary appointments by email for the next month. I had one priority, and one priority only, if I wanted to keep my job. I had to meet Harriet Chetwode-Talbot, persuade her that the National Centre for Fisheries Excellence was the only organisation that had any chance of coming up with a proposal for her salmon project, and I had to persuade her that I was the right man for that job.

I nodded. David stood up. He looked for a moment as if he was going to say something by way of apology or explanation. Then he checked his watch again and said, 'I mustn't keep the minister waiting.'

I left without saying anything further, I hope with some dignity.

Now, as I record these unpleasant events, I reflect that it would have been nice if Mary had been at home tonight. Sometimes one wants to talk things over with one's partner. Mary doesn't like long phone calls. She says phone calls are for information. The trouble is, she isn't often at home to have the conversations that she doesn't feel we should have on the phone. But I'm so proud of the way she is getting on.

I hope she will be proud of me when I tell her of the dignified way I stood up to David Sugden's bully-boy tactics.

## 15 June

I am writing this in the office.

Mary comes home tonight. I find I have been missing her. There is nothing to eat in the entire house. I must remember to call in at Marks & Spencer on the way home. I will buy some ready-to-eat meals. I must remember to get a new pair of pyjamas, as the elastic has gone in my present (Tesco) pair. I have kept a note of the mean time between failure (MTBF) of various things like socks – hole in the heel; pyjamas – elastic cord failure. I am afraid that I can detect a clear downward trend, almost a planned obsolescence, in some of these products. I am hoping Marks & Spencer will be more reliable.

No bowel movement this morning. A sure sign of stress. I did go for a run, however, and burned off some of the anger that has been churning inside me like bile.

This morning I received a phone call. Sally buzzed through to me and said there was a Harriet Someone on the line from Fitzharris & Price, and would I take the call? For a moment, glorious rebellion: I so nearly said, 'No, tell her I'm busy.' But instead I told Sally to put the call through – a girl's voice with what I would call a cut-glass accent asked if she was speaking to Dr Jones.

She was very polite. She apologised for disturbing me, told me she understood I had been very busy with some major projects and said she would not have disturbed me at present except that her client was being very pressing. Then she asked if I recalled her original letter about introducing salmon to the Yemen?

I made an assenting sound at the back of my throat. I did not trust myself to speak. She took this to mean yes and asked when we could meet. For a moment I was tempted to shout, 'Never!' but instead I found myself agreeing to go and visit her at her office in St James's Street the following morning.

'Will your client be there?' I asked.

'No, he is in the Yemen. But he is anxious to meet you on one of his future trips over here. That is, if you agree to take this any further after our meeting tomorrow.' We agreed on a time to meet at her office in St James's Street.

*Later*
Mary has just come home. She arrived at Heathrow this morning about seven and went straight to her office, and of

course she has overdone it. She looked at the Marks & Spencer Italian Selection I had purchased and said, 'I'm sorry, Alfred, I've just got no appetite.'

Naturally I didn't want to bore her with my problems when she was so exhausted. However, she revived over a glass of wine and talked for a while about US banking regulations. Most interesting. She has gone to bed now, and so will I in a moment.

It would have been nice if we could have talked a bit about my problems at work, but I must not be self-centred.


**16 June**

My meeting at Fitzharris & Price was not quite what I expected.

I cannot help but feel resentful towards these people who have disturbed the relative tranquillity of my life with their absurd ideas. My intention was to be damning without being rude, discouraging without being negative. I still feel, as I write this, that their proposal is so stupid that it will soon wither and die.

When I arrived at the F&P offices I found an elegant reception area, with an elegant receptionist commanding it from behind a large partners' desk. Opposite the desk were a pair of comfortable-looking leather sofas and a low glass table with *Country Life* and *The Field* laid out on it. Before I could sample any of these luxuries Ms Harriet Chetwode-Talbot came out to meet me.

She thanked me for sparing the time to come and see her. She was courteous, elegant, tall and slender. She appeared to me to be dressed as if she was about to go out to lunch at a smart restaurant rather than for a day's hard work in the office. Mary always says it is demeaning for working women to dress themselves up like that. She herself is a strong believer in sensible, practical working clothes which do not accentuate the wearer's femininity.

We went into Ms Chetwode-Talbot's office, which looked out over St James's Street. The windows were double-glazed and the room was quiet and full of light. Instead of going behind her desk she guided me to two armchairs facing each other across a low mahogany table on which were set out a white china coffee pot and two cups on a tray. We sat down, and she pulled the tray towards her and poured out two cups of coffee. Then she said, and I remember her exact words, 'I expect you think we are all absolute idiots.'

This was unexpected. I began to trot out some long-winded comments about the unusual nature of the project, how it was outside the mainstream of the centre's work, and how I felt a degree of concern that we might all waste quite a lot of time and achieve nothing.

She listened patiently and then said, 'Please call me Harriet. My surname is such a mouthful it really is too much to ask anyone to use it.'

I blushed. Perhaps Chetwode-Talbot has metamorphosed in pronunciation in the way Cholmondely has become Chumly, or Delwes Dales – one of those trick pronunciations invented by the English to confuse one other.

Then she suggested it might help if I understood some of the background.

I nodded; I needed to know who or what I was dealing with. Harriet – I don't think it is appropriate for us to be on Christian-name terms, but it is quicker to write just her first name in this diary – began to explain. I crossed my legs and clasped my hands over my knees and generally tried to assume the expression my tutor at university used to adopt when I had put in a particularly bad piece of work which he was about to tear to shreds.

Harriet gave me a faint smile and explained that I had probably gathered by now that Fitzharris & Price were chartered surveyors and property consultants, not fisheries scientists.

I told her I appreciated the point.

She bowed her head in acknowledgement and explained that for many years the business of her office had been acquiring agricultural or sporting estates in the UK on behalf of overseas clients – in particular, Middle Eastern buyers. Fitzharris had discovered quite quickly that its clients didn't just want it to buy the estates but also manage them in their absence.

That had led Fitzharris into providing technical expertise on a whole range of subjects, such as land agents' services and help with recruiting estate employees through to advice on farming practice, sporting lets, obtaining planning permission for building new country houses, and so on.

Of course, Harriet told me, most of their clients are very wealthy, and are fond of often quite ambitious projects to improve the properties they buy. Then she said, 'We have one such client who has been with us for a number of years. His wealth derives in part from oil, but if there is such a thing as a typical oil sheikh, he is not it. He is a most unusual, visionary man.'

Harriet paused to refill our cups with fresh coffee, and I found myself reluctantly admitting to myself that however foolish the project was, there was nothing foolish about this woman.

She added, 'I am not going to attempt to describe what my

client's motivation is. I think it is important you try and understand it, if you decide to help us, but it is for him alone to tell you about that part.' She continued, 'He is a man we hold in great respect in this firm. He is an excellent steward and landlord of the properties he has bought in this country, an employer everyone would want to work for, but people like working for him because of his personal qualities and not because he is enormously wealthy. Moreover, he is an Anglophile, which is perhaps less usual in the Yemen than in some other parts of the region, and his prominence in his own country means he is viewed as a key potential ally in Yemeni councils by the Foreign Office here.'

'Ah,' I said.

'Indeed, Dr Jones. I think you are aware there is a political dimension to all of this.' She did not attempt to call me Alfred. 'I know you will have had some pressure brought to bear on you from within government. Believe me, it was not of our doing and I very much regret it. We would rather you took on this job, impossible as it may seem at the moment, of your own free will, or else not at all. And that will certainly be the view of our client.'

'Ah,' I repeated, and then when she appeared to have stopped speaking, 'Well. You were speaking about introducing salmon into the Yemen.'

'And salmon fishing. I believe it is intended to be fly-fishing only, no spinning.'

'No spinning,' I repeated.

'Are you a salmon fisherman, Dr Jones?' asked Harriet. For some reason I blushed again, as if I was about to admit to something covert and slightly sinister. Perhaps I was.

'As a matter of fact, I am very keen. Perhaps not as unusual amongst us fisheries people as you might think. Of course I nearly always put back any fish I catch. Yes, I enjoy it very much.'

'Where do you fish?'

'Here and there. I like to try different rivers. I've fished the Wye, the Eden and the Tyne in England; the Tay and the Dee and a few smaller Scottish rivers. I don't get much time for it nowadays.'

'Well, if you take this project on I'm sure my client will ask you to fish with him at his place in Scotland.' Then she added with a smile, 'And perhaps one day you'll fish on the Wadi Aleyn, in the Yemen.'

I saw where this was going.

'Well, there are a few problems with that idea,' I suggested. This time Harriet crossed her legs, a movement that somehow caught my eye, and clasped her hands around her knees and looked at me critically, just as I had tried to do to her a moment or two earlier.

'Let's go through some of them,' she suggested.

'First, water,' I said. 'Salmon are fish. Fish need water.' Harriet only looked at me when I said that, so I had to continue. 'Specifically, as I said in my letter, salmon need cool, well-oxygenated water. The temperature should ideally not exceed eighteen degrees Celsius. The best conditions are rivers fed by snow melt or springs, although some varieties of salmon can live in lakes if they are deep and cool enough. So there's a fundamental problem, right there.'

Harriet stood up and went across to her desk, took a file from it and then sat down again.

Opening the file she said, 'Water. Parts of the Yemen have up to 250 millimetres of rainfall a month in the wet summer season. It is brushed by the monsoon, like parts of the Dhofar region in the south of Oman. On top of surface water run-off from the summer storms, there is constant recharging of the groundwater. People didn't use to think there was much groundwater in the Yemen but since they started looking for oil they have found one or two big new aquifers. So, yes, water is a huge problem, but there is water there. The wadis become rivers, and pools and lakes form in the summer.'

This was surprising.

'Then there is the question of water temperature. I suppose you're going to tell me the Yemen isn't that hot, but if it is, the oxygen will leave the water and the fish will die.'

Harriet looked at her file again and said, 'We're thinking mountains. That's where the rain is, and the elevations in the central highlands go up to over 3000 metres. At that height the temperatures are bearable. The night-time temperatures go down to well below twenty Celsius even in the summer. And Pacific salmon get as far south as California – as long as the water is aerated, they seem to be able to survive. I don't mean to be telling you your business, Dr Jones; just that it might not be as open and shut as you first thought.'

I paused, and then said, 'Salmon parr feed off certain types of fly life, and if we introduced salmon from English rivers they would only recognise food that came from those rivers.'

'Perhaps that can be introduced along with the fish? There are plenty of flies in the Yemen, at any rate. English ones might adapt if the local fly life didn't taste good.' She closed her file with a snap and looked at me with a smile.

'Then,' I said with mounting irritation, 'the salmon parr grow up into smolts, and the smolts want to find the sea, and the particular part of the sea they want to find is just south of Iceland – at least if the fish broodstock comes from an English or Scottish river. How do you suppose these fish will get there? Through the Suez Canal?'

'Well,' she said thoughtfully, 'that's one of the problems you would have to solve, of course. But if it was me, and of course I'm a completely non-technical person, I'd think along the lines of constructing holding ponds at the bottom of the wadis seeded with salmon, keeping the water cool, injecting it with oxygen if necessary, and confining the salmon there for three or four years. I read somewhere that in Canada salmon stay in the lake systems for that amount of time.'

'And what then?'

'Catch them all, then start again?' She stood up, looking at her watch. 'Dr Jones, I've taken up far too much of your time already. I'm very grateful indeed for you coming and listening to all this. I know how outlandish it is. But please don't dismiss it here and now. Take a couple of days to think about it, and then I'll call you again, if I may. Remember, all you have to commit to at this stage is a feasibility study. You're not going to be putting your reputation on the line. And remember too, if you will, that my client can commit very large financial resources to this project, should they be needed.'

And then I was back in the reception area, shaking hands and saying goodbye, almost without knowing how I got there. She turned and walked back to her office, and I couldn't help watching her as she went. She did not look back.


## 17 June

Last night I gave my talk to the local humanist society. My theme was that if we believed in God, we immediately created an excuse for tolerating injustice, natural disasters, pain and loss. Christians and other religionists argue that God does not create suffering but the world in which suffering occurs, and suffering allows us to rediscover our oneness with God.

27

I argued that such an approach stood logic on its head. All disasters, all loss, all suffering, demonstrate that there cannot possibly be a God, for why would a deity who is omnipotent create a universe so prone to disaster and accident? Religious faith, I argued, was invented in order to pacify the grieving multitudes and ensure they did not ask the really difficult questions, which if answered, would tend to lead to progress.

We were quite a big group that evening: seven or eight of us. Muhammad Bashir, a grizzled old Pakistani from down the road, is a regular attender. I think he wants to save me from myself. At any rate, he knows me well and likes me even though I am, by his lights, a blasphemer.

'Dr Jones,' he asked, 'you are a fisherman, are you not?'

'Yes,' I agreed. 'When I can.'

'And how many hours do you fish before you catch something?'

'Oh, I don't know,' I replied, not clear what he was driving at. 'Many hundreds of hours, sometimes.'

'So why do you fish? Is that not a bad use of your time?'

'Because I hope in the end I will catch one,' I replied.

The old man hissed with glee, rubbed his beard with his right hand and said, 'Because you believe. Hope is belief. You have the beginnings of faith. Despite all the evidence, you want to believe. And when you catch one, what do you feel? A great happiness?'

'A very great happiness,' I said, smiling at him. It did him good to win the occasional argument with me, so I let him. I didn't use the thousand logical and statistical arguments I could have done to put him down. I let him finish.

'You see, Dr Jones, you believe, and in the end your belief brings you great happiness. You are rewarded for your constancy and your faith, and the reward is much greater than the possession of a fish, which you could buy for little money at Tesco. So you are, after all, not so very different to the rest of us.'

## 18 June

This evening, after dinner, Mary looked up from the crossword and said to me, 'I'm going away for a fortnight to work in our Geneva office.'

This happened about once every year, so it wasn't a total surprise. I raised my eyebrows to register mild disappointment and asked her when she was going.

'On Sunday.'

I reminded her that we had booked in weeks ago for a weekend's walking and birdwatching with my brother in the Lake District.

'I know,' said Mary. 'I'm awfully sorry. But someone in the Geneva office has gone on sick leave, and they need me to cover and I know the office. Perhaps you could come with me and we could walk in the hills by Lake Evian?' But then she thought better of it and said that she would probably have to work Saturdays as well, to find her way into her the job. 'Anyway,' she added, 'you've got your weird fish project on, and you'd better stay with that to keep David Sugden happy.'

I told her rather stiffly that I had not decided whether to do that yet.

'You should,' she said.

The rest of the evening was a bit of a frost, but when we went to bed, I think Mary must have felt a little guilty about the way she had changed her plans. Suffice to say, my new Marks & Spencer pyjamas were not required for the early part of the night! A relatively rare event in our marriage of late.

Afterwards Mary said, 'There now, darling, that should keep you going for a bit,' and turned on her side and seemed to go to sleep. For a moment I felt a bit like a dog that has just been given a biscuit, but then drowsiness swept across me and I started to doze.

I fell into a waking dream, and saw the bright sunlight of the Yemen uplands and the glittering pools of water where hen salmon were laying their eggs amongst the gravel, 800 eggs per pound of body weight, and the cock salmon were injecting milt amongst them. The salmon eggs were fertilised. They hatched into little alevins. They wriggled about in the clear water and grew into fry, then parr. At each stage of their evolution the fish became larger and stronger, until they had smolted and were ready to make their journey to the sea. If we seeded a wadi in the Yemen with fish from an English river, would those fish head down to the sea in the summer rains, once they had grown? Would the smell of the saltwater lure them to the Indian Ocean, even if it was the wrong ocean? I rather thought so. And if we trapped them downstream and shipped them in purpose-built tanks back to the North Sea so that they could run to their feeding grounds in Iceland, what then? Would they overwinter there and then head back for their native English river, or would they try and find the Indian Ocean?

We could radio tag them. Imagine the excitement if we tracked them heading down the African coast, searching for their new home.

Suddenly I wanted this project. It was so strange that fundamental new science might be discovered. Our whole understanding of the nature of species migration might be transformed. We might witness, over time, the evolution of a new subspecies of salmon which could tolerate warm water, perhaps learn to feed itself in the rich soup of the Indian Ocean.

Then Mary said loudly, 'What?'

'What do you mean, what?'

'You were talking. In your sleep. About spawning. And egg production. Is that what you think about after we've made love? About your bloody fish and their reproductive cycles?'

She switched on her bedside light and sat up. She was for some reason wide awake now and very upset. I've noticed that guilt makes people go on the attack. Perhaps that was what it was all about. At any rate, I didn't want a row, about salmon reproductive cycles or anything else, so I said pacifically, 'Darling, I wish we could do a bit of reproducing of our own.'

'Don't be ridiculous,' she replied. 'We both know that until either I am earning more than £100,000 a year or you are earning more than £70,000 – which seems unlikely in view of your present relations with your department – then our after-tax income simply will not be sufficient to compensate for the additional cost of a child. Besides, I'm not ready to interrupt my career for three months, or even a month. Pregnancy might affect my chances of promotion, which right now I think are rather better than yours. You know all that. Why bring it up again?'

Then she yawned. At least she had forgotten what had woken her up originally. She looked a little bewildered.

I said, 'I know, darling. You're right. Switch out the light and let's get some sleep.'

But I couldn't sleep. I lay awake thinking about our

marriage, and wondering whether I was being unfair to Mary, or she to me. I asked myself whether things might have been different if we had had children. I thought about salmon spawning in the highlands of the Yemen. Round and round my head went these thoughts, chasing each other like salmon parr wriggling in the shimmering water of a stream.

I got out of bed and came next door. I thought that maybe writing up my diary would help me sleep.

It hasn't.

# 3

## Feasibility of introducing salmon into the Yemen

**Proposal submitted by Dr Alfred Jones of the National Centre for Fisheries Excellence (NCFE) to Fitzharris & Price, 28 June**

*Executive summary*

NCFE has been invited to advise and comment to Fitzharris & Price on the feasibility of introducing migratory salmonids into the wadi systems of the Yemen. The longer-term objective is to develop opportunities for good-quality angling tourism in the country. The Arabian peninsula has a rich natural fishery offshore which is harvested by all of the Gulf States. Fishery exploitation and, increasingly, good fisheries management is well understood in the region.

However, to date, angling for sport has not been accessible to most of the population. This could in theory change, if migratory fish such as salmon could be introduced into the river system. The proposal in this instance is to introduce salmon into the Wadi Aleyn in the western Yemen, as a pilot project. The longer-term objective is to develop a managed salmon fishery in this wadi, and subsequently in other watercourses where the right conditions can be found, or created.

It is accepted that the Yemen is, in many respects, not the ideal environment into which to introduce migratory fish whose natural breeding habitat is the northern edge of the temperate zone and whose feeding grounds are in the North Atlantic. Some obvious problems include:

- Watercourses go from dry to spate conditions for relatively short periods of time and then only in the wet summer months in those parts of the Yemen which experience monsoon weather.
- Mean average air temperatures indicate that water temperatures are likely to be significantly higher than those tolerated by the species *Salmo salar* without developing stress.
- The migratory journey of the salmon, assuming the upper watercourse could be seeded with juvenile fish in the wet season, would be somewhat more challenging than its normal journey to the North Atlantic, being several thousand miles longer and involving a journey around the Cape of Good Hope and up the west coast of Africa before entering waters where salmon are normally found. The previous southern limit of the Atlantic salmon is the Bay of Biscay, and the southern limit of the northern Pacific salmon is northern California.
- Once the rains end in September conditions in the watercourses would become dry and hot and it is unlikely any salmon still resident in the system would survive.

There are a number of other issues more technical in nature relating to the local ecosystem, lack of invertebrate life in the wadis (although there is an abundance of arthropods such as scorpions), bacterial issues, and the unknown question of predation. We speculate that buzzards, vultures and other local predators would quickly adapt to eating salmon stranded in relatively shallow water.

*

We have considered various closed-system models and our current proposals, based on desktop research only, are as follows:

1. Salmon from the North Sea would be trapped as they tried to enter their 'home' river and introduced into a cooled transport pod containing saline water from the North Sea. A condensation and recycling system would be installed to minimise evaporation losses. Means of controlling temperature and oxygen levels within the tank would also have to be found. The pod would be shipped by airfreight to the Yemen. The holding tank would be set up to have an outlet into the wadi which could be opened at need.

2. As fresh rainwater came into the wadi system, the outlet would be opened allowing it to flow into the holding tank. Salmon are anadromous – they adapt to both salt- and freshwater environments. We speculate that the salmon, on smelling the freshwater, would leave the saline environment and seek to migrate upstream to find spawning grounds. Although the salmon would not recognise the 'smell' of the water (the mechanism by which salmon at sea identify the estuarine water of the river in which they were hatched is still poorly understood) we believe there is a reasonable chance they would enter the freshwater. 'Strangers' are often found in English and Scottish rivers – salmon which have entered another river different to the one where they were spawned.

3. The upstream migration would depend on some civil engineering of the watercourse, subject to survey:
   a. to ensure that gradients and natural obstacles did not obstruct the movement of the fish along at least 10 kilometres of riverbed, regarded as the minimum

distance suitable for a meaningful pilot experiment

b. to ensure if possible some background level of flow from the aquifer to achieve a minimum level of water in the watercourse to avoid fish being stranded between spates

4. We understand that in the Wadi Aleyn there is an existing *falaj* system of stone conduits to allow the irrigation of a number of date palm groves which could be adapted for the purposes of the above.

5. Salmon seek gravel beds covered in relatively thin layers of well-oxygenated water for spawning. We understand there is an abundance of gravel in the Yemen, and in the Wadi Aleyn in particular. It is at least theoretically possible that fish could be encouraged to spawn, as we would be introducing summer/autumn-run salmon into the watercourse and they would be seeking to spawn at the end of their upstream journey if the right habitat presented itself. This gives rise to the exciting possibility that the introduced salmon could spawn naturally, or at least be electrofished and harvested for their eggs, either of which would allow a hatchery to be set up adjacent to the Wadi Aleyn in which the next generation of juvenile salmon would have an excellent chance of survival. This would create a generation of salmon whose true home was the Wadi Aleyn. How their migratory instincts could subsequently be managed must be a matter for further research. We speculate that the creation of a second holding tank filled with saltwater could be used to trick salmon returning downriver into thinking they smelled seawater, and trap and hold them in a saltwater environment.

*

At this stage we have not attempted to cost this project until the client has had a chance to consider and comment on the outline concept we have presented. We estimate that, excluding NCFE time and project management charges, the capital costs of this project would be in the region of £5 million. We have not yet considered operating costs.

We await the client's further instructions.

Fitzharris & Price
Land Agents & Consultants
St James's Street
London

Dr Alfred Jones
National Centre for Fisheries Excellence
Department for Environment, Food and Rural Affairs
Smith Square
London

6 July

Dear Dr Jones
Thank you for the project proposal, which was received here on 29 June. Our client, who is at present in the UK, has now had an opportunity to consider the document and wishes to discuss the matter with you in person. I may say that he was extremely positive about the professional and constructive manner in which you have addressed the brief.

Please would you be kind enough to sign the attached confidentiality agreement, to allow us to disclose further information to you regarding our client and the project. Once

I have received the signed copy I will then be in touch with you regarding a further meeting.

Yours sincerely

*(Ms) Harriet Chetwode-Talbot*


From: Fred.jones@ncfe.gov.uk
Date: 7 July
To: Mary.jones@interfinance.org
Subject: Yemen/salmon


I thought you would like to know that relations between myself and David Sugden are once again amicable. I have submitted an outline feasibility proposal on the Yemen salmon project to Fitzharris & Price. I have received a very warm and, frankly, enthusiastic response. I met David Sugden by the coffee machine today (by accident? he sort of turned up while I was dialling in a cappuccino, so he had one too and we chatted for a bit). He said, as far as I can remember, 'We were all pretty impressed by that paper you put up to Fitzharris & Price. Visionary stuff. This could be a very high-profile project in due course.'

I mumbled something, you know I can't stand flattery, and asked if it was OK to sign the confidentiality agreement before we go any further. He said yes, and actually patted me on the shoulder. He's not a very tactile person and that was really quite demonstrative for him.

The thing is, if I'd just rolled over for David when he first asked me to get involved in the project, he would just have taken my work for granted and not considered it anything special. Because I made a bit of a fuss – in order to test his own commitment to such an unusual project – he now thinks he has won a great battle and is one hell of a good manager. The reality is that if one knows how to handle these apparatchiks you can get them to eat out of your hand. Hope all is going well in Geneva, and that you will be home soon. Missing you.

Alfred XXXXX

From: Mary.jones@interfinance.org
Date: 7 July
To: Fred.jones@ncfe.gov.uk
Subject Dry-cleaning

Alfred

Could you go to the dry-cleaners in the High Street and pick up a load of stuff I didn't have time to collect before I got on the plane. Perhaps you could get it sent out here by Fedex or DHL as I am a bit short of things to wear and they haven't yet found anyone to replace the guy whose job I am doing? Thanks in advance.

Things are fine here, rather hard work, but I think I am being appreciated. I'm not quite sure when I will be back in the UK yet.

Love

Mary

PS Please make sure you collect the dry-cleaning tonight and send it latest tomorrow a.m.

PPS Glad to hear you are sorting out your problems with DS.

From: David.Sugden@ncfe.gov.uk
Date: 7 July
To: Herbert.berkshire@fcome.gov.uk
Subject: Yemen/Salmon

I thought you'd like to know that the (previously reluctant) scientist I wanted to work on this project is now eating out of my hand. I fed him some ideas on how to approach the work and he has come up with quite a reasonable first stab at the proposal, which has been welcomed by the client.
I'll keep you posted. Feel free to pass this on up the line if you think you should.
Yrs ever
David


**Memo**
*From: Peter*
*To: PM*
*Subject: Yemen/salmon*
*Date: 8 July*


PM
I thought it best to update you on the Yemen project (if you don't recall, it was to do with salmon). We've taken a step forward and it is ready to kick off. I don't think we'll talk to the media about it yet, though. I want to see whether it is really going to happen before we risk any exposure on what is, after all, a rather unusual story. On the other hand, we all know that most civil servants leak like sieves and no doubt fisheries scientists are no better or worse than the rest of them. We want to make sure that when this gets out, we tell

it in our own words and make it clear whose initiative it is (yours).

I'll update you as soon as I hear anything.

Peter

PS I never asked. Do you know how to fish?

# 4

## Extracts from the diary of Dr Jones: his meeting with Sheikh Muhammad

**12 July**

A very strange day.

I had arranged a meeting with Harriet (Chetwode-Talbot) at Fitzharris & Price in St James's Street first thing this morning. I must admit I was quite looking forward to finding out more about the project, and the client. I can even say I was quite looking forward to meeting Harriet again, as she has impressed me by the intelligent and professional way she has conducted herself thus far. Her people skills are in a different league to those of David Sugden, who by the way is now my new best friend. He and I had a drink in the pub on Friday night after work.

Anyway, I went round to St James's Street and announced myself at the reception desk. I was somewhat surprised to see Harriet come out of her office, carrying her briefcase and with a raincoat over her arm.

'Are we going somewhere?' I asked.

She greeted me good morning and suggested I follow her downstairs. I must note here she is really quite attractive-looking when she smiles, her face being a trifle severe in repose. We went out into the street, where a large black car was waiting. The driver jumped out and opened doors for us. Once in, Harriet turned to me and said, 'We are going to meet the client.' I asked her if she could tell me anything about him, but she simply replied, 'I think I'll let him speak for himself, if you don't mind.'

The car purred into Piccadilly and turned right. Harriet dug into her briefcase for some papers. Then she put on spectacles and said, 'You don't mind, do you? I need to go over some papers on some other business we are acting on for our client.'

She sat and read. Meanwhile the car was driving across Vauxhall Bridge. I was a little surprised; I had expected we would drive round to somewhere like Belgrave Square or Eaton Place. I sat back in the comfortable, new-smelling white leather seat and enjoyed the unaccustomed luxury. I do not own a car, myself. It's pointless with these congestion charges. We drove through south London. I began to wonder where on earth we were going. Surely the sheikh did not live in Brixton?

I said, 'Excuse me, Harriet, but are we going much further?'

She took her spectacles off, raised her head from looking at her papers, and gave me another smile. 'That's the first time you have used my Christian name.'

Not knowing how to respond to this I said something like, 'Oh, really?'

'Yes, really. And no, we are not going much further. Just as far as Biggin Hill.'

'Are we meeting your client at Biggin Hill?'

'No. His plane is meeting us.'

'We're not going to the Yemen?' I asked in alarm. 'I haven't got my passport. Or anything.'

'We're going to pay the sheikh a brief visit at his place near Inverness. He liked your proposal but he wants to speak about it with you face to face.'

'It is very kind of him to say he likes it,' I said.

'He is very kind, but he liked it because it gave him hope.' Then she said no more, and would not be drawn into further conversation until we arrived at the airport.

On any other occasion I would have found the experience of flying in a private jet overwhelming in itself; it's not that often I fly in any sort of plane. But really it was just a flight to somewhere. What was memorable was what happened after we arrived.

When we landed at Inverness airport another black car was there to meet us outside the terminal. This time it was a Range Rover. We drove onto the A9 and headed south for twenty minutes or so and then turned off down a single-track road and over a cattle grid. A sign read, 'Glen Tulloch Estate. Private'. We drove along the track towards some distant hills, down into a wooded valley and across an enchanting river full of appealing dark pools where fish might lie. We followed the river for another ten minutes until, surrounded by immaculate and damp-looking green lawns, a large red-granite lodge came into sight. There were turrets at each end of the front, and a central portico with pillars surrounding the massive front door, with steps leading down to the gravel.

As the Range Rover pulled up in front of the house, a man in a suit and tie came down the steps. For a moment I wondered if he might be the client, but as we got out of the car I heard him say, 'Welcome back to Glen Tulloch, Miss Harriet.'

Harriet said, 'How are you, Malcolm?'

Malcolm bowed his head in answer to this enquiry, made a respectful murmur of welcome in my direction, and then asked us to follow him inside. We entered the house and came into a large square hall panelled in dark wood. A round library table with a bowl of roses occupied the centre. A few dark pictures of stags were hung on the walls, and intimidating and massive casts of salmon mounted on wooden plaques, bearing the weight and date caught, occupied the spaces between the pictures.

'His Excellency is at prayer,' said Malcolm to me, 'and then he will be occupied for an hour or two. Miss Harriet, would you be kind enough to go to his office and he will join you there shortly.'

'Have fun,' Harriet said to me. 'See you later.'

'If you will follow me, Dr Jones,' said Malcolm, 'I will show you to your room.'

I was surprised to find I had a room. I thought I was coming for a brief meeting and back to the airport. I had imagined I would spend half an hour, perhaps an hour with the sheikh, and then he would have learned all I could tell him and I would be dismissed. Malcolm took me upstairs to a bedroom on the first floor. It was an enormous but comfortable room with a four-poster bed and a dressing table, and a large bathroom adjoining it. Through tall sash windows I could see heathery moors running up into the mountains. On the bed were laid out a check shirt, a pair of khaki-coloured trousers, thick socks and a pair of chest waders.

Malcolm surprised and delighted me by saying, 'His Excellency thought you might like to fish for an hour or two before you meet him, to relax for a while after your journey. He hopes these clothes will be comfortable. We had to guess your size.' He pointed to a bell push beside the bed and told me that, if I rang for him when I was ready, he would take me to meet the gillie, Colin McPherson.

Half an hour later I was walking along the bank of the river we had driven up with Colin beside me. Colin was short, sandy-haired, square-faced and taciturn. He looked gloomily at me when I was introduced to him, wearing the brand new Snowbee waders which had been left out for me and feeling rather foolish.

'You'll not have been after a fish before, sir?' he asked.

'As a matter of fact, I have,' I told him. His face brightened fleetingly, then relapsed into its scowl.

'Most of the gentlemen that comes to see the laird haven't had a rod in their hand before in their life.'

I said I would do my best, and we walked down to the river, Colin carrying a fifteen-foot rod and a landing net. He told me a little about the river, and about the fishing, as we walked along the bank. The river was about thirty yards wide and there was a good flow of water. 'We had some rain the night, and a few fish have maybe come up. But I doubt you'll see a fish today.'

At last we came to a dank pool fifty yards long or so, running out into white water over gravel shoals. Rowan trees and alders overhung the far bank, and I could see a few threads of cast hanging from the branches where over-ambitious fishermen had snagged their lines. 'You're no worse off fishing here than anywhere,' suggested Colin. He looked as if he doubted very much whether I would ever see let alone catch a fish. He handed me the rod he had put up for me. I tried it a few times to get the feel of it. It was beautifully balanced, stiff and powerful. I waded into the water a few feet, as Colin had suggested, and started to put line out.

'Put some line out, take a step, then put a bit more out and take a step,' Colin instructed me from the bank.

When I had got a bit of line out I tried a double Spey cast and saw with pleasure how the line shot out like silk, the fly landing on the water as gently as thistledown.

'I've seen worse casts than that,' said Colin, in a friendlier tone than he had used up until then. Then he sat down on the bank, took out a pipe and started to fiddle around with it. I forgot about him and concentrated on the fishing. A step, cast the line out, watch the fly come round gently on the dark water, strip the line, a step, and cast the line. Mesmerised by the flowing water and the silent beauty of the pool, I fished it down slowly and carefully. Once I saw a swirl and some bubbles just beyond my line, right beneath the opposite bank in the slow water, which I thought might have been a fish moving. But I did not dare lengthen my cast for fear of tangling my line in the overhanging branches. Once there was a flash of blue and bronze and I heard Colin, now some yards upstream, say, 'Kingfisher.'

At last I reached the end of the run, and the water was too slow to fish down any further, so I waded back to the bank. By that time I had almost forgotten where I was, I was so absorbed by what I was doing, so tranquillised by the absolute silence apart from the music of the water over the gravel as it ran out to the next pool below. Then Colin appeared at my elbow.

'I'll change the fly for something with a wee bit more colour. Maybe an Ally Shrimp. There's a fish showing beneath those alder trees.'

'I think I moved it,' I told him.

We walked back up the bank, and while Colin tied on a new fly I looked behind me. The road to the house ran past and beyond was the moor. I heard the shrill shouting of a pair of oystercatchers and, further away, the unmistakable cackle of a grouse. Colin handed me the rod, and I stepped into the head of the pool again. I fished down again as before, and just as I was coming to the place where I thought I had seen something move, I felt that prickling in the back of the neck we sometimes get when someone is watching us. I put the line out, and turned my head to look. About thirty yards behind me and a little bit above me, on the road, stood a small man in a white headdress and white robes. He looked absolutely out of place on that road, with the heather moor behind him. He stood very upright and quite still. He was watching me intently.

A tug on my line made me snap my attention back to the river. There was a swirl, then splashing, and suddenly line started screaming off the reel at a prodigious rate as the fish took the fly and ran. My heart beating, I lifted the rod tip and started to play my fish. It did not take long: after ten minutes I had brought a medium-sized silver sea trout to the water's edge, which Colin deftly landed in his net.

'Five pound,' he said. 'No bad.' He seemed pleased.

'We'll put it back,' I said. Colin did not approve of this idea, but he did as I asked and then we set out back towards the house.

*Later*

In the end it was not until this evening that I met the client. When I returned to the house I was handed over to Malcolm, who turned out to be the butler. I always imagined butlers wore black coats and striped trousers, looked like Sir John Gielgud and went everywhere with a glass of sherry balanced on a silver tray. Malcolm wore a dark suit, a white shirt and a dark tie. He looked sombre and discreet and moved noiselessly about the house. He showed me back to my room, where I changed back into the clothes I had flown up in. Then I was given tea in the library, with cucumber sandwiches with the crusts cut off and the day's papers to read – all of them, from *The Times* through to the *Sun*.

From time to time Malcolm would put his head round the door and apologise for keeping me waiting. His Excellency was engaged in a conference call that was taking longer than expected. His Excellency was at prayer again. His Excellency was in a meeting but would be free at any moment. Finally I asked, 'What time is our flight back to London?'

'Tomorrow morning, sir, after breakfast.'

'But I didn't pack anything – I didn't know we were expected to stay.'

'Don't worry, sir; you'll find everything is ready in your room.'

Malcolm's pager went off and he excused himself and left. A little while later he came back and said, 'I've taken the liberty of running your bath, sir. If you care to go upstairs and have a bath and change, His Excellency will meet you here in the library for drinks at seven o'clock.' I shook my head in disbelief and followed Malcolm upstairs again. He showed me to my room. By then I was beginning to know my way. I went in and had my bath, stretched out full length in steaming water infused with something that smelt of pine, wondering at the strangeness of the day.

As I lay gazing at the ceiling of the bathroom I felt a profound sense of peace steal over me. It was as if I was on holiday. I was away from the office, away from home, and I had had the wholly unexpected pleasure of catching a fish, something that happened to me about once every other year (Mary is not keen on fishing holidays; she says they are barbaric, a waste of money, boring for non-participants and therefore a self-indulgence on my part). I stepped out of the bath and dried myself with a huge white towel, and wandered

49

back into the bedroom. Although it was high summer, a fire had been lit and table lamps switched on. The bedroom was warm and softly lit, encouraging me to lie on the bed for twenty minutes' sleep. But I thought I might not wake up in time for dinner so I sat and wrote down a few words in my diary about the journey here, and the sea trout I caught.

When I had finished I inspected the clothes laid out for me on the bed. There were evening clothes, shirt and black tie, clean underwear, socks, which all fitted as if they had been made for me. On the rug beside the bed was a pair of black loafers, gleaming with polish. These also fitted like gloves. Somehow I was not surprised. I left my room and, as I came to the landing at the head of the stairs, I saw Harriet coming towards me from the other wing of the house. She was wearing a stunning black evening dress, with a gold belt around her waist. I have to admit she looked surprisingly glamorous. She saw me, smiled and said, 'I'm so sorry you have been kept waiting. His Excellency has many duties and unfortunately had to take time to deal with them this afternoon.'

I bent my head in acknowledgement. I no longer minded having been kept waiting all day. I felt curious and expectant, as if some important secret was about to be revealed to me. I was looking forward to meeting Harriet's client.

We went downstairs together. Harriet was wearing a perfume which, although faint, reminded me of the smell in a garden on a summer evening after rain. I found myself inhaling it as I walked down the stairs behind her. Mary says expensive perfumes are a form of feminine exploitation and no substitute for the frequent application of soap and water. We entered the library, and there standing in the centre of the rug in front of a log fire was the small man in white robes I had seen on the road earlier that afternoon. Now I noticed that the robes, and his headdress, were edged with gold. His face was dark-skinned with a grey moustache and beard beneath a hook nose and small, deep-set brown eyes. He had an air of stillness about him and stood very upright so that one forgot his height.

'Welcome to my house, Dr Alfred,' he said, extending a hand.

I went forward to take it and as I did so Harriet said, 'May I present His Excellency Sheikh Muhammad ibn Zaidi bani Tihama.'

I shook hands and we all stood and looked at each other, and then Malcolm arrived with a silver tray with a tumbler of whisky and soda and two flutes of champagne. Sheikh Muhammad took the whisky, and Malcolm asked me if I wanted something else, or would the champagne be acceptable?

'You are surprised,' said Sheikh Muhammad, in his clearly very good English, 'that I drink alcohol. In my homes in the Yemen, of course, I never do; there is none in any of my houses. But when I discovered that whisky was called the water of life, I felt that God would understand and forgive me a little, if I drank it in Scotland from time to time.' His voice was deep and sonorous, with few of the guttural sounds that Arabic speakers sometimes have.

He sipped his tumbler of whisky and made an appreciative, soundless 'Ah' shape with his lips. I took a sip of my champagne. It was cold, and delicious.

'You are drinking the Krug '85,' said Sheikh Muhammad. 'I do not drink it myself, but friends are kind enough to say it is palatable.' He motioned us to sit down, and Harriet and I settled side by side on one large sofa, whilst he sat opposite us. Then we began to speak about the salmon project. Although it is late now, I remember very clearly the sheikh's words. He is a man, I think, whose presence and words would not be quickly forgotten by anyone who met him.

'Dr Alfred,' said Sheikh Muhammad, 'I greatly appreciate the work you have done so far on the proposal to bring salmon to the Yemen. I read your proposal and I thought it most excellent. But of course you think we are all quite mad.'

I muttered something along the lines of 'Not at all' but he waved away my denials.

'Of course you do. You are a scientist – a very good one, I am informed. A leading light in the National Centre for Fisheries Excellence. Now come some Arab people who say they want salmon! In the Yemen! To fish! Of course you think we are quite mad.'

He sipped at his glass and then looked around. Malcolm appeared from nowhere with small tables for us to put our drinks on, then faded away to some corner of the room out of the light.

'I have observed,' said His Excellency, 'over the many years I have been coming to this country, a curious thing. Will you forgive me if I speak frankly about your countrymen?' I nodded, but he had taken my forgiveness for granted because he continued almost without a pause. 'In this country you still have a great deal of snobbery. In our country we too have many different ranks but everyone accepts these ranks without question. I am a sheikh from the *sayyid* class. My advisers are cadis. My estate workers at home are *nukka*s or even *akhdam*. But each knows his place and each talks to the other without restraint or fear of ridicule. Here in the UK this is not the case. No one seems to know what class they belong to. Whatever class they do belong to, they are ashamed of and want to appear as if they are from another. Your *sayyid* class put on the speech of the *nukka*s in order not to stand out, and speak like taxi drivers and not lords because they are afraid of being thought ill of. The reverse is also true. A butcher, a *jazr*, might make a great deal of money and adopt the speech of the *sayyid* class. He too is uneasy in case he pronounces a word wrongly or wears the wrong sort of tie. Your country is riddled with class prejudices. Is this not the case, Harriet Chetwode-Talbot?'

Harriet smiled and inclined her head ambiguously, but did not say anything.

'But I have for a long time observed,' said His Excellency, 'that there is one group of people who in their passion for their sport ignore all things to do with class. The *sayyid* and the *nukka* are united and stand together on the riverbank and speak freely and without restraint or self-consciousness. Of course I speak about salmon fishermen, indeed fishermen of all descriptions. High and low, rich and poor, they forget themselves in the contemplation of one of God's mysteries: the salmon, and why sometimes it will take the fly in its mouth and sometimes it will not.'

He sipped at his whisky again, and Malcolm was there at his elbow with a decanter and a soda siphon.

'My own people have their faults, too,' continued the sheikh. 'We are an impatient people, and sometimes violent, very quick to pick up a gun to finish an argument. Although our society is in many ways an ancient and well-organised one, we are first members of our tribe, and only second members of our nation. After all, my family and my tribe have lived in the mountains of Heraz for over one thousand years, but my country has existed for only a few decades. There are still many divisions in our country, which not long ago was two countries and much longer ago was many kingdoms: Saba, Najran, Qa'taban, Hadramawt. I have noticed in this country that although there is violence and aggression – your football hooligans, for instance – there is one group for whom patience and tolerance are the only virtues. I speak of salmon fishermen in particular, and all fishermen in general.'

Sheikh Muhammad's voice was gentle and quiet, but he had the gift of compelling attention and respect with every word he spoke. I said nothing, not daring or wishing to break his chain of thought.

'I have formed the view that the creation of a salmon river in the Yemen would in every way be a blessing for my country, and my countrymen. It would be a miracle of God if it happened. I know it. My money and your science, Dr Alfred, would not alone achieve any such thing. But just as Moses found water in the wilderness, if God wills it, we will enable salmon to swim in the waters of Wadi Aleyn. If God wills it, the summer rains will fill the wadis, and we will pump out water from the aquifer, and the salmon will run the river. And then my countrymen – *sayyid*, *nuqqa* and *jazr* and all classes and manner of men – will stand on the banks side by side and fish for the salmon. And their natures, too, will be changed. They will feel the enchantment of this silver fish, and the overwhelming love that you know, and I know, Dr Alfred, for the fish and the river it swims in. And then when talk turns to what this tribe said or that tribe did, or what to do with the Israelis or the Americans, and voices grow heated, then someone will say, "Let us arise, and go fishing."'

He sipped the last of his whisky and said, 'Malcolm, have they dinner for us?'

I am tired now and cannot remember much of the rest of the evening, but I remember those words of his exactly as he spoke them. I know that he is, as he says he is, mad, but it is a gentle even a noble form of madness, and one that cannot be resisted. What we ate and drank I cannot say, except that it was all delicious. I think we had lamb. The sheikh drank no wine with dinner, only water, and he ate little and spoke only enough to encourage Harriet and me to talk of this and that.

One other thing he said, as we drank small cups of cardamom-flavoured coffee in the library after dinner: 'If this project succeeds, then it will be God who has succeeded and God who should be thanked. If it fails, then you, Dr Alfred, can say that a poor, foolish, deluded man insisted that you tried to achieve the impossible. And no doubt some good will come from the work you do whatever happens. Some new thing will be known that was not known before, and you will be rightly praised for it and all else will be forgotten. And if it fails, the fault will be mine, because my heart was not pure enough, my vision not clear enough, my strength not great enough. But all things can be done if God wills it so.'

He put his cup of coffee down and smiled at us, preparing to bid us goodnight. Something made me say, 'But nothing bad will happen, Your Excellency, if this project does not work.'

'I have spoken to many scholars and imams about my dream of salmon fishing. I have told them how I believe this magical creature brings us all nearer to God – by the mystery of its life, by the long journey that it makes through the oceans until it finds the waters of its home streams, which is so like our own journey towards God. And they have told me that a Muslim may fish as well as a Jew or a Christian, without any offence to God. But that is not what the jihadis will say. They will say I am bringing the ways of the crusader to the land of Islam. If I fail, then at best they will ridicule me. If they think I might succeed, then they will certainly try to kill me.'

It is dark night now and the heavy curtains are drawn in my bedroom but I can still hear the owls shrieking in the woods. In a minute I will put down my pen but I must write these words: I feel at peace.


## 19 July

David Sugden called me into his office this morning. He waved me to a chair. He was beaming. 'You seem to have worked your charms on your Arab friend.'

'Sheikh Muhammad, I suppose you mean?'

He nodded and pushed a thick sheaf of documents across the desk. 'This arrived from Freshwaters this morning. They are the sheikh's legal advisers. Very expensive I should think they are, too.' He tapped the documents with his forefinger. 'Five million quid. Right there.'

It turned out that Freshwaters had sent us a draft contract to provide a legal and commercial framework for the Yemen salmon project.

'It's all there,' said David. 'Our legal people are looking at it, but it has everything we would want. No-fault clauses if it doesn't work, payment no matter what happens, bank guarantees to support it, milestone payments to keep the cash rolling in. It is,' he said, rolling his eyes at the ceiling, 'manna from heaven. If I can't get some of that five million into some of my underfunded budgets, then I've lost my touch.'

I said that I hoped we were not going to take Sheikh Muhammad's money under false pretences.

This must have sounded rather prim because David flapped his hands at me and replied, 'Don't be such an old woman, Alfred. You know what I mean. I meant every department in NCFE can charge time to this project for one reason or another. He'll get his salmon river in the desert – or not, as the case may be. We get five million pounds whatever happens. Now, let's talk about details. I'm going to head the project and take responsibility for communications with other departments ...'

'The Foreign Office, you mean?'

David tapped the side of his nose with his forefinger in a stagey gesture. 'The prime minister's office has become involved now; Peter Maxwell is keeping himself in touch with this. But you should forget I said that. In fact I must ask you to be very discreet about all this. The sheikh, the Foreign Office and indeed everyone wants to keep the lid on this project until we are certain we know what will come out of it. So, please remember, keep your mouth buttoned up.' He laughed to show he had intended a joke. 'Now then. Where were we? Yes. You are to be in charge of operations: I mean the research team and then project management. You will report to me.'

He turned his computer screen round so I could see it and led me through a project plan. What a bureaucrat! He has organised it so that I will do all the work and he will take all the credit (but not the blame, if there is to be blame). He really doesn't know what this is all about. He has no conception of how difficult it is going to be, how much scientific research has to be done, the ecosystem models that will have to be built, the environmental impact assessments, modelling the dissolved oxygen levels in Yemeni watercourses, bacterial sampling. My head feels as if it might explode when I think about the complexity of it all. And here is this idiot talking about 'milestones' and 'deliverables' and 'resource allocation'.

**23 July**

Mary came back from Geneva this afternoon. She's in the spare room asleep. Home for two hours, and we had a row.

First of all, when I tried to tell her about Sheikh Muhammad and his wonderful vision of salmon running the waters of the Yemeni wadis, she dismissed it by saying, 'The old boy must be insane. Are you sure you want to be associated with something quite as bonkers as that?'

'But you told me to,' I said.

'I told you not to throw over your job in a tantrum; I didn't tell you to attach your name to something that sounds like professional suicide. Still, I expect you know your own business best.'

'I hope I do,' I said stiffly.

There was a long silence and then she said she was sorry, it had been a long day.

Mary often says it has been a long day. She seems to think she is the only one who gets stuck late in the office, who has to sit through tedious meetings resisting the urge to drum one's fingers or doodle all over the agenda. We all get tired. I had a bubble of excitement inside me, a picture captured within that bubble of the sheikh in his white robes speaking of visions of shining salmon rivers in his quiet voice, of the black waters of his own river in the Highlands, of the sea trout that lurked there. I wanted to talk about the private jet that flew us there, of the grave and immaculate butler Malcolm, of the bubbles in the champagne. Somewhere in this picture, seen through the wrong end of a telescope, was Harriet, beautiful in her evening gown, head on one side, leaning forward to listen to the sheikh saying something. I wanted to share all this with Mary. I wanted to share my scientific excitement with her, the thought that with Sheikh Muhammad's money I could do something different, something that had never been done before; change the rules of the game.

But she wasn't interested, and the picture in the bubble darkened and went out, and I buried it deep within me. It's the first time I haven't shared something important with her. She just didn't want to know.

Later over supper I found out what was on her mind.

'They want me to move to Geneva,' she said. She didn't look at me when she spoke, but concentrated on getting her pasta round her fork.

'Move?' I asked, putting my own fork down.

'Move, yes, as in relocate.'

'Why?'

'Because the man who went absent on sick leave won't be coming back.'

'Why not?'

'Because he's dead.'

I considered this; it seemed conclusive. So I asked, 'For how long?'

'I don't know. At least for six months.'

'Well, obviously that is impossible,' I said, and then wished I hadn't.

'Why is it impossible?' asked Mary quietly, fixing me with a level stare and sitting upright.

'Well, I mean, how can you? We've got a life here. My work is here. Our home is here.'

Mary was silent and ate some more pasta. Finally she said, 'I've sort of told them I'll do it.'

Well, of course, after that I spoke my mind, and then Mary spoke hers. Now she is asleep in the spare room and I am sitting here writing my diary, and in a minute I will put down my pen and lie on our bed with my eyes open, grinding my teeth.

# 5

## Extracts from the diary of Dr Jones: marital issues may have clouded his judgement

**28 July**

Today, like the last few days, has been spent mostly in meetings with Fitzharris & Price, either with me going to Harriet's offices or she visiting NCFE. There were cost estimates to prepare, project plans to be drawn up, equipment suppliers to be located. At first we held our meetings in Smith Square, but David Sugden had a way of suddenly appearing in my office and asking to look at what we were doing. This took up a great deal of time, especially as he liked to explain to us how to do things which we had almost always already done.

He has a way of looking at Harriet that I do not quite like. This evening he said to me, after she had gone back to her own offices, 'Bright girl, that, don't you think?'

'Yes, she seems very able.'

'I suppose she's a chartered surveyor by profession. She must find all this is taking her a bit out of her depth?'

I don't know why I resented his remark. Perhaps it was the tone, not the words. 'I think she is coping. She has a well-ordered mind.'

'Attractive girl, too,' he suggested.

When I did not reply he rubbed his hands together for a moment, looking at the lino floor of the corridor where he had stopped me on my way from the meeting room to my office. Then he asked if Harriet was married. As a matter of fact, I knew the answer to that one and told David that she was engaged. He said nothing further and returned to his office.

The reason I know Harriet is engaged is that she took me out to lunch today. We had spent the morning looking at spreadsheets and both of us needed a break, so when she suggested lunch (a meal I do not normally indulge in) for once I was quite ready to accept.

We found a Middle Eastern restaurant nearby, which seemed an appropriate choice. I ordered a salad and some water. Harriet ordered a salad and a glass of white wine. When it came she held the glass up and looked over it at me and said, 'A toast – to the project.'

I raised my glass, but she wouldn't allow me to drink a toast with mineral water, so wine was ordered, despite my telling her I never drank in the day, and then we raised our glasses and both said, rather solemnly, 'To the project.'

Our eyes met as we sipped our wine together, and I looked away, embarrassed without knowing why. Harriet was undisturbed, and put her glass down and asked me if I was married. When I told her I was, she asked, 'What does your wife do?'

'Mary? She's in finance with a big international bank.'

'A career woman like me,' said Harriet, smiling.

But Mary wasn't like Harriet; she would never have ordered a glass of white wine at lunch, much less persuaded me to have one.

'Alcohol is all very well in its place,' Mary used to say, 'and as far as I am concerned, during weekdays its place is in a bottle and nowhere else.' And Mary didn't dress like Harriet or, frankly, smell like Harriet. Mary didn't believe in smart feminine clothes or perfume. Mary wore baggy brown linen work suits at home and grey ones at the office. She smelled clean, of rather antiseptic soap. She was always neat and tidy ... To my dismay I found I was comparing the two women and the comparison was unfavourable to Mary. What was so wrong with wearing an elegant calf-length dress, rather than a suit that looked as if it had been designed by a junior member of the Chinese communist party? What was wrong with smelling faintly of peaches ripening in a greenhouse, instead of something that recalled a mild industrial disinfectant?

We talked for a moment about Mary, and her endless travelling.

The salad arrived, and I concentrated for a moment on chasing an olive around my plate with my fork. Then I decided it was my turn to keep the conversation going and asked Harriet if she was married.

'No, but I will be next spring.'

'Oh, have you just become engaged?'

'It hasn't been in the papers yet, but it will be as soon as Robert comes back.'

'Comes back from where?'

Harriet put her knife and fork down on her plate and looked down for a moment, then said quietly, 'From Iraq.'

'What's he doing out there?' I said, watching her. Her smiling, easy look had gone and now her lips were compressed and she had turned pale. I suddenly realised she was on the verge of tears. In a panic I tried to make a joke: 'Well, perhaps we can get a contract to introduce salmon into the Euphrates, and then you can join him out there?'

Whatever the merits of this remark, it did the trick. Harriet looked startled and then smiled. I don't think she thought I was the sort of person who made jokes, and she would have been right. We talked about Robert and his adventures for a while.

'He wasn't expecting to go to Iraq,' Harriet told me. 'We were going to take a week's holiday in France together before I became totally buried in the salmon project. Then he got a call and the next thing I heard he was ringing me from Frankfurt airport, to tell me what had happened and that he was already on his way.' We sat in silence for a moment. Then she said, 'The worst thing is the letters. Either they arrive weeks late or not at all. And when you do get them they are so heavily censored it is impossible to know what Robert was trying to say.'

After that, she didn't seem to want to say any more about it. It was odd. A few minutes ago Harriet and I had been, in one sense, perfect strangers. I had spent time with her over the past week or two, quite a lot of time, but it had all been very professional. My admiration for her ability was unbounded, but I had been completely ignorant of her personal circumstances and perhaps would never have asked her a single question about herself if she had not suddenly suggested lunch.

Then I checked my watch and saw it was nearly two o'clock. We paid the bill and hurried back to the salmon project.


## 22 August

I'm working all hours, from seven in the morning until seven or eight at night. I'm mostly too tired to write up my diaries. I want to keep a record somehow now that, at last, I'm engaged in work of such immense significance. It's nearly a month since my last entry and the Yemen salmon project is growing. We are spending real money: not hundreds, not thousands, not tens of thousands; we are spending so much money, so fast, that a firm of accountants has been hired. They have put financial controls in place and they prepare budget reports which go to the sheikh which I feel sure he never looks at. I flew to Finland for two days of talks with some specialist manufacturers of fish farm equipment, to discuss the design of the holding tanks in the Wadi Aleyn. I flew to Germany to talk to a company which manufactures tanks used to transport tropical fish, and we discussed how to design and build the transport pods which would take the first salmon out by plane to the Yemen. Mary flew to New York, and then back to Geneva to attend enigmatic-sounding conferences on risk management. Harriet flew to Glen Tulloch to meet the sheikh and then out to the Yemen with him to discuss matters unknown to me. Everyone was flying everywhere. Everyone except David Sugden.

He was, I think, becoming a little jealous of the way the project was growing, sending its tendrils into every corner of NCFE. There were groups of people building mathematical models to show what happened to oxygen levels in water at high temperatures; others were investigating the possible microbiological impact on the salmon of local Yemeni bacteria; another group had formed a committee to write a paper entitled 'Vision 2020: can the Atlantic salmon *(Salmo salar)* colonise the southern Indian Ocean?' The idea was that my salmon in the Wadi Aleyn might one day run down the wadi to the sea and swim south across the equator, and down to the edges of the Antarctic Ocean, past the Kerguelen Islands, to feed on the giant shoals of krill at the edges of the polar ice cap.

I think it was that paper that tipped David Sugden over the edge. He came storming into my office today and said he wanted a word with me. I was on the phone to Harriet but told her I would call back, and hung up.

He pulled up a chair and sat down. He was angry, but trying not to show it. 'This salmon project is totally out of control,' he began.

I asked him in what way.

'People are spending money like water. You've been on three overseas trips this month alone.'

'It's not our money, of course,' I said. 'The sheikh sees all the bills and all the projected bills and the reporting accountants check everything, and I'm not aware that he's unhappy. And I can't invent a technology for transporting salmon to the middle of a desert without talking to the equipment suppliers. We can't buy this stuff out of the classified ads in *Trout & Salmon* magazine, you know.'

It gives me some pleasure to talk to David like this. I know there's nothing he can do about it. The sheikh is backing me first, the agency second. Harriet has made that clear several times, and David knows it as well as I do. Feeling unable to pursue the point about the money any further, David started to complain about the committee writing a vision paper on Atlantic salmon in the Indian Ocean. 'What happens if it all goes horribly wrong and gets into the press?'

'If all what goes horribly wrong?'

'This stuff about Atlantic salmon actually spawning in the wadis of the Yemen and then migrating to the edge of the Antarctic Ocean. The idea of Atlantic salmon swimming around somewhere south of the Cape of Good Hope is such an outrageous proposition, it could destroy the credibility of our centre for ever if the press got hold of it.'

I looked at him. This was the man who a few weeks ago had told me he would fire me if I didn't come up with some ideas for the salmon project.

I was saved from answering by the phone ringing. I picked it up to tell the switchboard to hold my calls but a smooth voice said, 'It's Peter Maxwell here, director of communications from the prime minister's office. Is that Alfred Jones?'

I said hello and put my hand over the mouthpiece and mouthed 'Peter Maxwell' at David Sugden. He sat up straighter in his chair and reached for the phone.

Maxwell said, 'I gather David Sugden's in there with you?' then asked to be put on the speakerphone.

I hit the button and put the phone back in its cradle. Peter Maxwell's voice came from the speaker now – oily but somehow also steely. 'Hi, Fred. Hi, David. Can you hear me okay?' We both said we could.

'Guys, I'm going into the prime minister's morning briefing meeting in a few minutes. Can you give me a heads-up on the project? How's it all going?'

David said, 'We're on track, Mr Maxwell.'

'A little more detail would be good.'

'I'll let Alfred talk you through that. He's more involved with the nuts and bolts than I am.'

'Nuts and bolts are what I want,' said Peter Maxwell cheerfully. So I gave him a quick summary of the work going on.

'Good stuff, Fred. Can you put all that in an email to me just after we finish this conversation. Have you got a pen? Here's my email address.'

I wrote it down and then Maxwell said, 'The PM is interested in this project. He wants to see it succeed. I'll get myself more involved once you're a bit further down the road with it all. David, for the moment I want you to come and give me a monthly briefing, starting one month from now, or sooner if there are any dramatic developments. Talk to my secretary and get dates and times from her. And I want everyone in your centre to keep away from the press. Nothing about the Yemen salmon project must get into the public domain unless my office clears it first. Okay?'

After that conversation with Peter Maxwell, David Sugden's mood changed. Monthly briefing meetings at Number 10 were not something he had ever dreamed would come his way.

He left my office glowing with pleasure.

*Later*

Tonight Mary was back home before me. I am writing this in the spare bedroom. At first she was sweet. When I arrived home there was the smell of something delicious coming from the kitchen. Mary can be quite a good cook when she wants to be, which is not all that often. She was whisking up a sauce and wearing an apron. I kissed her hello and asked her what she was cooking. She told me it was pasta with scallops, and that there was a bottle of white wine in the fridge.

This was unprecedented. As I have noted, Mary never drinks in the week and not often at weekends.

'I'll just go and change,' I said. 'You must have come home early?'

'Yes, I'm off to Geneva again in the morning so I thought it would be nice for us to have a proper dinner together before I go.'

Ah, so that was it. When I came downstairs dinner was

ready, and two glasses of white wine were misting on the kitchen table.

'This is really good,' I said, after a mouthful. And it was. Mary shook her head and said something about being out of practice.

I sipped my wine and asked, 'Do you still have no idea how long you are in Geneva for?'

'Well, that's just it,' she said, putting her fork down. 'I told you before that I'm standing in for someone who fell ill and died. They want me to stay there for at least a year, not just on a temporary basis. They've been very impressed with my work.'

I said it seemed a bit hard on me that she was the only person in the bank they could find to send out there. Mary frowned and said, 'Why not me? I'm very good. It's a great opportunity. It's promotion, even if the salary isn't very different.'

It was happening again. Mary could have been one of Napoleon's generals: for her, attack was not just the best form of defence, but the only form of defence. We began to argue. Despite my intention to keep the conversation at the calm, rational level I prefer I too became annoyed. I remember saying, almost shouting, that I didn't think she had spent five minutes considering what my feelings might be. So she told me how selfish I was and how little account I took of her career, and how I was always impossible to talk to because I thought of nothing but my bloody, bloody fish.

'I must have told you a dozen times, if I get offered the job in Geneva as a permanent position, the next step is almost certainly a senior posting to London. I've told you a dozen times,' she repeated.

'At least a dozen,' I said. This was not helpful of me, but I couldn't stop myself.

'Oh, I'm sorry if I've been boring you. Well, here's a bit of news which I won't repeat too often because I won't be here to repeat it. I'm going to Geneva tomorrow. I will be away for at least six months before I am entitled to any leave. I can't come home at weekends because they work Saturday mornings in the bank. If you want to come and see me, my address and some other notes for you are on my desk in the study.'

She was really angry now. She told me I didn't care; I was buried in my own career, and now on our last evening I was being sarcastic and self-centred. She pushed her plate away and I heard her run up the stairs and slam the bedroom door.

I haven't the nerve to go in there tonight. I'll try and catch her in the morning before she leaves.


**23 August**

This morning I made a last effort. I felt shattered by the evening before. These emotional exchanges take it out of me, and I felt bilious all night long. Despite that I was up at five, and went downstairs in my pyjamas to find Mary's cases in the hall. Mary herself was sitting drinking a mug of tea at the kitchen table.

She looked at me in a not very friendly way and asked me what I was doing up at that time of day.

'To say goodbye, of course,' I said. 'Darling, don't let's part on a sour note. I'm going to miss you.'

'Well, you should have thought of that before you were so unpleasant to me last night.'

The front door bell buzzed. It was her taxi.

Mary stood up. She allowed me the faintest peck on the cheek by way of a kiss, and then in a few moments she, her cases and the taxi had gone. Gone for how long, I wonder. For a year? For good?

# 6

## Correspondence between Captain Robert Matthews and Ms Harriet Chetwode-Talbot

*Written and posted in Frankfurt airport*

10 May

Darling Harriet

I don't know how to tell you this. I tried you on your mobile and left a message, but by the time you pick it up I will be out of the country and not contactable by phone or email.

I was rung by the adjutant and given about five minutes' notice to get packed and out to the airport. We flew commercial to Frankfurt, which is where I am now. I'm writing this in a little coffee place in the departure lounge. We have a few minutes before our connecting flight out to Basra.

Yes, I'm afraid I'm going to Iraq and that means our week together is in ruins. Darling, I feel as sick about this as you will do when you read this. One thing I have already decided: I'll do my tour here, which is meant to be about twelve weeks, but when I come back I'm going to put in my papers. I'm going to leave the forces. I'm not especially ambitious for promotion – I can't be bothered to go to staff college. I only joined up because Dad wanted me to, and I was never going to get to university. I just wanted a few years of fun. Well,

72

I've had lots of fun and they've looked after me very well, so I suppose when they tap me on the shoulder and send me somewhere slightly unpleasant, I can't object.

But now I've met you, as a way of life the marines are no longer for me. It's just as you say. It would be so good to settle down and become part of somewhere again, instead of constantly passing through.

That's small consolation for a bust holiday, but I hope you will understand. Don't worry about Iraq, it's just a routine rotation of people. I wasn't on the list but someone had a slight accident so I was pulled in to replace him. We won't be doing any dangerous stuff. The place has calmed down a lot over the years. It's more public relations than anything else. I'd almost prefer it if we saw some action, because otherwise it can be a very dull place to be stuck, particularly at this time of year when it's almost too hot to go outside.

Anyway, I'll be thinking of you. We'll go away the minute I get back. That's a promise.

Write to me as soon as you can c/o BFPO Basra Palace, Basra, and it should reach me pretty quickly. Don't worry if you don't hear from me for a while. If I'm on the base at Basra I should get letters almost straight away, but if I'm in-country there might be some delay before I have a chance to see them.

So don't ever worry about me. I'll be all right.

Love

*Robert*

Captain Robert Matthews
c/o BFPO Basra Palace
Basra
Iraq

12 May

Darling Robert

You can imagine my first reaction when I picked up your message on my voicemail. I went in a rage to my desk and pulled out the file with all the copies of the hotel and car hire reservations and tore them up. Then I burst into tears.

In other words, I behaved just as badly as you might have expected, but I think you will admit I had some excuse. I was looking forward to our holiday in France together *so much*. Now I've got over that I spend all my time imagining something ghastly might happen to you, but I know that's just me being stupid again, plus a hyperactive imagination. I don't think you have any imagination at all, and never worry about anything. Or at least that's what you always tell me, and of course you will be perfectly all right with your friends around you, and because you've done it all before.

Now I sort of accept it, and I just want you to know I'm thinking of you every minute, and when I'm asleep I dream about you. You can't ask for more than that, can you?

Don't leave the marines just because your girlfriend whines at you every time you have to go away. If that's really what you want to do, then of course it's right. But don't do it for me if it's a sacrifice, because then you'd blame me when you got bored and restless and then we'd end up divorced five minutes later. I don't want to divorce you; I want to marry you. Anyway, what would you do instead?

We'll talk about it when you come back. Don't do anything until then.

Masses of love

*Harriet*


Captain Robert Matthews
c/o BFPO Basra Palace
Basra
Iraq

15 May

Darling Robert

I wish I knew where you were and what you were doing. It would mean I could worry a bit less. I hope, wherever it is, you are not too uncomfortable and it is not too dangerous. I tried to look your unit up on the Internet but, of course, I found nothing.

Isn't it strange, writing letters to each other? Because I'm not allowed to email you and I can't speak to you by phone, I am left with no choice. Apart from a few thank you letters and one or two to you I haven't written any letters to anyone since I used to write to my mother when I was away at school. Even then it was mostly to ask her to send me more money. And because I haven't the least idea what you are doing in Iraq, thank God, we can't talk about that. So I suppose I'll have to bore you to death, and tell you about me.

Our client, a sheikh from Yemen (I'm not supposed to tell anyone his name – I would tell you, but it wouldn't mean anything to you anyway) has come to see us with the most extraordinary idea. He wants us to commission the best UK fisheries scientists to introduce salmon into the Yemen. He has an estate up near Inverness we helped him buy a few years ago, with a few miles of river which are apparently quite good fishing in June and July. You would know about all that sort of thing. The sheikh has become rather good at it, and enjoys going up there to fish more than almost anything. He also takes beats on other rivers whenever he can. He is almost obsessive about his fishing, much more so than his shooting or stalking. I've seen him at it, and he seems to know what he is doing.

He is a very impressive character. He is quite small, but stands very upright and communicates a sense of power which you cannot ignore. I don't mean I fancy him, and he certainly doesn't fancy me – tall, thin European women are not his type. He is happily married, anyway, with wife number four being the current favourite.

I don't know what we are going to do about his request. He has clearly got a bee in his bonnet about fishing and the Yemen salmon project in particular. It seems almost wrong to take any money from him for something as dotty as this, which is bound to fail, but it is a *lot* of cash and our project management fees would be serious money just on their own.

Anyway, darling, I just wanted to write to let you know I was thinking about you and missing you.

Love you lots

*Harriet*

5 Scarsdale Road
London

15 May

Darling Harriet

So good to hear from you. I'm sure this letter will take ages to get to you but where we are now is about a ███████████ miles from anywhere *Under Security Regulations Chapter XII Section 83 all references which might indicate the location, intention or capability of a unit must be deleted from correspondence. Security Office, BFPO Basra* and the heat is at least ████ degrees in the shade *See above. Security Office, BFPO Basra*. I am not allowed to tell you what we are doing but it is not a whole lot of fun, and conditions are ████████████ █████████████████. The Iraqis are either very friendly or absolutely murderously ████████████ ████ █████████████ █████. So a letter from home is a chance to escape and forget all this for a few minutes. Keep writing. Each letter you send me is like a long cool drink of water.

I'll stop now. The ██████████████ censor at Basra will probably delete most of this anyway. *Sir or Madam, as noted earlier, under Chapter XII Section 83 we are required by military regulations to delete references in private correspondence which might compromise the unit concerned or otherwise act against the interests of British forces. Security Office, BFPO Basra*

Loads of love


*Robert*
XXXXX

Captain Robert Matthews
BFPO Basra Palace
Basra

10 June

Darling Robert

Your letter took *weeks* to reach me, and some awful man in the censor's office in Basra had crossed out lots of what you wrote, and then scribbled over the letter. Awful to think someone else is reading everything we both write. Otherwise, there are all sorts of things I would like to say to you but won't or can't, because nothing is private any more.

The papers are full of stuff about Iraq again. It seems to have got worse again after years of relative calm: children being shot, people being blown up by car bombs or shot at from helicopter gunships. I shudder when I think you are in the middle of all that. Why does it all have to start up again just as you arrive there?

I don't suppose you will ever tell me what it is really like, even when you come home. I can't wait for you to come home.

We had a meeting in the office a few days ago, and decided we would try and help our sheikh with his salmon fishing project. Everyone was saying things like 'It's not our job to tell the client what he can or can't do – our job is to help him do it.' The fact is it is ages since we had a really big deal. Things have been slow for a while. So I was deputed to write to some man that our contacts in DEFRA tell us is one of the top fisheries scientists. The pompous little man did not even bother to reply himself – he got his secretary to write a short note containing ten good reasons why the whole idea

78

was a waste of time. Naturally I wasn't going to stand for that so I rang up an old friend of mine who works in the Foreign and Commonwealth Office and told him what was going on. I said, 'Look, with all this bad news coming out of the rest of the Middle East, isn't this a potential good news story? Shouldn't we be encouraging our client to spend his money, however mad it may seem? Isn't this a good news story about Anglo-Yemeni cooperation?' I thought it was rather clever of me to think of that angle, don't you? It only occurred to me because you had just been sent out there.

Anyway, the idea seemed to ring a bell with my old friend. He said, 'You know, Harriet (yes, I know – former boyfriend but a *very* long time ago), I think you might have a very good point. Let me talk to some people.' The next thing I knew I had someone on from the prime minister's office in Downing Street, asking for more details of the sheikh's idea. Then the next morning I had some grovelling man on the phone called David Sugden who said he was the 'immediate superior' of the man I had written to, a Dr Jones, and that Dr Jones had now 'come to terms' with the project. And finally, this morning, I was visited by Dr Jones himself. If ever someone walked into my office with his tail between his legs, it was Dr Jones.

He looked just as I had imagined him after speaking to him on the phone. He wasn't very tall, about my height, say five foot ten. He had sandy hair and a square, pale, indoors sort of face, and didn't look as if he told many jokes. He also looked as if he was going to make things as difficult as possible for me. But I had done my homework and managed to show him I knew a little bit about what I was talking about, and after a while he became almost reasonable. I could see the scientist in him thinking 'This can't be done' when I started talking. When I finished I could see he was thinking 'Just in theory, is there any way in which this could be done?' So at least he was honest enough to accept he might have been wrong, and in fact he wasn't really that pompous after all. He did look henpecked, though.

I hope you never look henpecked when we get married. I will try not to peck too hard.

Love you lots

*Harriet*


5 Scarsdale Road
London

15 June

Darling Harriet

███████ ████████ we drove down a street and suddenly ███████ ████████ ██████ █████ ████ guns were pointing the wrong way. ████ ██████ ████ ███ █████████ ████████ and the helicopter arrived after a few anxious minutes, ██████████ ███ ███ ██████████ █████ █████ █████ a very beautiful old mosque with blue tiles ██████ ███████ █████ ████ pieces as a result of an error by a US Cobra pilot. Apart from that nothing exciting has happened, it is mostly the heat and the flies that get us down. Yesterday we drove into a village near ██████ █████████████████████ and came across a small boy in the street. There had been a visit by the Sunni insurgents ██████ ██████████ ███████ ████ ████ ████████

80

███████ ████ ███ ████ lost his
mother and stood in the middle of the street screaming.
Sunday papers arrived at last four weeks late but before we
had a chance to clean up and read them we were given new
orders.

██ █ ████ ███ ██ ████

████ ███ ███ ███ I didn't think we
were supposed to be that close to the ████████.
Anyway, orders is orders and I suppose we've got to go there.
I haven't even been allowed time to go back to base and get
a change of clothes. A clean shirt would be nice.

Thinking of you all the time, much love

*Robert*


Captain Robert Matthews
c/o BFPO Basra Palace
Basra
Iraq

22 June

Darling Robert

I couldn't make much sense of your last letter. The censor
had attacked it with his pen and obliterated nearly all of it.
But keep writing anyway. At least I know then that you are
well and still thinking of me. Sometimes I ache with worry
for you. One hears so many dreadful stories from the newspapers and much worse ones if one ever meets anyone with
family out where you – where I think you are.

I'd better go on with my salmon story. My Dr Jones has

come up trumps. He has written an absolutely brilliant proposal about introducing salmon into the Yemen. It is too technical to go into here and anyway it would bore you to death if I went into all the details, but the upshot is, he thinks, in theory, that something can be done. When I passed this on to my client he was thrilled. He rang up in person, something he never does, and said, 'Bring Dr Alfred Jones to my house in Scotland. If I like him, I will give him whatever money he wants to make this thing happen. He is a clever man, but I need to meet him to know if he is an honest man, and if he can have the faith to do this.'

So I rang up Dr Jones, and the client sent his car to take us to a little airport in south London where he keeps his Learjet, and we flew together up to Inverness. Dr Jones was rather overawed and didn't say much. His eyes kept on darting round the cabin of the plane in a nervous way as if he couldn't quite believe what was happening. I have flown in the client's private jet at least twice before, so of course I could pretend that it was all part of a day's work.

We got to Glen Tulloch about lunchtime but then I had to go and sit with the factor and deal with all sorts of trivial problems about the estate. The sheikh joined us for a few minutes, issued a few instructions and then disappeared again. When he came back he said, 'I have sent your Dr Jones to fish with Colin. I have been watching him from the road for a while. He is a true fisherman, not just a scientist. I am pleased with your choice, Harriet Chetwode-Talbot.' When he calls me this I am never sure whether there is irony in his voice, or whether he is simply being correct in his manner of address, as he sees it.

I said that was good luck. 'It is not luck, Harriet Chetwode-Talbot. It is God's wish. He has set this man in my path, the right man at the right time, *insh'Allah*. I will talk to him later at dinner, but already I know what I needed to know.'

And later at dinner he did talk to Dr Jones. It was all very simple and somehow very moving. My client is, I think, more than a little mad, but it is a charming form of madness, almost a divine form of madness. He believes that the salmon and its long journey through endless oceans back to its home river is, in some strange way, a symbol of his own journey to become closer to his God. You know, a few hundred years ago, the sheikh might have been called a saint, if there are saints in Islam?

Dr Jones called me Harriet tonight. He never looks me in the eye. I think he fancies me, but he is a married man and so feels guilty. Don't worry, darling. As far as I am concerned, there is only you.

Love

*Harriet*


*Undated and unsigned letter from the Family Support Group at the Ministry of Defence*

Dear Harriet Chetwode-Talbot

Copies of your correspondence with Captain Robert Matthews have been forwarded to this office by Security, BFPO Basra Palace.

Captain Robert Matthews is now, for operational reasons, in an area where postal services cannot be guaranteed. Further correspondence will not therefore be forwarded to him. Nor will any postal facilities be available to his unit until further notice.

Please note the call centre number below will access the Family Support Centre, who will provide counselling to enable you to cope with any trauma arising from loss of contact with a close friend/relation/spouse.

0800 400 1200

This counselling service is provided free of charge by the MoD but calls will cost 14p per minute.

MoD

# 7

## Press comment

*Article in the* Yemen Observer, *14 August*

### Fishing project for western highlands

Sheikh Muhammad ibn Zaidi has surprised the Arab world with his decision to introduce salmon fishing into the Wadi Aleyn in the Heraz. Yemenis may understandably ask many questions about the legitimacy of this project. We say that we should wait and see what the scientific reality of the salmon project turns out to be.

The project is being debated in a lively manner at family dinners and at khat chews. There are many who think that the introduction of salmon into a desert country is neither a realistic nor an economic proposition. Others however state that the project is being supported by a leading fisheries scientist from the UK and that there is a real prospect in future years of our tourist industry being boosted by the sale of salmon fishing permits.

The agriculture and health ministry declined to comment but we understand that the present Aquatic Law No. 42 does not expressly forbid the development of a salmon fishery in the Yemen. Therefore Sheikh Muhammad is entitled to develop such a fishery without the need to seek further consent from the government.

## Yemeni sheikh plans new ecosystem for wadis

*Sana'a, Yemen Republic*

Sheikh Muhammad ibn Zaidi, a key figure in Yemeni political circles, has long been noted for his pro-Western views in a country whose relationship with Western states has sometimes been troubled. On Sunday he urged President Saleh to lend his backing to a revolutionary eco-project that has received some support in UK government circles.

Sheikh Muhammad is planning to spend millions of pounds sterling with the British government to introduce wild Scottish salmon into a wadi in the western Yemen. In stark contrast to US policy, which currently involves further military build-ups in Saudi Arabia and Iraq, the UK now appears to be shifting its political ground. Although British government officials deny any formal relationship with Sheikh Muhammad, nevertheless a UK government agency, the National Centre for Fisheries Excellence, has taken a leading role in this environmentally challenging project. British policy in the region now appears to be looking for ways to take cultural and sporting images, likely in an effort to soften the impact of recent military actions in southern Iraq.

The funding will be provided by Sheikh Muhammad. UK government officials today distanced themselves from the project, claiming it was a private-sector initiative. However, it is likely that such a major scheme involving some of the world's most prestigious fisheries scientists could not proceed without sanction from Prime Minister Jay Vent's office.

Some observers speculate that Sheikh Muhammad's initiative may not be universally welcome in his own province. The area is home to several radical Wahhabi *madrasas*, religious training schools, and it is understood that salmon fishing is regarded as an unacceptable activity by some Wahhabi imams. Water is also a scarce resource in the Yemen, and its diversion into the wadis to support a run of salmon will not be universally popular in a country where the availability of water is often a matter of life and death.

*Article in* The Times, *17 August*

**British fisheries scientists in major row**

Concerns were raised yesterday in Parliament that a key Government agency, the National Centre for Fisheries Excellence (NCFE), is going outside its mandate. Set up a decade ago to support the work of the Environment Agency in monitoring and improving the health of rivers in England and Wales, NCFE is now said to have diverted over 90 per cent of its resources into a project to introduce Atlantic salmon into the Yemen.

The Department for Environment, Food and Rural Affairs (DEFRA) confirmed that the funding for the Yemen salmon project is not coming from the UK taxpayer but has been met entirely from private-sector sources. However, questions are being asked as to whether this is an appropriate use of a key government department at a time when so many environmental and other challenges face rivers in England and Wales as a result of global warming and the risks from agricultural and industrial pollution to our rivers. A spokesman for the RSPB confirmed that, if the Yemen salmon project went ahead, the society would seek to have English cormorants exported to the Yemen, to ensure that the natural checks and balances on any salmon river were maintained.

*Extract from* Trout & Salmon, *18 August*

## Comment

We acknowledge that we have, from time to time, sung the praises of the National Centre for Fisheries Excellence. This organisation had established for itself within the angling community a reputation for good science and common sense.

Fly-fishing has become 'cool' in the USA, and even in the UK we are discarding our waxed jackets for the latest in clothing technology from Orvis, Snowbee and many other manufacturers. Films are made about fishing, once regarded as the most boring of sports. This trend was firmly set by the making of *A River Runs Through It* in 1992, while television programmes about fishing such as *A Passion for Angling* and *Go Fishing* attract prime-time audiences and are repeated endlessly on satellite channels.

So, fishing is fashionable, and its appeal crosses borders and it is becoming truly international, but nothing so far has prepared us for the idea that the mountains of the Heraz, in the Republic of Yemen, are soon to become the next playground for internationally minded game fishermen seeking the latest salmon fishing thrill.

Who is making this happen? A prominent and wealthy citizen of the Yemen has teamed up with the National Centre for Fisheries Excellence, an organisation we would not have anticipated would become involved in an adventure of this kind. But money talks and the millions of pounds that Sheikh Muhammad of the Wadi Aleyn is spending are talking loudly enough to grab the attention of the NCFE and even (it is rumoured) the director of communications at Number 10 Downing Street.

We have looked back through our files to find a similar instance of such absurdity from a government department, but we are unable to find anything to parallel this. At a time when the health of English and Welsh rivers is so fragile, and stocks of salmon and sea trout, not to mention brown trout, appear threatened by climatic change, our best fisheries scientists have been committed to a hare-brained scheme which is of absolutely no benefit whatsoever to our own angling community here in the UK.

*Extract from the* Sun, *23 August*

### 'Chest' wader

Glamorous Harriet Chetwode-Talbot, the dreamy blonde who is masterminding the crazy plan to bring salmon fishing to the Yemen, refused to talk to our reporter when we rang her today. We contacted her at exclusive West End estate agents Fitzharris & Price, to ask her to comment on her wacky idea – let's all go salmon fishing in the desert! She couldn't tell us too much about how it would all work, and refused to say anything about her Yemeni boss, Sheikh Muhammad. So we asked if she would like to get her kit off for our photographer and pose for us in 'chest' waders. We're still waiting for her answer!

*Letter to the editor of* Trout & Salmon

Dear Sir

I feel compelled to respond to the recent article about introducing salmon into the wadis of the Yemen.

Whilst I applaud the intention to introduce the sport of angling where fishing for sport has not so far been widely practised, I am bound to ask what is wrong with coarse fishing? Wouldn't it be more practical and, dare I say, more affordable for the average Yemeni to have dace or perch introduced to their rivers? What about considering stillwater fishing for rainbow trout in the Yemeni reservoirs, an even more accessible and economical sport for the average fisherman? To me, the decision to introduce salmon into the wadis of the Yemen without any consultation is characteristic of the elitist attitude which still prevails far too often in fishery circles in this country and, it appears, in the Yemen as well.

Yours

*(Name withheld)*

*Letter to the editor of the* Daily Telegraph

Dear Sir

I understand that there has been a lot of fuss about a plan to introduce salmon into the Yemen. I served in the Yemen in the 1950s. I was based in Aden and had the opportunity to see local fishermen going after everything from anchovies to sharks. I can well remember the Yemeni fishermen standing with perfect balance on the prows of their boats, setting out to sea to catch all manner of fish. I know that the Yemeni people are natural fishermen, and I am sure would make fine anglers, given the chance.

I applaud the imaginative nature of this project.

Yours sincerely

*(Major) (retd) Jock Summerhouse*


*Letter to the editor of* The Times

Dear Sir

The Republic of the Yemen has much expertise in the management of its fisheries. The Ministry of Fish Wealth is the responsible party, and the legal framework for our fisheries management is Aquatic Law No. 42 (1991).

The Yemen fishing industry is second to none, being responsible for an annual catch of 126,000 tonnes per annum of different species, pelagic and non-pelagic, both by artisanal and by industrial means. Our annual consumption per capita of fish is 7.6 kilos per head.

It has been reported in your press that certain individuals are seeking to install a salmon fishery in our Yemeni watercourses. We have no official knowledge at this time of such proposals but we can confirm that such proposals would be entirely in accordance with the excellent Yemen traditional skill and expertise in fishing and fishery management.

Aquatic Law No. 42 makes no reference to the management of a salmon fishery and would have to be amended in due course to include the possibility of a such a fishery. We respectfully conclude that such a project, if true, would be in the national interest and would be symbolic of Anglo-Yemeni co-operation.

*Hassan bin Mahoud*
Assistant to the deputy director
Ministry of Fish Wealth
Aden, Republic of Yemen

# 8

## Intercepts of al-Qaeda email traffic (provided by the Pakistan Inter-Services Intelligence Agency)

From: Tariq Anwar
Date: 20 August
To: Al-Qaeda members in Yemen
Folder: Outgoing mail to Yemen

I send you my greeting from beyond the swamps to your country where there is progress and civilisation – here we have many problems with our brothers the Taliban and they are not always acting in the best way according to the wishes of Abu Abdullah and the whole Nation of Islam. Also we have many adversaries who press from every side – the crusader special forces, even our brothers in Pakistan who have forgotten the true faith and chastise our people with guns and whips.

We have heard that the Sheikh Muhammad ibn Zaidi bani Tihami is now consorting with the English crusader prime minister and spending many millions of dollars on absurd and dangerous projects to bring salmon fish to the Yemen, and to persuade our brothers in the Yemen to fish for sport and not simply to feed the mouths of their families as is their duty. Moreover since all people in the Yemen must work from dawn until dusk, for six days of the week, just to keep the bread in their mouths and the mouths of their children, it follows that the sheikh will be expecting them to fish on the sabbath, which is expressly forbidden in the Koran.

This project is evil because it is not Islamic in its nature and because it is intended to distract attention from the greater evils that the crusaders are carrying out against the whole Muslim nation in Iraq, Iran, Afghanistan and Palestine. Therefore it must be stopped.

Abu Abdullah enjoins you to start an operation against Sheikh Muhammad ibn Zaidi. You must call on one of our brothers in Finchley, London. He must carry out an operation against the sheikh with extreme urgency to liquidate him and stop the salmon coming to the Yemen. We have wired $27,805 which is the operational budget, to the usual account.

We ask God to lead you to the good of both this life and the afterlife.

Peace be upon you and God's mercy and blessings
Tariq Anwar


From:   Essad
Date: 20 August
To: Tariq Anwar
Folder: Incoming mail from Yemen


Kind brother Tariq

We don't have any people in Finchley any more – they have all been arrested or dispersed by the British police. It would be necessary to send someone from here to Scotland to find the sheikh, unless the sheikh should return to his palace and his village here.

We don't think this operation will be very popular. The Sheikh

Muhammad is known everywhere as a man who follows God's teaching very closely. The people in his *wilayat* all revere and adore him. It will be hard to find one who will liquidate him and certainly not for the operational budget you have mentioned.

Peace be upon you
Essad

From: Tariq Anwar
Date: 20 August
To: Essad
Folder: Outgoing mail to Yemen

Brother Essad

Abu Abdullah doesn't want to hear your thoughts concerning Sheikh Muhammad. You forget our brother Abu Abdullah himself has family in the Yemen and is very well informed about who is, and who is not, a follower in the true path of God. He considers it very necessary for the sheikh to be liquidated, and at once.

Operational budget: flights $1000 (one way), car hire $500, food $25, disguise $200. Reward is $30,000 payable to the family of the operative assuming he is himself caught or liquidated by the security service. We will provide a clean mobile. We will provide papers. Total: $31,725, which is an increase of many dollars on what was first proposed. There is no more.

The needful operational sums will be made available at the Finchley post office in an account in the name of Hasan Yasin Abdullah. They only watch the banking system, not the post office. The reward will be paid when the deed is done.

Please confirm. Abu Adbullah wants to know your answer.
In the name of God
Tariq Anwar

From: Essad
Date: 21 August
To: Tariq Anwar
Folder: Incoming mail from Yemen

Brother Anwar
Peace be upon you.
We have found a brother here in the Hadramawt who speaks some English. His thirty goats have all just died from the foot and mouth. Now he has no food, no money and no goats. He will do it. Please send the money and then we will commence the operation.
In the name of God
Essad

# 9

## Interview with Peter Maxwell, director of communications, prime minister's office

**Interrogator:** Please describe the initial reasons for your involving the prime minister in the Yemen salmon project.

**Peter Maxwell:** Do you know who I am?

**I:** You are Mr Peter Maxwell. Please describe the initial reasons for your involving the prime Minister in the Yemen salmon project. Please bear in mind it is in your own best interests to cooperate fully with this enquiry.

**PM:** Okay. I see. Of course I will cooperate. Why shouldn't I? It's in everyone's interests to get the fullest possible picture of what happened. I am writing a book about it. Or at least I was, until one of your lot took the manuscript away.

**I:** Your manuscript is considered to contain material which might constitute a breach of confidentiality and its status will have to be reviewed by this enquiry before a decision can be taken as to whether it can be returned to you.

**PM:** I'm deeply, deeply hurt by what happened. I'm traumatised. I want that put on the record. I'm traumatised.

*The witness here broke down in tears and required mild sedation. The interview recommenced the following day and is transcribed here verbatim, as far as possible. Operational security details have been withheld from the public record.*

**PM:** My name is Peter Maxwell and I am – I was – the director of communications, prime minister's office. I had held that post for two years. I am an old, old friend of the prime minister. That's not why I got the job; I got the job because, false modesty aside, I am absolutely the best guy they've got at this sort of thing. I could have held Cabinet office. If I'd been elected as an MP, that is. But that whole ego trip of front-line politics was not for me. I wanted to serve my party from the sidelines, from the shadows. That's where I operate. In the shadows. Let other people take the credit. Don't be the story, shape the story: that's my motto.

Jay [*Prime Minister the Right Honourable James Vent MP*] was a godsend for our party. He's the best prime minister this country has had since Churchill. Since Gladstone. Since Pitt. He lifted this country up out of the Second Division and put it back in the Premier League, world affairs-wise. Right at the top. In the Champions' League. He had total mastery of the House of Commons. Members bowled seamers, spinners, yorkers – it didn't matter what – Jay put his bat to them all and carted them out of the ground. Every shot was in the bullseye.

**I:** You appear to be quoting from the first chapter of your book. Please can you direct your reply to the question that was asked. How and when did you decide to recommend to the prime minister that he should become involved in the Yemen salmon project?

**PM:** If you'd just let me answer in my own time, thank you very much, I was coming to that. You see, everyone has an off day. Everyone can get blindsided, sideswiped, no matter how good they are. That's when I can add some value. That's what I do. If the news is bad, I present it in the best possible light. If the news is *very* bad, I come up with a different story. The attention span of most of the media is about twenty minutes, and a new story, a new angle, normally tempts them to drop the bone you want them to drop, and look at the new bone you're offering them. That's off the record.

I: I am afraid everything you say here is *on* the record. Please, can we proceed to discuss how you first became involved with the Yemen salmon project.

PM: It was one of those bad news days you sometimes get. That was when the Yemen business first came up. I can't remember what it was that had happened. I think someone had held a map upside down and bombed a hospital in Iran instead of a militants' training camp in the Iraq desert. Not ideal from a presentational point of view, so I did what I usually do. I have a little email group of friends and right-minded people around the Foreign and Commonwealth Office and one or two other departments, so I sent out the usual 'Anyone got a good news story for me?' emails.

Usually what I get is stuff I have to work very hard at to turn into something I can use. You know, we have opened a new sewage treatment plant in south Basra, picture of a general standing by a ditch. The British Council has sent a group of morris dancers on tour in the Sunni Triangle. Hard work to sell that sort of story at a press conference – some of my colleagues in the trade are a touch cynical these days. But this story sold itself. Herbert Berkshire from the FCO rang me and asked, 'What do you think of the idea of salmon fishing? In the Yemen?'

'How's that again?' I said. I remember reaching for the

*Bartholomew's School Atlas*, which is never very far from my desk in these days of ethical foreign policy. We have got ethical in so many places I begin to wish I had not given up geography at school. I flip the pages, and the atlas more or less opens itself at the Middle East. Sure enough, there's the Yemen, and sure enough it's mostly coloured yellow and brown. 'It's desert,' I said. 'You won't find many salmon there.'

I don't know anything about salmon fishing. I like cricket, darts, football, salsa dancing, physical fitness stuff like that. Salmon fishing: isn't that what old men in tweed caps and rubber trousers do in the rain in Scotland?

'That's the story,' said Herbert. And he told me about Sheikh Muhammad from the Yemen. Herbert said that the sheikh had always been pro-British. He owned an estate in Scotland and had a power base in the Yemen that included a share of oil revenues. Money is a key driver in these situations. If there's a pot of money somewhere in any project, you've cracked it almost before you start. Herbert told me that the sheikh had an obsession about fishing, in particular salmon fishing. He had a strange theory that fishing is a sport which has a calming and beneficial effect on people, and he wanted his own people in the Yemen to have the benefit of that. He actually believed that, said Herbert. I must say, it sounded like *total* crap to me but, who cared, it would make a good story. He wanted to spend a lot of money with UK fisheries scientists to work on a project to seed Yemeni watercourses with Scottish salmon. With live salmon, that is. He believed that if he spent enough money, he could create conditions in which salmon could be caught during the rainy season in the Yemen.

Herbert said that the sheikh had both the will and the money to make something happen. The sheikh wanted to spend the money funding a development project by some outfit within DEFRA called the National Centre for Fisheries Excellence. I didn't realise it still existed; I thought we had reallocated all its grant funding to a programme of building swimming pools in deprived ethnic-minority-type inner-city areas. I remember making a mental note to check that later. My view was, fish don't vote. When would people get that simple point?

'Herbert, this is going to fail. It has D for disaster written all over it.'

'Think about it for a moment,' said Herbert. He started to number his points and I could see him in my mind's eye spreading the fingers of his left hand and then bending them over double with the forefinger of his right hand. It's an irritating, schoolmaster-type thing which he does in meetings. 'One: all the news coming out of the region has got worse again just now and it doesn't make the government look good. This is a chance to get a picture on the front covers that *does* have the words "Middle East" in the caption, and *doesn't* have bodies in the picture. Two: we've only just repaired our diplomatic relations with the Yemen after recent terrorist incidents in which Yemeni groups have been involved. Here's a chance to be constructive and open up a new, non-political dialogue with the Yemen. We can show water with fish swimming in it, in a desert country. It doesn't matter whether it works or not. The point is, it can probably be made to look as if it works, even if only for five minutes. We put a few fish into a stream, take pictures, then move on.'

'Good point, Herbert,' I said.

'Three: the president of the Yemen is not part of this, nor is his government; this is a private initiative. Your office, and the boss, can get involved or not, as you wish. FCO doesn't need to be. Either your office can decide to support this, or it can decide not to, depending on how things stack up when you take a closer look. But it could just look very good if the PM could be seen to be promoting something scientific, something sporting, something cultural, like this. And there's a terrific story about how Western ideas and science can transform the harsh desert environment and the lives of the people who live there. I think you ought to run it past the boss.'

The more I thought, the more I liked it. It was win-win. 'Herbert, thank you for this suggestion. I like it. I'll take it to the boss, as you suggest.' How I wish I'd hung up on him, when he first said the words 'salmon fishing'.

I: So your initial interest in the salmon project was for purely political reasons?

PM: Hey, politics is what I do. I wasn't paid to think about fish; I was paid to think about what would make the boss look good. So, anyway, that is how it started. I wrote to the PM and the PM got it, immediately. He didn't ask questions. He just said, 'Go for it, Peter. Nice work,' or something like that, and then I had to run with it. The first bit of press exposure, we were a bit off balance. I mean, something came out in the *Yemen Observer*. How am I meant to anticipate that? Then the *International Herald Tribune* picked the story up, and from there it got into the UK broadsheets, then the tabloids. So we had to get into the act, keep control of events, make sure the story spun our way. You saw the interview on breakfast TV, didn't you? Now I'm very tired. I don't want to answer any more questions today.

**I:** For the record, I am now switching off the tape.

# 10

Transcript of interview with the prime minister, the Rt Hon. Jay Vent MP, on BBC1
*The Politics Show*

**Andrew Marr** [*in vision, facing camera*]: Today we're going to consider the question of salmon fishing, which makes a refreshing change. More specifically, we are going to talk to Prime Minister Jay Vent about salmon fishing in the Yemen. Earlier this week I spoke to the prime minister about this at Number 10 Downing Street.

*Studio link to 10 Downing Street. Shot of prime minister and Andrew Marr seated in armchairs opposite each other, a table with a bowl of roses between them.*

**AM:** Prime Minister, isn't the very thought of salmon fishing in the Yemen an idea from way out on the lunatic fringe?

**Jay Vent:** You know, Andy, sometimes someone comes up with an idea that is improbable but truly, truly heroic. I think that's what we've got here, with my old friend Sheikh Muhammad. He has a vision.

**AM:** A lot of people, perhaps not knowing enough about it, would describe it as more of a hallucination than a vision.

**JV** [*turns to camera*]: Yes, Andy, maybe to some people it does sound a little crazy, but let's not be afraid of thinking outside the box. My government has never stepped away from challenging new ideas, as you know. You know,

Andy, if you'd been a reporter when the first ship was built from iron rather than from wood ...

AM [*faces camera*]: Sometimes it feels like I have been doing this job rather a long time, Prime Minister.

JV: Ha ha, Andy. I think you get my point, though. My point is, it probably sounded a little crazy when someone said, 'I'm going to build my next ship out of iron and not out of wood.' It probably sounded a little crazy when someone said, 'I'm going to lay this cable across the Atlantic and send telephone messages along it.' People laughed, Andy. But now the world has been changed for the better and all because those people had that heroic, extra bit of vision.

AM: Yes, Prime Minister, that's very interesting, but those were great inventions that changed the lives of millions of people. Salmon fishing in the desert sounds more of a minority sport. Isn't a great deal of money going to be spent for no particular good reason? Why is your government supporting such an apparently bizarre project?

JV: Andy, I don't think that's the question you should be asking.

AM: [*inaudible*]

JV: I think the question you should be asking is, what can we do to improve the lives of those troubled people who live in the Middle East—

AM [*interrupts*]: Well, perhaps, Prime Minister, but that was not the question that I just asked. The question I ...

JV [*interrupts*]: ... and, you know, Andy, isn't it just a little bit special that we're sitting here talking about changing a Middle Eastern country, and the lives of its people, so much for the better [*camera on prime minister*] without talking about sending out British troops and helicopters and fighter aircraft. Yes, we've done that in the past, because they've asked us to, some of them, and so we've had to. But now it is different. This time, we're going to send out fish.

**AM:** So, is exporting live salmon to the Yemen now official government policy?

**JV:** No, no, Andy. Not everything I do or say is official government policy. You chaps in the media attribute all sorts of powers to me, but life isn't really like that. Official government policy is ultimately the business of Parliament. No, I'm merely sharing with you my personal view that the Yemen salmon project is rather a special project that I feel deserves some sympathy and encouragement. That's not the same thing as official government support, Andy.

**AM:** And why do you personally support this project, Prime Minister. What is it that especially appeals to you about salmon fishing in the Yemen when there are so many other political and humanitarian crises that demand your attention?

**JV:** Andy, you're right that there is an endless list of problems out there that need dealing with. And no government has devoted so much of its time to global issues of the kind that you mention than mine has. But what's so special about salmon fishing in the Yemen? Isn't this project a different way forward? Isn't it a form of intervention that is so much kinder and gentler and somehow ... more transforming? Water in the desert? Isn't that a powerful symbol of ...

**AM:** [*inaudible*]

**JV:** ... of a different sort of progress? Yemeni tribesmen waiting for the evening rise by the side of a wadi with fishing rods in their hands. Isn't that an image we'd rather have in our mind's eye than a tank at a crossroads somewhere in Fallujah? Salmon smokeries on the edge of the wadis. The introduction of a gentle, tolerant sport that unites us and our Arab brethren in a new and deep way. A path away from confrontation.

All this is going to be achieved with the help of UK scientists. And that's another thing: we're a world leader in this fisheries science business. Thanks to the policy of this government. If we can manage to introduce salmon into the Yemen, where else can we do it? Sudan? Palestine? Who knows what new export opportunities this will open up, and not just for the scientists, but for our world-class manufacturers of fishing tackle, fishing wear and salmon flies.

So, you see, Andy, maybe it's a little crazy as you say. And maybe, just maybe, it might work.

AM [*turns to camera, prime minister out of shot*]: Thank you, Prime Minister.

# 11

## Continuation of interview with Peter Maxwell

**Interrogator:** Did that interview indicate official government support for the salmon project?

**Peter Maxwell:** God, no. The boss was too clever to be pinned down like that. No, what he was trying to do was create a climate of approval for the project, and the impression that he, personally, liked the idea. It went down extremely well, that cameo speech. It made the news that night and stayed top of the news for several days in one form or another.

I can't remember the rest of the interview but I remember that bit because I wrote a lot of it the night before, sitting downstairs in the kitchen at Number 10, cracking a bottle of Australian Chardonnay with Jay. And I remember the letters we got for the next few weeks from all the fishing rod manufacturers and wader manufacturers. We could have kitted out half the Cabinet with the free samples we got. As a matter of fact, I think we did.

Jay turned the media round with that interview. We had spun the story our way. We got good leaders in the *Daily Telegraph* and *The Times*. We even got a faintly patronising but not entirely negative leader in the *Guardian*. Suddenly the stories about dead bodies in the Middle East were on pages four and five. The front pages were about fish, and even the review and magazine sections were all doing pieces on fishing, what a wonderful sport it was and what terrific old characters fishermen were. They even interviewed the sheikh's fishing guy up in Scotland, Colin McPherson. I talked to him myself at one point. I'll come back to that later. I never understood a word the man said when I met him, and I imagine the journalists didn't either, and just made the interviews up.

The important thing I want to say here is that, suddenly, Jay started to believe his own press. He started to believe it was his idea, it always had been his idea, just as it said in the newspapers. I think he half believed, although he never came out loud and said it, that he'd gone up to Sheikh Muhammad ibn Zaidi at some Number 10 reception and cocktail party and said, 'Muhammad, hey, have you ever thought about salmon fishing? In the Yemen?' That happened a few times with some of the stunts I organised for Jay. He took them over, and they became his ideas, his initiatives. I didn't mind. That was the game. Shape the story, then step back into the shadows.

Can I have another mug of tea? I'm thirsty. And some more of those biscuits?

*The interview was interrupted. The witness became emotional after the consumption of custard creams and was incoherent. The interview resumed after a break of four hours.*

PM: It was decided at the highest level that I would stay with the project, make sure something happened and that we had a good understanding of who the players were and where they were coming from. At the right moment we would drag the story back into the headlines, get the photo opportunity for the PM, and see where we could take it next.

Nothing much happened for a bit. I asked for a briefing from the head of NCFE, a man called David Sugden. He came and gave me an hour-long PowerPoint presentation during a very busy day, and talked about timelines, and milestones and deliverables, but he didn't actually seem to know anything about anything. So then I took him out of the loop and put myself in touch with the man who was actually doing the work, a man called Jones.

**I:** Was that the first time you communicated directly with Dr Jones?

**PM:** It was the first time we had met. I have to say I wasn't very excited the first time I met him. He didn't look like the sort of man who would tell many jokes. But Dr Jones made more sense than his boss. He struck me as a bit of a pedant to start with, and when he came to see me in Downing Street I gave him a hard time, just to let him know who was in charge. But after a while I realised he wasn't so bad. It was just his manner, mixed with quite a lot of apprehension at finding himself in my office, at the very heart of power in the United Kingdom. He seemed bright enough. I think he was honest too, in a naive sort of way. Politically, he was just an innocent, of course.

After I had listened to him outlining the work NCFE had done on the project, which was mostly conceptual stuff, I interrupted him as he began to talk about dissolved oxygen levels and water stratification, and said, 'Fred, is this going to work? Are future generations of Yemenis going to catch salmon in the wadis during the summer rains?'

He blinked and looked at me in surprise, then said, 'I shouldn't think so, no.'

I asked him, if that was his opinion, why we were doing all this.

He paused and thought for a moment and then he said, as far as I can remember, 'Mr Maxwell, I've often asked myself that question over the last few weeks. I don't really know the answer. I think there's more than one answer, anyway.'

'Try some of them on me,' I suggested, tilting my chair back and putting my feet on the desk.

Dr Jones told me that, in the first place, while this project probably won't succeed, it may not entirely fail either. We may achieve something, such as a short run of salmon up the wadi when it is in spate. That in itself would be so extraordinary as to justify all the effort we are putting into it – providing of course we don't have to defend what we are doing in economic terms. And we don't. Sheikh Muhammad is being liberal with his money. He questions nothing, he always responds to funding proposals and cost overruns by writing another cheque, and the project is now well outside original estimates.

Secondly, whatever happens, it will have moved forward the boundaries of science. We will understand many things we did not know before we started this project. Not just about fish, but about the adaptability of species to new environments. In that sense, we have already gained something.

Then, too, said Dr Jones, there is something visionary about Sheikh Muhammad. For him, this isn't just about fishing. Perhaps, at one level, it isn't about fishing at all, but about faith. 'You've lost me there, Fred,' I told him.

'I mean,' said Dr Jones, taking off his spectacles and

polishing them with a clean white handkerchief, 'that what the sheikh wants to do is demonstrate that things can change, that there are no absolute impossibilities. In his mind it is a way of demonstrating that God can make anything happen if he wants to. The Yemen salmon project will be presented by the sheikh as a miracle of God, if it succeeds.'

'And if it fails?'

'Then it will show the weakness of man, and that the sheikh is a poor sinner not worthy of his God. He has told me that many times.'

There was a silence. I didn't go for this religious stuff, but the boss might like it, and I scribbled some notes to myself to talk to him later. While I did this there was a silence, and I almost forgot Dr Jones was there. Then he startled me by asking, 'Have you ever met Sheikh Muhammad, Mr Maxwell?'

I shook my head. 'No, Fred, I have not. But I'm thinking that maybe I should now. Can you fix it that we go up to his Scottish place together, some time soon?'

'I might be able to arrange that,' said Dr Jones. 'He returns to the UK tonight. I will try and speak to him in the morning, and let you know.'

'Talk to my secretary on your way out and check my availability,' I said.

Dr Jones stood up and said mildly, 'Mr Maxwell, the sheikh is not a UK citizen. He is a very simple man. He will either want to see you or he will not. If he wants to see you, he will send his plane, and if you get on it, he will see you. If you do not, he will not bother any further with the matter.'

As he turned and left I said, 'Thanks for your input,

Fred,' to his retreating back, but he left without any further words.

**I:** So when did you next meet Dr Jones?

**PM:** I'll come to that. I've just remembered something else, something that happened right after Jones left my office.

I still can't believe that was how it all started. I should never have allowed myself to become involved. As soon as Jones started talking about the sheikh and faith and all of that, I should have terminated the interview, closed the file and told the boss to drop it. After all, what did it amount to at that point? A little story to keep the papers happy, a photo opportunity with a difference? I blame myself, all the way. I should have stuck to our core agenda and not been distracted. Salmon fishing in the Yemen? What does that do for hospital waiting lists or late trains or gridlocked motorways? How many Yemenis are registered to vote in our party key constituencies? Those are the questions I should have been asking myself, if I'd been doing my job.

But I didn't. Instead I sat chewing the end of my biro and I daydreamed. I thought about quiet Dr Jones saying, 'Perhaps, at one level, it isn't about fishing at all, but about faith?' What did he mean by that? What does faith really mean? I keep faith with my party and my boss. How does salmon fishing come into that? It was all rubbish. Faith is for the archbishop of Canterbury and his dwindling congregations. Faith is for the pope. Faith is for Christian Scientists. Faith is for the people stranded in the last century and the centuries before that. It doesn't belong in the modern world. We are living in a secular age. I live at the heart of the secular world. We put our faith in facts, in numbers, in statistics and in targets. The presentation of these facts and statistics is our labour, and winning votes is our purpose. I am a guardian of our purity of purpose. We are the rational managers of a modern democracy, taking the optimum decisions to safeguard and enhance the lives of busy citizens who haven't got the time to work things out for themselves.

I remember thinking there was a speech there. I took my biro out of my mouth and started to muse, thinking that later I would jot some notes down to run past the boss. And, as I mused, I had a waking dream.

**I:** You wish to record a dream as part of your evidence?

**PM:** I'm trying to tell you what happened. I'm still trying to understand it myself.

I sat at my desk and I had a waking dream, as clear as if I had been watching it on Sky News. The boss and I were standing by the side of a broad and shallow river, a river of many glistening clear streams winding around islands of gravel or tumbling over boulders. Along the fringes of the river a few green palms waved their fronds. Beyond the river, mountains of staggering savagery and beauty rose precipitously into a sky of a blue so dark, it was almost indescribable as a colour. The boss and I were in shirtsleeves and I felt the heat like a dry flame on my face and forearms. Around us were men in white or coloured robes, tall thin men with bright turbans and dark bearded faces, gesturing at the river. In my dream I heard the boss say, 'Soon the water will rise in the wadis. And then the salmon will run.'

# I2

Email correspondence between David Sugden, NCFE, and Mr Tom Price-Williams, head of fisheries, Environment Agency

From: David.Sugden@ncfe.gov.uk
Date: 1 September
To: Tom.Price-Williams@environment-agency.gov.uk
Subject: Yemen salmon

Tom
As you know the Yemen salmon project has received semi-official support from the Foreign Office and from Number 10. You may be aware one of my colleagues has scoped the project following some guidance from me. He has now asked me to explore with the Environment Agency how best to procure live salmon for the project.
Please consider this correspondence at this stage as informal and off the record, but we are preparing a request for the agency to supply us with 10,000 live Atlantic salmon, for shipment to the Yemen some time next year (dates to be agreed).
Of course it is up to the agency to say how best this might be achieved, but I would have thought – if you don't mind a suggestion from an old friend! – that you might consider netting an agreed percentage of the average salmon run from a number of the main English and Welsh rivers and

transporting them to a collection centre we would set up
for this specific purpose with specially designed holding
tanks.

That way no one river would lose a significant proportion of
its total catch, and I am sure most of the angling community
would be delighted to contribute to such an innovative and
groundbreaking project.

Of course I am contacting the Scottish Environment Protection
Agency, the Scottish river boards and the Tweed
Commissioners with a similar request. A meeting may be
necessary to decide how many salmon are harvested from
each river.

Yours ever
David


From: Tom.Price-Williams@environment-agency.gov.uk
Date: 1 September
To: David.Sugden@ncfe.gov.uk
Subject: Re: Yemen salmon

David

I cannot think of a less acceptable request than the one you
made to me in your last email. Have you any idea what an
outcry there would be within the angling community and
amongst the owners of fisheries in England and Wales, let
alone amongst my own colleagues, if you formally approached
me along the lines you suggest? King Herod, when he
suggested that the firstborn of every family in Palestine might
be killed, could be regarded as launching a charm offensive,
compared to NCFE's proposal. You can have no idea of the
depths of emotion felt by fishing clubs and anglers generally

(let alone my colleagues in Fisheries) about the salmon run in
their rivers, for which they feel a stronger attachment than
I often think they do for their own children.

My life would not be worth living if this proposal of yours
ever became public, not that I would for a minute contemplate
stripping English rivers of native salmon so that they could
be shipped to a Middle Eastern desert. You may recall that
the mandate of this agency, and my department, is to protect
the environment, and to conserve our fish stocks, not export
them. I really cannot imagine anyone here at any level
accepting such a request unless it was backed by an act of
Parliament, and even then we'd probably all resign on the
spot.

How on earth have you allowed yourself to become entangled
in this affair?

Tom


From: David.Sugden@ncfe.gov.uk
Date: 2 September
To: Tom.Price-Williams@environment-agency.gov.uk
Subject: Re: Re: Yemen salmon


Tom

I was disappointed by your reply to my last email, which I
though was a trifle flippant and even irrational, if you don't
mind me saying so. Perhaps you may have got the matter into
perspective by now. Ten thousand salmon is not that many
to sacrifice for a cause supported by the prime minister and
will do so much good for international relations. The loss of
these fish can easily be replaced by production from one of
your hatcheries.

I repeat, to ensure you get my point, *this project has the support of the prime minister*.
David


From: Tom.Price-Williams@environment-agency.gov.uk
Date: 2 September
To: David.Sugden@ncfe.gov.uk
Subject: (no subject)

David
Then the prime minister had better send a couple of regiments as well, if he wants our salmon. In either case, over my dead body.
Tom

# 13

## Extract from the diary of Dr Jones: his return to Glen Tulloch

**3 September**

When I returned to Glen Tulloch this morning it was raining. As we arrived, the sky was grey and claustrophobic. The mist was coming in, the drizzle constantly pattering against the windows. It was so dark. In the house today the lights were on all the time, even in the middle of the day. And I was still upset, since Mary had gone to Switzerland. I felt a sense of desolation I had never before known. I remembered that old song, 'Raining in My Heart'. That's how I felt today, that it was raining in my heart.

It had been arranged a few days ago that I would accompany Peter Maxwell on a visit to Glen Tulloch to meet Sheikh Muhammad, as Mr Maxwell had requested. We flew up to Inverness and were driven to Glen Tulloch to meet the sheikh, and of course the sheikh wasn't there. He had been delayed in Sana'a or missed his connection in Riyadh, or something. I spent a long time looking out of the windows as we stood around, waiting for the sheikh to return. Outside, on the soft green lawn, glistening in the fine drizzle that fell steadily from the lowering sky, stood a dozen or more Yemeni tribesmen in flowing white robes and bright emerald turbans. Each had a fifteen-foot salmon rod in his hand and, as I watched, was being drilled by the gillie, Colin McPherson, in the art of casting out a line. It looked as if they were being instructed in the double Spey. There was much laughter among the men as yards of line wound themselves in every direction around their legs and arms and necks. One man seemed in imminent danger of being strangled. Colin watched with an expression changing from dour to thunderous. Through the glass I could see him mouthing instructions, but could not hear the words. One of the Yemenis must have been translating for him. I found myself wondering how easy a task that was. What was the Arabic for 'Drag the fly across the water'?

'What are those idiots doing?' asked Peter Maxwell morosely. He was obviously unaccustomed to being kept waiting.

'Colin is trying to teach them to cast,' I said. Peter Maxwell shook his head in disbelief and walked across the room to a large round table and began flicking through the pages of *Country Life*, looking at the advertisements.

'Where do you think the sheikh is?' asked Maxwell, pushing the magazine away from him abruptly. 'How long will we be kept waiting like this?'

'I am sure he will be along shortly,' I said. 'He has probably landed at Inverness by now.'

'Doesn't he know who I am?' Peter Maxwell asked me. 'Haven't you made it clear—' There was a soft sound, the swishing of robes.

'Gentlemen, Mr Maxwell, I am sorry to have kept you. Welcome to my home.'

The sheikh was standing in the doorway. I introduced Peter Maxwell even though the sheikh quite clearly knew who he was, and then stood apart, feeling detached and miserable, while they talked.

It was raining in my heart. The trite words of the song rattled around my head and would not leave me. I felt hollow inside, all that time after Mary left for Geneva. And while I should have been thinking about the problems of the Yemen salmon project, problems so vast and complex they should have engaged every moment of my time, every last calorie and atom of energy, I was thinking about Mary.

When Mary left for Switzerland, there was a vacuum in my life.

I had always thought of myself as a sensible, stable person. When we did our annual performance appraisal forms at work, we had to write about our colleagues. I know that when my colleagues wrote about me, the first word they put down was always 'steady'. The next was 'sensible'. Sometimes I was described as 'committed'. Those words were a true picture of Dr Alfred Jones, as I once was.

I still remember the first time I met Mary. It has been in my mind often, since she went away. We were both at Oxford at the same time, towards the end of the 1970s. We met at an Oxford University Christian Society evening in our first term. It was a wine and nibbles evening, a very good way of socialising for those of us who felt we could not spare the time to go to parties every night.

I remember that I first caught sight of Mary as she stood by the door with a glass of white wine in her hand, casting an appraising glance around the room. She looked – but I can't remember how she looked. Sharp-featured, slim, intense, I suppose – much as she is now. She has not changed much over the years, physically or in any other way.

She saw me clutching a glass of soda water and she smiled and said, 'Don't you trust the wine?'

'I have an essay to finish tonight,' I replied. She looked at me with approval.

'What are you reading?' she asked.

'Marine biology. I am specialising in fisheries science. And you?'

'I'm an economist,' she said. She did not say, 'I am reading economics,' or, 'One day, I want to be an economist.' In her mind she had already become what she wanted to be. I was impressed.

'Is this your first term?' I asked.

'Yes.'

'Are you enjoying it?'

Mary sipped her wine and looked at me over the rim of the glass. I remember that look, level, challenging.

She replied, 'I don't think enjoyment is relevant. If you asked me, am I managing it, I would reply that on an allowance of forty pounds a month I am finding it difficult but not impossible. My view is that if I cannot successfully budget even on such a small sum of money as that, then really I should not be studying economics. After all, economy starts at home. And you, are you enjoying what you do? I know little about zoology. I imagine it is a very relevant and valuable subject. Do you know, in my year at college nearly every other girl is reading English literature or history. What can be the point of that?'

And so we were off. We went out to supper together that night, somewhere very economical, and Mary talked about her wish to do a thesis on the Gold Standard and I went on, I fear at great length, about the possibility that one day England's great industrial rivers would become clean again, and the salmon runs would return.

By the end of the summer term we were going out together regularly, and so it was not a major surprise when Mary suggested I take her to a May ball. It was perhaps a little unusual for Mary to depart from her normal frugality, and spend money on a new ball gown (even if it was from the second-hand shop) and having her hair done. But then, as with everything in Mary's life, it was all part of the plan.

We went with a group of friends and dined and danced together. We spent most of the evening in the marquee set up in the college quadrangle. The DJ played a song that night over and over again – 'I'm Not in Love' by 10CC.

At some point early in the morning I found that Mary and I were somehow sitting alone at a table apart from all the friends we had come with. Mary was looking at me with more intensity than usual. We had both drunk a great deal more wine than we were accustomed to and had stayed up much later than was usual for either of us. I felt that light, feverish feeling that can overtake one in such circumstances. A sense of unreality combines with the feeling that anything might be possible, sometimes with unlooked-for results. Mary reached across the table and took my hand. It wasn't the first time she had done so, and we had even kissed once or twice, but unnecessary emotional display was not something she approved of on the whole.

'Fred,' she said. 'We get on well together, don't we?'

For some reason this remark made me swallow. I remember my throat going dry. 'Yes, pretty well, I think,' I said.

'We have so much in common. We both believe in hard work. We both believe in the power of reason. We are both achievers in our different ways. You are more academic; I am more ambitious in a worldly way. I want to go into the City, and you want to become a professional scientist. We both want many of the same things from life. Together we make a great team. Don't you think that's true?'

I began to see where this might be going, the feeling of

unreality I had sensed earlier grew stronger, and I spoke and felt and thought as if I were in a dream.

'Yes, I suppose it is, Mary.'

She squeezed my hand.

'I could imagine spending my life with you.'

I didn't know what to say, but she said it for me. 'If you asked me to marry you ...'

The DJ was playing 'I'm Not in Love' again, and I wondered what those words meant. The truth is, I didn't know about love just as I didn't know about fear of death or space travel. It was something I hadn't encountered or, having encountered it, had not known it for what it was. Did that mean I wasn't in love, or did it mean I was in love, but didn't know? I remember feeling as if I stood at the edge of a great cliff, tottering towards the precipice.

I knew I had to say something, and then I felt Mary's foot press against mine, hinting of other possibilities, so I said, 'Mary, will you marry me?'

She flung her arms around me and said, 'Yes, what a good idea!'

There was a burst of cheering from some of our friends at the nearby tables, who had either worked out, or had been forewarned of, what had just happened.

Of course ours was a sensible engagement. We agreed that we could not get married until we had both graduated and were in employment and our combined salaries had reached more than £8000 a year. Mary had calculated (as it turned out, accurately) that this would be enough to pay the rent on a small flat somewhere on the outskirts of London, plus an allowance for travel, a week's holiday a year, and so on. Long before Microsoft Excel Mary had intuitive software in her brain that allowed her to see the world in numbers. She was my guardian and my guide.

We were married in her college chapel a little more than a year after graduation.

Ours was a stable marriage for many years, at least on the surface. We had no children because Mary felt, and I have never disagreed with her, that we needed to invest in our careers first, and only when these had achieved a certain momentum, in our family. But time has marched on, and we still have no children.

She rose effortlessly through the pay grades in her bank; for Mary, there was never a glass ceiling. I made my reputation as a fisheries scientist and although as the years went by I fell far behind Mary in my earning power, I knew she respected me for my integrity and growing reputation as a scientist.

And then, as slowly as the light fades on a calm winter evening, something went out of our relationship. I say that selfishly. Perhaps I started to look for something which had never been there in the first place: passion, romance. I daresay that as I entered my forties I had a sense that somehow life was going past me. I had hardly experienced those emotions which for me have mostly come from reading books or watching television. I suppose that if there was anything unsatisfactory in our marriage, it was in my perception of it – the reality was unchanged. Perhaps I grew up from childhood to manhood too quickly. One minute I was cutting up frogs in the science lab at school, the next I was working for the National Centre for Fisheries Excellence and counting freshwater mussel populations on riverbeds. Somewhere in between, something had passed me by: adolescence, perhaps? Something immature, foolish yet intensely emotive, like those favourite songs I had recalled dimly as if being played on a distant radio, almost too far away to make out the words. I had doubts, yearnings, but I did not know why or what for.

Whenever I tried to analyse our lives, and talk about it with Mary, she would say, 'Darling, you are on the way to becoming one of the leading authorities in the world on caddis fly larvae. Don't allow anything to deflect you from that. You may be rather inadequately paid, certainly compared with me you are, but excellence in any field is an achievement beyond value.'

I don't know when we started drifting apart.

When I told Mary about the project − I mean about researching the possibility of a salmon fishery in the Yemen − something changed. If there was a defining moment in our marriage, then that was it. It was ironical, in a sense. For the first time in my life I was doing something which might bring me international recognition and certainly would make me considerably better off − I could live for years off the lecture circuit alone, if the project was even half successful.

Mary didn't like it. I don't know what part she didn't like: the fact I might become more famous than her, the fact I might even become better paid than her. That makes her sound carping. I think what she really thought was that I was about to make the most gigantic fool of myself: to become linked forever with a project derided by the scientific community as fraudulent and unsound, to be marked forever as a failure who had been turned from the path of virtue by the lure of unlimited budgets, to appear on her personnel record as a black mark. 'Mary Jones is a sound enough colleague. It is unfortunate that her husband turns out to be a publicity-seeking scientific charlatan. That could have negative public relations implications for the bank. Perhaps we'd better pass her over this time.'

Yes, that's why I have to write about Mary. When they pushed me into working for the sheikh, they pushed me out of the far side of my marriage. She saw an opportunity in Geneva and, with characteristic ruthlessness, she took it. Or perhaps that had been the plan all along, and she decided that the moment had come to do something about it.

And I could like it, or lump it.

And yet I write as if I did not love her. I must have loved her, because when she went I felt so empty.

Our marriage is not over, it has just become an email marriage. We communicate regularly. She has not asked for a divorce, or suggested we sell the flat or anything like that. There she is in Geneva, and here I am in London, and we have no plans to meet in the near future. I feel as I write this that my life has no meaning now. And if it has no meaning then perhaps everything over the last forty-odd years has been a waste of time. As I write this entry in my diary, I myself feel like a diary which has been left out in the rain, from which the moisture has washed away the cramped inky writing, the record of thousands of days and nights, leaving only a blank and sodden page.

# 14

## Interview with Dr Alfred Jones: his meeting with Mr Peter Maxwell and Sheikh Muhammad

**Interrogator:** Describe the circumstances of Mr Peter Maxwell's interview with Sheikh Muhammad.

**Dr Alfred Jones:** It wasn't so much an interview. This is what I'd call an interview, with all these endless questions you chaps want to ask. I don't know what good it will all do.

**I:** Of course we'd like to conduct these interviews in a friendly and cooperative way, Dr Jones. But we can do this all quite differently, you know.

**AJ:** Well, I didn't say I wouldn't cooperate, but let me tell you about it in my own way. It was quite a long time ago now, you know. I can't always remember every little detail.

**I:** You tell it any way you want to. But miss nothing out.

**AJ:** I'll do my best. As far as I remember, after the sheikh arrived he and Peter Maxwell had a private conversation. I wasn't included. This was political stuff, I imagine, and I was simply a humble fisheries scientist. I was left to myself for an hour or two. As far as I remember, I went up to my room and wrote up my diary, which you have already helped yourself to. I can't remember exactly what I wrote but I know I was feeling fairly depressed. It was a gloomy day and I was feeling wretched. My wife hadn't exactly walked out on me, but it felt as if she had.

Even Harriet wasn't considered important enough to be included in that part of the proceedings, although she was around. She was up at Glen Tulloch before Maxwell and I got there.

I: Harriet? You are referring to Ms Chetwode-Talbot?

AJ: Of course. Then we were called into the sheikh's office and I was given to understand that I was expected to make a formal report to the sheikh on the progress of the Yemen salmon project to date. I wasn't looking forward to it. A few days before, I'd received some email correspondence from my boss David Sugden which indicated a fundamental obstacle. David had told me he would manage the supply side of the project, that is, the supply of live Atlantic salmon. Of course, as usual, he hadn't a clue what he was talking about. He had no idea where we were going to get the salmon from at all.

I: So you went into the sheikh's office? Who was present at this meeting?'

AJ: Yes, we went into the sheikh's office and sat down around a long mahogany table. It was more like a dining-room table than an office table, and the only thing at all office-like in the room was a large desk with a plasma screen on it in one corner of the room. Malcolm the butler served us all with tea in china cups and then withdrew, and the sheikh gestured to me to start talking. So I did my best to bring him up to date. Peter Maxwell told us he was there as an 'observer'. He had apparently already told the sheikh of the prime minister's support and enthusiasm for the project, but he repeated this for the benefit of Harriet and me, and the sheikh murmured some word of thanks. Then Maxwell sat back in his chair looking bored and impatient while I made my report.

'The pods for the transport of the salmon have been designed and tested. We are using Husskinnen, a Finnish environmental engineering specialist, to do the feasibility and test work. Broadly speaking, we are comfortable with our estimates on cost and we believe the salmon will survive the journey without undue stress from vibration or noise, as the design insulates the pod from the aircraft itself.'

I ticked an item on my list and looked around for questions. Apart from the sheikh, Harriet Chetwode-Talbot and Peter Maxwell were the only other people in the room, as Malcolm had left by then. Nobody said anything.

'We have analysed the water samples sent to us from the Wadi Aleyn and from the aquifers. Of course I need to take a team out there on a field trip to get a proper idea of conditions and the challenges we will face, but the initial samples suggest no factors, other than extreme heat and lack of dissolved oxygen, which might pose a threat to salmon.'

Peter Maxwell took out his Blackberry and started scrolling through his emails.

'The design of the holding pens is now in its fifth revision, Sheikh, and I regret to say that our original estimates on cost look a bit optimistic. There is a probable overrun of 20 per cent on our original budget for this phase. The engineering firm Arup is in charge of this part of the project.

'Broadly speaking, we envisage a series of concrete basins adjacent to the wadi. These will fill from rainwater, and the water levels will be maintained by additional water pumped from the aquifer. The basins will be partly covered by an aluminium mesh canopy, which will allow some sunlight through but reflect most of the heat, and this should help keep the water temperature within a manageable range. In addition, we will have heat exchangers along the walls of the basin to help take out excess heat. We have to ensure a balance between keeping the salmon comfortable and ensuring the temperature gradient when they finally enter the wadi is not too steep. We will have bubblers around the walls of the basin to ensure there is enough dissolved oxygen in the water to keep the fish alive. Interestingly, both Air Products and BOC have bid for the oxygenation equipment on a below-cost basis, as they want the publicity. We will need planning permission to install these basins and I presume we will also need an environmental impact assessment carried out.'

With a slight gesture of his hand, the sheikh indicated the absurdity and irrelevance of an environmental impact assessment. Then I reached the part of the project that concerned me most. It was a real snag. We couldn't get hold of any salmon. I think I already told you that David's confidence he could deliver on this part of the project had been misplaced.

I: We have seen the relevant email correspondence.

AJ: Then you'll know how David managed to upset in a very short time most of the people who could have helped us. We had been in talks with the Environment Agency and the Scottish Environment Protection Agency, and we couldn't find a single river in England, Wales or Scotland prepared to allow us to take away any of their salmon. I remember Tom Price-Williams, the man I spoke to at the Environment Agency, turning pale when I suggested it at one of the meetings David sent me to . . . to try and smooth things over after he'd already made a complete hash of things.

'Take salmon out of their rivers and send them to Saudi Arabia?' said Tom. 'You don't know the fishing community. They'd sooner sell their children into slavery.'

'It's the Yemen, actually,' I told him.

'They'd be up in arms,' he said. 'They care more about those fish than anything. I wouldn't rule out guerrilla warfare if we attempted any such thing.'

I described all this to the sheikh. Peter Maxwell looked up from his Blackberry and the sheikh frowned. Harriet already knew, as I had told her about it on the plane. There was more bad news. Even if the Environment Agency or the Scottish Environment Protection Agency let us take some salmon parr from some of the more abundant rivers, there was another fundamental snag.

Those salmon parr will have never been out to sea, and if we grow them to smolts, their instincts will urge them to head for saltwater, where all salmon spend two to three winters before returning to their home river to spawn. So we might spend millions on rearing salmon from juvenile fish and sending them out to the Yemen, and find that when we release them into the wadi, instead of turning upstream they might, as it were, turn left for the Indian Ocean and vanish for ever. This would ruin the whole project.

I said, 'So the next thing was, we discussed with the environment agencies the prospect of trapping returning salmon which have grown up in the Tyne or the Tweed or the Spey, have matured and have come back to their rivers to spawn. The agencies absolutely refused to contemplate this. Firstly, to trap mature salmon and then export them to the Middle East would be in breach of the agencies' statutory duty to protect their fisheries. It would require an act of Parliament to amend their mandates in order for them to do this. And, as Tom told me, there would probably be a popular uprising.'

'Let's not go there,' said Peter Maxwell. He was now following the discussion, and the words 'act of Parliament' had him sitting bolt upright, his ears twitching like a hare's. 'That's not an option.'

'I'm sure not,' I agreed, 'and in any case, the agencies wouldn't apply for one. The other problem the agencies would encounter if this course of action was suggested is open warfare from the angling community. Not a fisherman in the country would allow a single returning salmon he is hoping to fish for to be extracted from the river before he has had a chance to try for it, and then be shipped to the Yemen. It simply couldn't happen.'

'And,' said Peter Maxwell, 'the whole point of this project, as far as the government is concerned, is to win goodwill in the Middle East. I'll be perfectly frank about that, Sheikh Muhammad. And that only works if, while we are doing that, we don't create a corresponding or greater amount of ill will at home. Ill will among voters. So, the bottom line is, we need another solution or else we need to scrap the project.'

There was a silence around the table. Harriet looked at the papers on her desk and said nothing. Peter Maxwell looked from face to face as if daring anyone to challenge him.

'Mr Maxwell,' said the sheikh mildly, 'of course this project will continue, and of course it will succeed. I have great confidence in Dr Alfred. If he comes to me with a problem, I know that he will already have found the solution to that problem. Is that not so, Dr Alfred?'

'Oh, yes,' I said. 'I have a solution. But I'm not sure if you will like it.'

**I:** And what was that solution?

**AJ:** I'll get to it. After the meeting we went upstairs and bathed and changed, and then came down for dinner.

**I:** Did Peter Maxwell say anything further that you can recall over dinner?

**AJ:** I don't think anybody spoke a great deal that evening. Dinner was a formal, silent occasion. Malcolm waited on us, treading soft-footed behind our chairs and serving us with what I remembered from my last visit to Glen Tulloch: the most delicious food accompanied by the best wines. For me, it might have been ashes on my plate, vinegar in my glass. I pushed the food around and sipped at my wine without tasting it. Even Peter Maxwell didn't have much to say, after one or two unsuccessful attempts to draw the sheikh on the subject of his feelings of friendship towards the UK.

I saw Harriet glance at me once or twice, and I realised my expression must be giving away something about how miserable I felt. I have never been very good at hiding my feelings. For a while there was no sound except the clink of cutlery. The sheikh never minded whether one spoke or not; he did not feel the need to entertain, or to be entertained. The sort of social conversation we need, like we need air to breathe, was foreign to him. There were things to be discussed or there were not. There were stories to be told or there were not.

Peter Maxwell couldn't stand it. I could see he liked being the centre of attention, and one or two further conversational gambits, this time mostly directed at Harriet, had gone nowhere.

Finally he said, 'Sheikh, as you know, the prime minister is a passionate fisherman. That is to say, he would be, if he ever got the free time.'

The sheikh smiled and said, 'I am sorry he has not the time. It must be very sad to love something so much and never do it.'

'Well, the prime minister is a very busy man. I'm sure you understand. But, if you get the salmon project to work, he'd really love the chance to come and see it in action.'

'Your prime minister is most welcome, if he ever finds some free time,' said the sheikh.

'What I really mean is,' said Peter Maxwell, 'that an official invitation from you some time nearer the launch date would be looked on very favourably by Number 10.'

'Who is this Number 10?' asked the sheikh, pretending to look puzzled.

'I mean by the prime minister's office.'

'Of course, the prime minister is most welcome then or at any time. He has only to say, and we will receive him in our modest home and he can join with us and enjoy his passion for fishing for as much time as his busy life will permit him to stay. You, too, are most welcome, Mr Maxwell. Are you also a passionate fisherman?'

'I don't know how,' said Mr Maxwell. 'Never had the time to try. I'd like to come, though. May I take it that we have your invitation to attend the opening of the Yemen salmon project, whenever that might be?'

'Of course, of course,' said the sheikh. 'We would be greatly honoured.'

'And, Sheikh,' said Peter Maxwell, 'of course I don't know how long Jay can stay until we can look at dates with you, but I presume if I give you some dates he currently has free, we could work the project launch timetable around that?'

'Dr Alfred and Ms Harriet Chetwode-Talbot are the guardians of the project, Mr Maxwell, and you must speak with them about dates and arrangements of that kind.'

Peter Maxwell looked at me and said, 'You'll keep me in the loop, Fred.' It was an order, not a question. Then he turned back to the sheikh and said, 'One last thing, Sheikh. Jay – the prime minister, I mean – thinks it would be a great idea for the project if he could be photographed beside you with a rod in his hand. Maybe we could organise for him to catch a salmon, or something, while he's there. We sort of imagine that if he can fly into Sana'a, catch a helicopter down to the site, maybe spend twenty minutes meeting the project team and getting a few handshake photos, maybe present some sort of award, then twenty minutes with you guys – I mean you, Sheikh, and some of those people we saw out on the lawn earlier today – all with fishing rods. We could get some more group photos. It would be great if everyone was wearing full tribal dress with those dagger things. Maybe Jay could do a quick change into some sort of kit, you know, like he was an honorary tribesman ...'

I felt myself blushing on behalf of Peter Maxwell but the sheikh only smiled and nodded. 'And will the prime minister be able to spare twenty minutes to catch a salmon with me?'

'We'll have to work up a schedule but, yes, we need a good photo of Jay catching a salmon. Maybe the first salmon ever caught in the Arabian peninsula. That would be great publicity for the project. Of course, we'd let you use the photos in all your marketing literature.'

'Sometimes it takes a little longer to catch a fish,' said the sheikh. 'Even here, in Glen Tulloch, where we have many salmon, it may take hours or days before one is caught.'

'I'll leave that to Fred,' said Peter Maxwell. 'He's the salmon expert. But, Fred, the prime minister is going to expect to hook a fish. I don't much care how you do it, but you need to make sure that happens.'

I just stared at him, but the sheikh spoke before I could say what I felt like telling Peter Maxwell to go and do. 'I am sure Dr Alfred will find a way of keeping your prime minister happy. If he is a passionate fisherman, as you say, then he will be happy whatever happens, and it will give me great pleasure to greet him in the Wadi Aleyn and to welcome him as our guest, and to fish with him on our new river. Perhaps Dr Alfred can find him a fish. It will be as God wills.'

'Great,' said Peter Maxwell. 'We think this project is an excellent idea, Sheikh, very imaginative and innovative, and the prime minister is delighted you are using British engineers and scientists to achieve your goals. We very much want to be a part of it, so that the Yemen nation can understand that we British are a sympathetic ally, pro-democracy and pro-fishing, ready to share our technology to help aspiring Yemeni anglers fulfil their dreams.'

He looked around the table as if he had made a speech, to see what effect it had had on us. I suppose it was a sort of speech. The sheikh nodded and said, 'I am not a political man, Mr Maxwell, just someone who wants to share the joy of salmon fishing with a few of my tribe, and show them what can be done if there is faith enough.'

'With your faith and our technology, we will have salmon leaping all over the place,' said Peter Maxwell, 'and you can expect a lot of high-rolling, big-spending tourists coming in to benefit from the Yemen salmon experience, I am sure. It will repay your investment many times. Now, if you'll excuse me, I have a few emails I need to deal with before I go to bed.' And he picked up his Blackberry and went upstairs.

'I do not think Mr Maxwell quite understands us yet,' said the sheikh when Peter Maxwell had left the room. 'But perhaps, one day, God will reveal himself to him and help him understand.'

The three of us sat together for a while longer, the candles on the dining-room table burning low. Being with Sheikh Muhammad had a calming effect on me, especially now we were without the abrasive presence of Peter Maxwell. For a while no one spoke.

I wondered if the sheikh would say something more about Peter Maxwell, for although he had shown not the least sign of it, I was sure he disliked him. Instead he surprised me by turning his eyes upon me and saying, 'You seem sad, Dr Alfred.'

I did not know what to say. I flushed again and was thankful that in the candlelight the change in my colour was probably not obvious. I saw Harriet look from the sheikh to me, intently.

'Oh ... nothing. A few problems at home, that's all,' I said.

'You have illness in your home?'

'No, it's nothing like that.'

'Then do not tell me, for it is not my affair. But I regret to see your sadness, Dr Alfred. I would rather see you with an untroubled spirit and with your whole heart and mind bent upon our project. You need to learn to have faith, Dr Alfred. We believe that faith is the cure that heals all troubles. Without faith there is no hope and no love. Faith comes before hope, and before love.'

'I'm not very religious, I'm afraid,' I said.

'You cannot know,' said the sheikh. 'You have not looked inside yourself, and you have never asked yourself the question. One day, perhaps, something will happen that will cause you to ask yourself that question. I think you will be surprised at the answer that comes back.'

He smiled, as if he realised the conversation was getting a little deep for the time of night, and then made a gesture with his hand. Malcolm materialised from nowhere, startling me, for I was absorbed in what the sheikh was saying, without understanding him. The butler must have been standing in the shadows of the dining room, watching, perhaps listening. He pulled back the chair as the sheikh stood up. Harriet and I both got up at the same time.

'Good night,' said the sheikh. 'May your sleep bring you peace of mind.' Then he was gone.

Harriet and I walked slowly up the staircase together without speaking. On the landing, she turned to me and said, 'Fred, if ever there's anything you want to talk about ... talk to me. I can see things are not right with you. I hope you can count me as a friend. I don't want you to be unhappy either.' She leaned forward and kissed me on the cheek and I smelled her warm perfume. Her hand brushed mine for a moment. Then she turned away.

'Thanks,' I said to her, as she walked down the corridor to her room. I don't know if she heard me.

I thought for a while about my life as I undressed in my bedroom. It was warm, and a fire still burned low in the grate. I hung my borrowed evening clothes in the wardrobe and changed into my borrowed pyjamas and, having brushed my teeth, climbed between the white linen sheets of the enormous, soft bed.

What a strange evening it had been.

I remember thinking as I lay in bed that everything about my life is strange now. I am sailing in uncharted waters and my old life is a distant shore, still visible through the haze of retrospection, but receding to a grey line on the horizon. What lies ahead, I do not know. What had the sheikh said? I could feel sleep coming upon me fast, and the words that came into my mind, my last waking thought, were his but also seemed to come from somewhere else: '*Faith comes before hope, and before love.*'

I slept better that night than I had done for a long time.

I: Describe how you found the salmon?

AJ: It is not my happiest memory. The chartered helicopter came to pick us up after breakfast the next morning and the sheikh, Harriet, Peter Maxwell and I climbed in and buckled our straps. The blades started turning and then, in a moment, the grey roofs and soft green lawns of Glen Tulloch were slipping sideways below us. We flew amongst the scurrying rain clouds and over the brown moors beyond the house, which sloped gradually upwards to become craggy mountains.

Then the helicopter found a line of lochs heading southwest. I think it must have been the Great Glen. Low clouds brushed against the helicopter and obscured the view from time to time until suddenly the sky cleared and it seemed as if we were flying straight into a brilliant sun. Below us now, sheets of water alternated with the spongy greens and browns of headlands, and I saw we were losing height and approaching the shore of a sea loch. I glimpsed the structures I expected to see below us.

We landed in an empty car park next to some Porta-kabins. Beyond them was a jetty with a couple of boats tied up, and beyond that, metal structures in the loch glinted in the sunlight. As the rotors stopped spinning, a door in one of the Portakabins opened, and two figures in oilskins and hard hats came out to greet us.

When we were on the ground the first of them shouted above the engine noise, 'Dr Jones? Dr Alfred Jones?'

The pilot cut the engines and I said, 'That's me. Archie Campbell?'

'Aye, that's me. Welcome to McSalmon Aqua Farms, Dr Jones.'

I presented Peter Maxwell and Harriet and the sheikh to him. The sheikh was wearing a beret and a military-looking pullover with epaulettes, and khaki drill trousers. Harriet and I were in waxed jackets and jeans. Peter Maxwell was wearing a white trench coat over his suit and looked, I thought, like a private detective from a bad film.

Archie Campbell gestured behind him to the cages moored in the loch.

'You want a tour?'

'That was rather the idea.'

We went into the Portakabin and were handed cups of hot Nescafé. Then Archie Campbell said, 'Well, now. Let me tell you what we do here. We raise the finest, freshest salmon that money can buy. Don't believe what they tell you. There's nothing wrong with farmed salmon. And at least you know where they've been, not like the wild ones which could have swum through anything!'

He roared with laughter to show it was a joke. On the wall of the cabin was a laminated chart showing the different stages of rearing farmed salmon: the freshwater hatchery where the broodstock was reared to become alevins, then fry; the cages where the salmon parr were released and grown to smolts; the big cages further out in the saltwater of the loch where the smolts were ranched to become mature salmon. Archie led us through all this and then, when it was obvious we hàd had enough, suggested a tour by boat.

There was a converted fishing boat tied up to a jetty; we climbed in and slowly chugged out into the middle of the loch. Now that we were close we could see the metal structures were a series of booms which formed the tops of deep cages moored to the bed of the loch. The water inside these booms was frantic with movement, boiling with the desperate churning of tens of thousands of fish which all wanted to be somewhere else. Every few seconds a fish would leap out of the water as if it was attempting to escape or climb some fish ladder or run up some waterfall that its instincts or its race memory told it should be there. I could hardly bear to look. Here was a creature whose most profound instincts urged it to swim downriver until it could smell the saltwater of the ocean and then find the feeding grounds of its ancestors in the far north of the Atlantic, where it would live for the next two or three years. And then, by an even greater miracle, it would return south, travelling past the mouths of all of the rivers where it might have been born until something made it turn north again, searching the coastal waters until it smelt or sensed in some other way the river waters that led to the place where it had been spawned. But these salmon spent their whole lives in a cage a few metres deep and a few metres wide. 'Look at the little darlings,' said Archie Campbell fondly. 'Look at all the exercise they get. Don't tell me they aren't every bit as fit as wild salmon.'

The water around the cages was cloudy with effluent, debris of all sorts floating past. The sheikh looked around him with growing dismay. Then he turned to me and said, 'This is the only way? The only way?'

'Yes,' I told him. 'The only way.'

'And how many was it you will be wanting, Dr Jones?' asked Archie Campbell.

'We're still working on numbers. Think along the lines of five thousand, if you can.'

'It's a big order. We'll need notice.'

'I know,' I said.

On the flight back to Glen Tulloch the sheikh said nothing for a while. I knew this was not what he had envisaged. He had imagined silver fish which had run home from the storm-tossed waters of the North Atlantic, fresh as paint, surging miraculously up the waters of the Wadi Aleyn. He had not imagined these sea lice-infested creatures, born and raised in the equivalent of a gigantic prison.

But that was what we were going to have to use; there was no other solution. Eventually, the sheikh smiled a bitter smile, turned to Peter Maxwell and said, 'You see, Mr Maxwell, how our project answers to the wishes of your government? How well it matches your policies? We will liberate these salmon from captivity. We will give them freedom. And we will give them a choice. We will release them into the waters of the wadi, and they can vote to turn one way to the sea, or the other way to the mountains. I think that is very democratic, is it not?'

Peter Maxwell, I remember, chewed his lip and said nothing.

# 15

## Peter Maxwell is interviewed for the 'Time Off' column of the *Sunday Telegraph*, 4 September

*An occasional series of articles in the* Sunday Telegraph Magazine *in which Boris Johnson interviews well-known public figures to find out what they do in their spare time. This week, it's Peter Maxwell, the director of communications at the prime minister's office in Downing Street.*

**Boris Johnson:** Peter, you're going to tell me that you never do take any time off, aren't you?

**Peter Maxwell:** Boris, you are absolutely right. I almost never do. That's the trouble with my job. You've got to be available 24/7 because things around the world happen 24/7 and they need dealing with 24/7. Whether I'm in my office or travelling, I've got to be connected. I'm watching live feed from at least three news channels most of the day, and picking up maybe a couple of hundred emails on my Blackberry. Then there's the meetings. You wouldn't believe how many meetings I have to go to. That's just a normal working week, Boris, and my working week doesn't end until Sunday night and usually starts again on Monday morning. But it's when the unexpected happens, as it constantly does, that the pressure really comes on.

**BJ:** You mean, 'Events, dear boy, events?'

**PM:** I'm not with you there, Boris.

**BJ:** Harold Macmillan once said that.

**PM:** Then Harold knew what he was talking about.

**BJ:** But just suppose you had a few days or even a few hours to spare, what would you do with them? What about holidays?

**PM:** It's a long time since I had a proper holiday, Boris. My colleagues are always suggesting it, but I don't think any of them have the faintest idea of what would happen if I wasn't there to look after their interests. I did go to Ibiza, once, for a weekend, and I suppose I'd like to go back there again if ever I had the time.

**BJ:** And what about time off for a bit of exercise?

**PM:** Well, as you probably know, I'm a bit of a fitness freak so if I can take a few hours off, often it's all about physical exercise. I think it's well known I'm a keen salsa dancer. It's probably less well known I got into the Islington area finals two or three years back. I'm not saying I'm any good at it, but I suppose I can't be doing everything wrong, to nearly win the North London Salsa Cup.

**BJ:** Any other sports or recreational activities of that sort which appeal to you?

**PM:** I suppose the boss and I play tennis a bit ...

**BJ:** The boss being the prime minister, I suppose?

**PM:** Exactly.

**BJ:** And who wins?

**PM:** Well, Boris, I think my job might be at risk if I told you that! Seriously though, it's pretty even between us, which is great. I think when you have a fairly intense desk job – on the phone or watching the screen all the time – anything that gets you outside and takes your mind away from the daily pressures and stresses has to be good.

**BJ:** *Mens sana in corpora sano* – all that sort of thing, you mean?

**PM:** I'm not following you there again, Boris.

**BJ:** Any other interests outside work you can tell us about, Peter, apart from sports?

**PM:** I like music a lot. Of course I like salsa music, that goes without saying. But I also like the classics. The 'Ride of the Valkyries' is one of my absolute favourites. I think it is a fabulous piece, so evocative.

**BJ:** What exactly does it evoke for you?

**PM:** It always makes me think of that wonderful scene in *Apocalypse Now* when they play it from loudspeakers on the helicopter gunships while they napalm a Cong village. A really moving bit of cinema history, and the music to go with it.

**BJ:** We've moved on a bit from those days, Peter, haven't we? I mean, napalming insurgent villages isn't anything we would do nowadays, is it?

**PM:** Are we straying from the subject here, Boris?

**BJ:** Possibly. What about reading? Do you have any favourites?

**PM:** *Hansard*.

**BJ:** But what about works of fiction? Novels and so on?

**PM:** I don't really get a big kick out of novels. I admire people who can organise their lives so well they have the time to curl up in a chair and read a few pages of a novel. Personally, I don't have the time. I've kind of got a restless mind, Boris, and reading a novel has always seemed to me to be a terrible waste of my waking hours.

**BJ:** But there's a rumour, Peter, which must have reached your ears, that you yourself are writing a book ...

**PM:** Well, political biography is something I do read when I get the time. As for writing a book about myself and my own time in politics, I suppose at some point in the future when I'm less busy than I am now, it might be interesting to look back and reflect on things that happened during my watch. I've had a very interesting position for the last few years, in the eye of the storm, Boris, and I've seen and heard a lot. There's certainly material there for a book if I ever I had the time to write one. But it wouldn't be about me, Boris, because I'm a very private and quiet man. I would be more likely to write about some of the events I've witnessed.

BJ: Well, let's hope you do write that book one day, Peter. I, for one, would certainly queue up in a bookshop to buy a copy. But have you any other thoughts about things you would like to do in the future? If the pressure ever eased up for a bit, is there anything you've never done that you would like to try – sort of unfulfilled ambitions for your spare time?

PM: Chance would be a fine thing, Boris. However, it's funny you should ask me that because, yes, there is something I've never done before that I would like to do. It's no secret that I have been acting in a kind of informal liaison role for the boss with respect to the Yemen salmon project, and while I've been doing that, I've come to feel I might like to try salmon fishing. You know, it's a rather wonderful sport. I visited a place very recently where there were literally thousands of salmon leaping about, and they are the most wonderful creatures to watch. They can – I don't know if you knew this, Boris – jump several feet out of the water into the air. It's quite something to see, and if you've never seen a salmon leaping, let me know and I'll put you in touch with this particular place.

148

**BJ:** Thank you, that would be a very interesting experience. Have you any immediate plans to fish for salmon, then?

**PM:** Well, we've arranged for a few to be put into an old gravel pit filled up with water near Chequers, so that the boss can practise his casting. He's keen on the idea, too. And if we get the hang of salmon fishing, as I'm sure we both will, I'm hoping Sheikh Muhammad ibn Zaidi will ask us both to come and fish with him some time soon in the Yemen. Wouldn't that be great? You ought to come, Boris!

**BJ:** I can't wait. I hope they ask me. Until then, Peter, thanks for talking to me.

# 16

## Interview with Ms Harriet Chetwode-Talbot

**Interrogator:** Describe your first meeting with Mr Peter Maxwell.

**Harriet Chetwode-Talbot:** Yes, I remember that visit to Glen Tulloch with Fred and Peter Maxwell. It was horrendous.

Peter Maxwell – is this being recorded? Well, I don't care – is the most ghastly little man. How people like that get into such positions of power is quite beyond me. Did you read that appalling interview in the *Sunday Telegraph* he gave when he returned to London from Glen Tulloch?

**I:** It will be included in the evidence. Please describe your first meeting with Peter Maxwell.

**HCT:** He didn't exactly make a favourable first impression. He can't be five foot six. He wears suits that are years too young for him, nipped in the waist, shoulder padding, scarlet silk lining peeking out everywhere, which obviously cost a fortune in tailor's bills. Candy-striped shirts with huge cufflinks. And the ties! And *what* is that stuff he puts on his hair! It reeks!

Sorry, I had to get that off my chest.

It was funny, though, to see him mincing across the wet lawns at Glen Tulloch in his Gucci loafers. The sheikh made him do it. He had to go outside in the rain and inspect the sheikh's honour guard, or whatever they are.

Two dozen tall Yemeni tribesmen – skinny, hawk-nosed, fierce-eyed men who look as if they would kill you for the price of a goat. Or less. And Peter Maxwell had to walk past and pretend to inspect them while they stood to attention in their *thobe*s, their long warm wraparound robes, with jackets over them, clutching their curved daggers in one hand and their fishing rods in the other. If only I had remembered to bring my digital camera. Couldn't I have sold *that* photo to the *Sun*!

His loafers were wet through. Ruined.

I remember wondering if the sheikh might not have rather a well-developed sense of fun. He never appeared to make jokes. But I wonder.

We had the stickiest evening imaginable. Fred was down in the dumps. The sheikh told me before we came up on the plane that Fred's wife had left him. Or not left him, exactly, but decided to go and work in Geneva. It sounded like much the same thing. I don't know how the sheikh knew. But he always seemed to know everything.

Poor Fred. Poor me, come to that. I hadn't heard from Robert, my fiancé, for weeks. His letters stopped coming and then mine started being returned unopened, with the message that it had not been possible to forward them. So I was lonely and miserable and worrying to death about what might be happening to Robert. You can understand why.

Oh, God.

*The witness became emotionally disturbed for a brief period. The interview resumed an hour later.*

I: Please continue, Ms Chetwode-Talbot.
HCT: I was very stressed out by the project. It had become

too big. I was seconded full-time by my firm to support it. There was an immense amount to do. Fred did a good job, don't get me wrong. The science and the engineering studies and proposals that he produced, or had produced for him, were brilliant. No one will ever know the amount of work that man put in. But at the end of the day Fred was a scientist, not an administrator. So I was spending twelve hours a day talking to contractors, talking to auditors, running a project team, talking to bankers, talking to Peter Maxwell's office, talking to Fred's boss to keep him off Fred's back, writing reports, writing letters, writing spreadsheets for my partners, who were hypnotised by the fees rolling in. Then at seven o'clock at night I'd get off the phone and start dealing with the hundred or so emails that had come in.

Some of them were from other teams working on the project, but some were from fishing-rod manufacturers, and wader manufacturers, and fishing-wear manufacturers wanting us to use their products. Some were from people wanting work as consultants: retired oilmen from Saudi who knew a thing or two about wadis, indigent fisheries experts wanting to advise us on the science, an expert in ancient Arabian irrigation systems who believed that our project had been forecast and described in hieroglyphs on the interior walls of the Great Pyramid. I was emailed by people wanting to buy a week's fishing on the Wadi Aleyn, people wanting to ask the sheikh to speak at their next fly-fishing or angling association dinner, people wanting a timeshare in a villa in the Yemen. I received daily and hourly requests for donations from the Retired Drift Netsmen's Association, the Retired Gillies Association, the North Atlantic Salmon Foundation, the Atlantic Salmon Trust, the Rivers Trusts – from just about everyone you could imagine except for Oxfam.

Come to think of it, I think Oxfam asked for money too. Why not? We were spending it like water, to coin a phrase.

The project had taken over every moment of my waking life. I was exhausted, and anxious about whether we would succeed. I was worried about what would happen to my job when it was all over; I had completely lost track of the rest of the business and someone else had been given all my other files. I had one client and one only: the sheikh. It was only his calm certainty that kept me sane.

It wasn't surprising that Fred and I were such poor company that evening. Fred's workload was as enormous as mine, and as far as I knew he wasn't getting paid any extra for it. He was on secondment from NCFE, still drawing the same miserable salary. At least I would bank my partner's share of the profits. And Fred was more exposed than I was. If the project failed, his reputation would die with it; there would always be plenty of people to point out where he had gone wrong. If it succeeded, I didn't know what would happen. For all I knew he might be created a life peer. Or made a freeman of the city of Sana'a.

I: Can you focus your remarks on what was actually said that evening?

HCT: I've got off the point, haven't I? Yes, that was a dreadful evening. Peter Maxwell was either pompous or provocative. I don't know which I found the most awful. He dominated the conversation, such as it was, and kept trying to goad the sheikh into saying things about the Middle East. He wanted the sheikh to say something

153

unmeasured, incautious. Then Peter would have something on him. He wouldn't use it. He'd file it and keep it as ammunition for some other day.

Then he started making patronising remarks about how the prime minister wanted this photo opportunity and that photo opportunity. He actually turned to Fred at one point in the evening and told him to make sure the prime minister caught a fish, and to bear in mind he would only allow twenty minutes in his schedule to do so. I think he imagined that salmon could be driven to the fishermen, like grouse over guns.

Of course the sheikh took no notice of him. He was endlessly polite, and also managed to deflect Fred from saying something he might have regretted afterwards. I could almost see steam coming out of Fred's nostrils at one point in the evening. The sheikh is a very subtle, intelligent man. He won't be manipulated by people like Peter Maxwell. He just lets them make fools of themselves.

Eventually Peter took himself off – to go and play with his Blackberry, I expect. The sheikh then turned to Fred and told him, not quite in these words, to pull his finger out and get a grip of himself. And he said something else too, about faith, and love. I can't remember the words he used then, either. It was a typical sheikhism. A mixture of down to earth and practical with a strong dash of the mystical.

At any rate, it had the most extraordinary effect on Fred. He jerked upright in his chair as if he had been poked with an electric cattle prod. After a moment his expression began to change. He stopped looking so Eeyorish and sorry for himself. His face took on a distant look, as if he was seeing something he thought he rather liked, but a long way off, too far away to be certain of what he was looking at.

When Fred wasn't being gloomy, or pompous, I thought he looked rather nice. I walked upstairs with him and, on the landing, I kissed him goodnight, on the cheek. Perhaps I shouldn't have done. Maybe that was less than professional, but I didn't care. I felt a little sorry for him, and a little sorry for myself, so I kissed him on the cheek. He looked at me when I did that. He didn't try to make anything of it, for which I was grateful. He just said, 'Thanks,' very quietly and as if he really meant it.

When I first met Fred and we were still at the stage of calling each other Dr Jones and Ms Harriet I'm-not-quite-sure-how-to-pronounce-your-surname-so-I'll-just-mumble-it, I think I would rather have kissed a salmon than Fred. Now, I was not so sure. I went to bed wondering what would have happened if I had kissed him properly, on the lips.

The next morning we took a helicopter down to see the fish farm. Fred had told me about this and kept saying, 'The sheikh will hate it. He'll hate it.'

But there was nowhere else to get the fish, you see. We needed so many and it seemed as if trying to rear fish from wild stock would meet with so many objections and obstacles that it would take for ever, perhaps never. I couldn't see the difference – then. Salmon farms breed salmon. We needed salmon, and lots of them. What was the problem?

So Fred gave me a long lecture about genetic integrity, and why wild salmon have it and farmed salmon don't. I couldn't see why it mattered. A fish is a fish, isn't it? I had to pretend to be interested for half an hour. At the end of his speech I told him, 'If this is the only way to get the salmon we need in the time we've got, let's please just get on with it.'

The sheikh did hate it. I hated it, too. I hated seeing those poor fish crowded together like that in those cages, swimming in their own dirt. I hated the way they leaped into the air all the time as if they were trying to escape from a vast prison camp, which is of course what it was. I know they were only fish. But still.

Peter Maxwell took a few pictures; otherwise he said nothing until we were back in the helicopter. I think he thought that was how salmon always lived because he said how fascinating it was to see wild creatures so close, and what a marvellous tourist attraction they could be. Then he started to muse about whether one couldn't sell tickets for people to row alongside the cages and hook fish out of them. He took out his Blackberry and wrote a note to himself to talk to the Scottish Executive about it. I saw Fred give him a look of such contempt and loathing it was lucky Peter did not see it.

When we got back to Glen Tulloch the helicopter dropped us off and took Peter Maxwell on to Inverness airport, so he could fly back to Downing Street and tell his boss all about it. He said, 'The PM will be very impressed by what I have to tell him.' There was more about being 'deeply gratified by the progress made' and 'how delighted the prime minister will be to share the moment of the launch'. Then he turned to Fred and me and instructed us to keep him posted. He wanted weekly updates by email; he wanted us to keep at our work on the project night and day. I must say I felt like giving him a piece of my mind. Fred was a civil servant, so perhaps that gave Peter the right to give him instructions although I don't really see why. But he had no right to tell me what to do. I was working as a partner in a private firm, and the sheikh was my client and the sheikh was the only person who could tell me what to do.

Then Peter Maxwell was gone. I saw later that he went straight back to London and gave that interview to the *Sunday Telegraph Magazine* about what a great salmon fisherman he was going to be.

I: Please describe the events which followed Mr Maxwell's departure.

HCT: Well, Fred was almost incandescent with rage after Peter left. He turned to me as the helicopter headed for the airport and said, 'That man...' a little too loudly, because the sheikh overheard him and said, 'I am so pleased your prime minister is interested enough to send such an important man as Mr Maxwell all the way to my modest home in Scotland to meet me. I am so glad he came. His contribution was very valuable.'

I: Describe the alleged incident on the river.

HCT: The sheikh decided that, as we had a few hours before we needed to get back to London, we would go and fish. I was invited to sit on the riverbank and watch. So that was how we came to be on the river that autumn afternoon, with the leaves turning buttery yellow on the rowans, and the clusters of gleaming red berries reminding one that winter was coming. There was enough warmth in the sun for it still to be pleasant to sit on the fine, soft grass. I knew I would be covered in pine needles and leaf mould when I stood up, but I didn't care.

The dark waters of the Tulloch flowed below me. On each bank were scrubby woodlands of birch, rowan, and

Scots pine. A few rhododendrons provided some cover. I heard a pheasant sounding its alarm call, not far away. I watched the two men fishing.

In his waders the sheikh lost some of his majesty. He was just a simple fisherman, at one with the river, his whole being concentrated on his next step and his next cast. I saw him form the double loop of his cast and heard the hiss of the line as, without apparent effort, a great length of it shot out silkily and the fly landed on the water with a kiss. Thirty or forty yards below him was Fred. On land, Fred was a little wooden in his movements at times. In the water he was graceful, moving easily, casting, as the sheikh did, with an economy and skill that were somehow surprising if you were used to seeing him behind a desk. They had both forgotten me, forgotten the project, forgotten everything except the immediate moment and the riddle of the dark waters that hid the fish they sought. Somewhere round a bend in the river was Colin, fishing as well, perhaps as recompense for a trying few days training the sheikh's Yemeni future corps de Gillies, but I knew that if the sheikh so much as touched a fish with his fly, Colin would appear miraculously at his elbow with a landing net, ready to help bring the fish onto the bank.

It was so peaceful. My eyelids felt heavy. I was tired: shattered from weeks of work, exhausted by weeks of worry about Robert. I could hear the musical sounds of the river, the hiss of the line as it went out, the occasional chirrup of some small dipper or other wading birds balancing somewhere on a stone, its tail going up and down. A sense of deep calm flowed through me, a feeling that everything would be all right: the sheikh would have his salmon river, Robert would ring me from an airport saying he was on his way home, and everything would be fine and I would be happy again. Then I heard the alarm call of the pheasant again. It made me look up.

Coming between the trees towards us was a small, dark man in a kilt and stockings. His top half was encased in a bulky leather jacket. On his head was some kind of beret, perhaps more reminiscent of a French onion-seller than a Highland clansman. I heard his feet scrunching on the first fallen leaves of autumn, and I realised I had been half listening to that noise for a few moments before I saw him. Then I realised that the little man was not fat. He looked very thin, in fact half starved. What had made him look so big was some kind of pistol with a long barrel that he swept from underneath his jacket.

Everything then took on the aspect of an underwater ballet. I had all the time in the world to watch him cock the gun, all the time in the world to scramble to my feet, and all the time in the world to shout a warning to the sheikh. Except my voice froze in my throat, and the first person to speak was the little dark man. 'Allahu akhbar,' he said conversationally, in a clear high voice.

The sheikh turned in the river at this sound and saw him, and without any sign of alarm replied, 'Salaam alaikum,' raising the tips of his fingers to his brow and then opening his hand in a gesture of greeting. The little man raised his gun and sighted it on the sheikh, and the sheikh stood still in the river waiting to be shot.

All this happened very slowly, it seemed to me at the time, and took perhaps five seconds. Then everything speeded up again. I found my voice and a shriek came out, not the words of warning I had wanted to shout. Out of the corner of my eye I saw Fred moving towards the bank, wading through the waist-deep water with the fluency of an otter. But he had no chance of reaching us in time. And if he did, the little man would most likely have shot him too, and me. That was probably the plan. There were no bodyguards around. The sheikh never allowed anyone near the river to disturb the tranquillity of his fishing. I closed my eyes and then opened them again as the first shots were fired.

They went straight up into the air as the little man jerked inexplicably backwards, howling and grabbing at his face. The gun fell to the ground from his hand as he clutched at something invisible. Somewhere behind I glimpsed Colin straining on a big fishing rod bent nearly double. He had somehow cast and hooked the little man, and was now reeling him in.

Then I fainted, or at least somehow disconnected from the proceedings. When I became aware of events again I was lying on the grass and Fred was bending over me, patting the back of my hand and saying, 'Harriet, Harriet. Are you all right?' Or was he saying, 'It's all right'? There was a buzzing in my ears and I couldn't quite hear. Then things came slowly back into focus, and I was able to sit up and look around me while Fred supported me with his arm around my shoulders.

The little man was now sitting on a bank some yards away, clutching his cheek with a bloodstained hand-kerchief. He was talking volubly to the sheikh in Arabic, and weeping at the same time. Four of the sheikh's Yemeni guards stood nearby. They had abandoned their fishing rods, and stood with their hands on the hilts of the great, curved *jambia* daggers that they wore. I had no doubt they would cut the little man into shreds given the slightest encouragement to do so by the sheikh.

I heard Colin say, 'Aye, I seen him come up the glen on the other bank, but I had just had a tug on my line from a fish, so I didn't take much notice for a wee minute. Then I knew he was wrong. His kilt was a Campbell tartan. There's nae Campbells in this glen. They were all chased away many hundreds of years since. So I left my fish for another day and came and cast my hook at the wee man, instead.' Then he laughed and said, 'He didn't put up as much of a fight as the fish would have. I had him on the grass in three minutes.'

I never saw the little man again. I believe from what I heard from Malcolm later that a few days after that he was flown back to the Yemen inside a hamper marked 'Harrods', on the sheikh's jet.

The sheikh told us that evening on the plane to London, 'Poor man! He was no assassin. He was a goatherd whose goats had died. He had been told his family would be killed if he did not do this thing, and that they would be given thirty goats as *diyah*, blood money, if he did. How he got this far is a mystery. He spoke little English, and he was wearing the most extraordinary clothes.'

'What will happen to him?' asked Fred.

'Oh, that is not up to me. He begged my forgiveness, and of course I forgave him. He is not an evil man. The people who sent him are another matter. Long ago we pushed them out of our country, but still they are a danger. See how they can try and strike me from their caves in Afghanistan or Pakistan. But the man himself will be tried by a *sharia* court, and I am afraid the penalty may be severe. I will take care of his family when I return. It is all I can do.'

'At least you are safe now, thank God,' I said. The sheikh looked at me fondly.

'Yes, we should thank God for this escape. But they will try again, Ms Harriet. They will keep trying until I am dead.'

# 17

## Extract from *Hansard*

*House of Commons*

*Thursday 9th October*

*The House met at half past eleven o'clock*

*PRAYERS*

*(Mr Speaker in the Chair)*

*Oral Answers to Questions*

*The Prime Minister*

**Mr Hamish Stewart (Cruives & The Bogles) (SNP):** If he will list his official engagements for Thursday 9th October?

**The Prime Minister (Mr Jay Vent):** Later this morning I will be in meetings with ministerial colleagues, and for most of the rest of the day.

**Mr Hamish Stewart:** Will the Prime Minister find time during the course of his meetings with colleagues to explain his support for yet another example of how this government and recent governments have considered it appropriate to interfere with the political, cultural and religious affairs of a sovereign Middle Eastern country?

**The Prime Minister:** I presume the honourable gentleman is referring to the Yemen salmon project?

**Hamish Stewart:** That is correct. Will the Prime Minister explain to the House why this government is sponsoring the export of live Scottish salmon to die miserably in a desert country? Is he aware that salmon fishing is not a recognised activity in the Muslim world? Does he appreciate the gross religious and cultural intrusion this project represents? Has the export of salmon been in any way regulated by appropriate agencies such as the Food Standards Agency? Is the RSPCA aware of this project? Can the Prime Minister assure us that he is content these Scottish fish will not suffer as they die from heat stress in the sand?

**The Prime Minister:** That is quite a lot of questions to answer at one time. However, if the honourable member for Cruives & The Bogles has paused to draw breath, I will respond as best I can. The Yemen salmon project is a privately funded project which does not involve this government in any way. Nor does it constitute interference, political, cultural or otherwise, with the affairs of the Republic of the Yemen. On the contrary, it is a vindication of this government's multicultural policies that a Yemeni citizen has come to think of this country as his second home, and that as result of his UK residency he has developed an interest in salmon fishing and as a result of that, has involved UK scientists and engineers in this project.

Of course we are also aware that a government agency, the National Centre for Fisheries Excellence, has been selected as the primary source for the science for the project. And that is why this government can rightly be proud of its continuing support for environmental science and environmental projects, something that does not appear to be a priority for the party opposite.

**Mr Andrew Smith (Glasgow South) (Lab):** Is the member for Cruives & The Bogles aware that the export of salmon to the Yemen actually represents a very large order with the respected Scottish firm of McSalmon Aqua Farms? As a result of that order I believe six more Scottish jobs are being created in a region where unemployment has always been high. Of course, these jobs are not in the member for Cruives & The Bogles' constituency, nor are they in mine, but I welcome this tribute to Scottish environmental engineering and this boost for Scottish jobs. I am surprised the member for Cruives & The Bogles is not more supportive of such matters.

**Mr Hamish Stewart:** The right honourable member for Glasgow South might do better to become more familiar with the affairs of his own constituency before he offers me advice on the affairs of others. [*Cries of 'Shame!' The House is called to order by Mr Speaker.*]

Will the Prime Minister explain to the House, if the government is not involved in this project in any way, as he has just stated, why his director of communications, Mr Peter Maxwell, has recently spent two days as the private guest of Sheikh Muhammad ibn Zaidi bani Tihama on his estate in Glen Tulloch? Is the Prime Minister not aware that Sheikh Muhammad is the chief financial sponsor of the Yemen salmon project? [*Interruptions from the Opposition benches*]

**The Prime Minister:** The right honourable gentleman correctly refers to my colleague Peter Maxwell's job title as director of communications. As such, his job is not only to communicate with the nation about this government's policies and its many achievements [*Cheers from Government benches*] but also to communicate to my office and to me personally matters in which I take an interest. I am personally interested in this project not only because I have always been a keen angler [*Laughter from Opposition benches*] but because I think it is a splendid example of how, despite the many differences that exist between our nation and some Islamic nations in the Middle East, cultural and sporting values can transcend such religious and political differences as may exist. And that is why I have instructed my director of communications to make it clear to my friend Sheikh Muhammad that while the government has no official position on this matter, we would not wish any unnecessary obstacles to be placed in his way, and would wish to be kept informed at all times of his progress. That is the reason for Mr Maxwell's recent visit, except I might add I believe he used his influence to ensure that the order for salmon, to which my right honourable friend Mr Smith alluded a moment or two ago, was placed with a Scottish firm rather than a Norwegian one.

**Mr Gerald Lamprey (South Glos) (The Leader of Her Majesty's Opposition):** Would the Prime Minister consider whether it is not odd, at a time when 30 per cent of the armed forces budget is spent supporting military operations in Iraq, and now in deployments to defend the Saudi Arabian oilfields and the oilfields in Kazakhstan, that Mr Peter Maxwell, this government's highest-ranking unelected and *ex officio* Cabinet member – [*Interruptions from government benches. Mr Speaker calls the House to order.*] – I say, Peter Maxwell, should be spending significant amounts of his time thinking about salmon? Surely this government needs to consider the consistency of its policies? We have been told too often in this House that democracy can flower from the barrel of a gun, but we have never yet heard of democracy being hooked on the end of a fishing line. [*Laughter*]

**The Prime Minister:** I do not know whether the honourable member opposite expects a serious answer to his question, if indeed there was a question there. But yes, this government and the preceding governments from this party are proud of their record in introducing democratic ideals through the mechanism of political and sometimes, regrettably but inevitably, military intervention in the Middle East and central Asia. And history will show us to be right. In the matter of the Yemen salmon project, which I believe has led somehow to this line of questioning, if private individuals who share an interest in the sport of angling wish to come together and create what will be, I may say, a miracle of science and engineering, a veritable flowering of the desert, then speaking as an individual, I can only applaud such efforts. I might also add, I believe such efforts will lead to greater harmony between nations, just as the sports of cricket and, perhaps more widely, football have done. [*Interruption: 'The Prime Minster wasn't at the game between England and Holland last Friday night then?'*]

**Mr Hamish Stewart:** I am grateful to the Prime Minister for his clarification of the government's position, although I regret to say I am not much clearer about what the government's position in this matter is, or is not. Would the Prime Minister find time today during his meetings with ministerial colleagues to discuss with them the failed assassination attempt last week on the life of Sheikh Muhammad ibn Zaidi bani Tihama by a member of the al-Qaeda network at his residence in Scotland? Would the Prime Minister not agree that, in terms of his earlier statement when he referred to the government's wish to remove any unnecessary obstacles to the Yemen salmon project, the successful assassination of Sheikh Muhammad would perhaps have represented a significant obstacle to the project? [*Uproar on all sides of the House*]

[*Pause while the Prime Minister consults with the Home Secretary.*]

**The Prime Minister:** I refer the question to my honourable friend and colleague, the Home Secretary.

**The Home Secretary (Mr Reginald Brown):** My department is not at this time aware of any such attempt, and I would be grateful if the honourable member would in due course share with my officials any sources he has for such allegations.

**Mr Hamish Stewart:** The Secretary of State may read a report of the incident on the inside page of the last week's edition of the *Rannoch and Tulloch Reporter*. I am sorry he does not find time to read such an excellent paper, which is published weekly in my constituency. Would the Prime Minister find time, when he discusses matters with his ministerial colleagues later today, to consider whether a person who is an absentee landlord who appears on his Scottish estate for only a few weeks a year and who, when he does appear, has become a magnet for international terrorist activity, is a suitable person for his director of communications to wine and dine with? Would the Prime Minister and his colleagues care to explain to this House, after duly informing themselves of events of which they should have been aware, why the attack was never officially reported, and what happened to the attacker? We are aware that it is necessary from time to time to arrest and hold suspected terrorists without bail pending further investigations, but in this case the matter seems to have been taken out of the Home Secretary's hands. Would he care to explain why? Would he care to explain what the extradition policy is between this country and the Yemen, and if so what the due process is, and whether those processes were followed in this case? And if they were not, could he tell this House what did happen, and where the alleged al-Qaeda terrorist now is?

# 18

## The termination of the employment contract of Dr Jones

*Extracts from government memoranda and emails*

**Prime Minister's Office, 10 Downing Street**
*From: Peter Maxwell*
*To: Herbert Berkshire, Foreign & Commonwealth Office*
*Subject: Yemen salmon project*
*Date: 14 October*

Herbert

The PM was asked about the Yemen salmon project in the House yesterday. It is not an issue he wants to take up any parliamentary time. Our concern is that the involvement of a government agency (NCFE) may be wrongly construed as suggesting that this project has official government backing.

You will, I am sure, understand that our posture has always been supportive with respect to the Yemen salmon project. *If it works*, then I am sure the PM will be happy to endorse it, and perhaps make a personal visit as a private guest of the sheikh to see the salmon running. Meanwhile we need more deniability.

I suggest that the scientist Jones, who is doing all the work at NCFE, is disemployed from the agency with immediate effect. If you think this can be done by a word in the right ear, he could perhaps be re-employed by Fitzharris, the consultants who are project managers for the sheikh. That is a matter for them. The important thing is that no civil servant or government official should be directly connected with this project. NCFE should, in my view, be discouraged from being so close to the project. Whilst NCFE is part of DEFRA, this essentially is a matter of foreign policy and that is why I am airing the matter with you.

This memo is only a suggestion, of course. I leave it to you in your wisdom to decide the right course events should take.
Peter


**Memo**
*From: Herbert Berkshire*
*To: Peter Maxwell*
*Subject: Salmon/Yemen*
*Date: 14 October*

Peter
Thank you for your suggestion of today's date. I think it is wise that the Yemen salmon project should be perceived as a wholly private-sector project, and I will make appropriate noises in appropriate ears in due course.
Herbert

From: Herbert.Berkshire@fcome.gov.uk
Date: 14 October
To: David.Sugden@ncfe.gov.uk
Subject: Yemen salmon project

David

There is a degree of concern in (senior) government circles
with respect to current NCFE management issues. There is
a view developing at ministerial level that NCFE may have
embraced the Yemen salmon project a little too
enthusiastically. I think you need to be aware that Foreign
Office policy is to maintain a neutral stance with respect to
the Yemen, which is in a politically sensitive region of the
world. Policy is not to, or be perceived to, do anything that
might be interpreted as religious, political or cultural
interference with that country by the UK government. I recall
speaking to you about NCFE giving some limited technical
support to the Yemen salmon project as a goodwill gesture,
but I cannot imagine that your own department or mine ever
envisaged at that time the level of involvement NCFE now
has. However, I think you should know my own department
has advised, and will continue to advise, government that it
is important there are no grounds for a perception being
formed by the media and others that the project in any way
has official backing. Some ministers, I know, feel a concern
that NCFE is now overdependent on the income stream
from the Yemen salmon project, and might be said by
uninformed observers to be somewhat in the pocket of a
private Yemeni individual.

Whilst no one (as far as I know) wants the project to be
stopped, it might be a creative and responsible course of

action if you were to put a little more distance between your
agency and the project and its sponsor.
Herbert

> From: David.Sugden@ncfe.gov.uk
> Date: 14 October
> To: Fred.joncs@ncfe.gov.uk
> Subject: (no subject)

Fred, please come to my office asap.

> From: Fred.jones@fitzharris.com
> Date: 14 October
> To: Mary.jones@interfinance.org
> Subject: New job

Dear Mary
I have lost my job.
There were, apparently, some awkward questions in the House
of Commons about the Yemen salmon project last week. As
a result of that someone called Herbert Berkshire from the
Foreign Office rang my boss to say it might be better if I
ceased to be on the Civil Service payroll. Apparently Peter
Maxwell wants 'clear blue water' between the government
and the Yemen salmon project.
So, the bad news is, I have had my employment contract with
NCFE terminated. David called me into the office and
explained that it was 'no longer appropriate in all of the
circumstances' for me to continue. 'There was concern in the
department at imbalances in workload and priorities caused

173

by the growing demands of the project.' I have received an appallingly small redundancy cheque and a month's pay in lieu of notice. David Sugden handed me both yesterday, and explained I had the right to go to an employment tribunal if I did not like the circumstances in which my contract had been terminated.

Needless to say, there was a bit more to it than this. At almost the same time the lady who manages most of the sheikh's affairs in the UK (a Ms Chetwode-Talbot, I can't remember if I have mentioned her name before) sent me an offer of employment. The contract will run for an initial three years and my salary will be – wait for it – £120,000 a year!!! On top of that I will receive a car allowance, plus pension, plus health insurance, plus special hardship allowances for travelling and time spent working in the Yemen.

The bottom line is, the project will continue, but now I will be working for Fitzharris & Price, the firm that manages the sheikh's UK affairs, and the government will be able to say there is no official UK involvement in this project.

I don't know what to think about it all. On the one hand I am sad to leave the NCFE, where I have spent most of my working life, and I feel sure that once I am out I will never get back in, at least not in the same position. On the other hand, now I am working for the sheikh I am no longer bound by all our departmental procedures – I can just get on with the project, and to be honest that is what I most want to do.

So, Mary, I am now a very well paid and independent fisheries scientist. Well paid enough that you could afford to give up your job in Geneva and come back home to me. I know it isn't just the money, but maybe you could think about it?

I miss you.
Come back home.
With much love
Your Fred
XXX


From: Mary.jones@interfinance.org
Date: 16 October
To: Fred.jones@fitzharris.com
Subject: New employment

Fred

I don't know what to say. It appears you have been forced
out of a respectable if not overpaid position which you have
worked hard to get in order to make some politician or other
feel more comfortable. What will happen about your pension?
It was a final salary scheme, wasn't it? What are your new
pension arrangements? I doubt the private sector will give
you anything as generous as you got as a civil servant. Now
you tell me you are working for Fitzharris & Price. I looked
them up on their website. They appear to be estate agents.
What is a (once) eminent fisheries scientist doing working for
people whose main business appears to be managing and
selling property?

I feel very sorry for you. I suppose the money is some
compensation while it lasts, but how long will it last? What
happens to you when the project is complete or, more likely,
stopped? As for me coming back, I am amazed you think so
little of my career and what I might want to do. I am afraid
I am not as whimsical about career changes as you have
become. I have plans for my own career which now depend

on me doing at least two years in the Geneva office, and I am afraid I am not coming home just so that you get the washing and ironing and cooking done for you. Life doesn't work like that, not in modern marriages between professional people. Anyway, won't you be spending half your time in the Yemen? Your project can't all be managed from behind a desk, can it?

So, I am sorry, but your abrupt job change, far from making me feel more secure about our joint income, suggests to me that it is more important than ever that I consolidate my position as the main breadwinner, notwithstanding the (I am afraid, probably temporary) elevation in your salary.

No, you did not mention 'Ms Chetwode-Talbot' to me before. Who is she? Is she your new boss? I looked her up when I checked out the website. Her photograph is shown there. She does not look much like a businesswoman, does she? Is she qualified in anything?

Love

Mary

PS I am conscious I have been a little brief with respect to personal matters. I appreciate your saying you miss me. I have been too busy of late to reflect as deeply on personal issues as I should. I recognise that a work–life balance has to be sustained, and that to wholly subordinate one's personal life to one's career is self-defeating and just as likely to damage one's career path as the other way round.

Therefore you might like to make a diary note that I have some leave coming up next June, which is only eight months away. Perhaps it would be appropriate to spend a few days together to reassess our lives, jointly and individually.

From: Fred.jones@fitzharris.com
Date: 16 October
To: Mary.jones@interfinance.org
Subject: Re: New employment

Mary

Are we married or aren't we?

Fred

PS What are you implying about Harriet Chetwode-Talbot?
She is an extremely able manager running a project whose
budget runs into millions.

From: Mary.jones@interfinance.org
Date: 17 October
To: Fred.jones@interfinance.org
Subject: Re: Re: New employment

Fred

I suggest we resume communications when you are in a more
temperate frame of mind.

Mary

PS I am not implying anything about Ms Chetwode-Talbot.
Or Harriet, as you referred to her just now. I know my own
personal life is free from blame or complication. I trust you
can say the same.

*Article in the* Daily Telegraph, *1 November*

**Prime minister has other fish to fry**

Following the reported assassination attempt on a Yemen sheikh in the Scottish Highlands, in a statement today a spokesman for the prime minister distanced his office from the Yemen salmon project. The spokesman denied there had been any such incident and cited the absence of any involvement by local police forces.

The Yemen salmon project was officially launched in June this year. It initially received technical support from the National Centre for Fisheries Excellence. Now NCFE has announced it has ceased advising the salmon project team. David Sugden, director of NCFE, stated: 'It is not a priority for the centre. We did carry out some advisory work in the early stages of the project, but the centre's mandate has always been, and will continue to be, scientific work to support the Environment Agency and others in their task of looking after fisheries in English and Welsh rivers. Getting salmon to run up watercourses in the Yemen has never been high on our agenda, and although we were delighted to make an initial technical contribution, the project falls well outside the mainstream of our work.'

In July this year Prime Minister Jay Vent indicated his support for the Yemen salmon project, although the project never achieved official inter-governmental status. Sensitivities about other British and US initiatives in the region have resulted in the prime minister's office backing away from a closer association with salmon fishing in the Yemen.

The spokesman from Number 10 Downing Street added, 'The prime minister is always supportive of sporting and cultural initiatives such as this one, but at the moment he has other fish to fry.'

**Prime minister casts doubt upon the veracity of our reporter**

Last week we published a detailed account of an alleged attempt on the life of an eminent local resident, the Laird of Glen Tulloch, Sheikh Muhammad.

Eyewitness reports which reached us suggested that the individual concerned in this attempt was wearing a Campbell tartan which we feel sure he was not entitled to wear but no doubt was intended to help him avoid detection until he was close enough to make the attempt. We understand that this individual may have been of Arab extraction and that his attempt to pass himself off as a native of this glen was not notably successful. We are given to understand that the alleged would-be murderer was only restrained at the last moment by the intervention of one of the sheikh's employees, the respected and enterprising Colin McPherson.

We understand Mr McPherson detained him with a size 8 Ally Shrimp treble hook on a 15-pound line, and took less than five minutes to play him. After that achievement, it is unclear what the subsequent fate of the individual was. We make no allegations, but merely speculate that if he is not in Glen Tulloch, then he is somewhere else, possibly somewhere with more sand than Glen Tulloch.

No doubt events in remote Scottish glens are of little interest to the London or even the Edinburgh press these days, but we were surprised that no other paper saw fit to reproduce our scoop. Indeed the first notice that anyone outside of our regular readers took of this event was when an official from the prime minister's office rang up and asked us what our source for the story was. It is not this newspaper's policy, and never has been, to identify a journalistic source without consent. In this case we have no such consent. We also note from the national press that the day after we broke the story it was labelled a 'hoax' by a spokesman from the prime minister's office. We are not given to hoaxes in this paper. We are here to report the facts, and we are appalled and alarmed by the casual slur by the prime minister's spokesman on the integrity and competence of the *Rannoch and Tulloch Reporter*, which has been faithfully reporting on events up and down the length of Glen Tulloch for the last hundred years.

*Editorial*, Trout & Salmon

**Traditional British common sense**

We are pleased, even delighted, to record a rare victory for common sense in the world of British fisheries science. Readers will recall our dismay earlier this year at the way the National Centre for Fisheries Excellence had been drawn into supporting the Yemen salmon project. We commented that there were enough unsolved problems in our own rivers without diverting scarce resources to what sounded like a scientifically impossible project to introduce salmon into non-existent watercourses in the Middle East.

It is therefore with some pleasure that we saw David Sugden (the director of NCFE) quoted in the national press as saying that NCFE was no longer involved in this project. We might all speculate as to the reasons behind this apparent change of heart by the government, whose interest, we suspect, led to the involvement of NCFE in the first place.

Now NCFE has freed up the considerable resources it was devoting to the Yemen salmon project, could we, through these pages, urge Director David Sugden to allocate time to some scientific issues in the real world? We desperately need more research into the effects of rapid changes in water temperature on the hatching of dace eggs.


*Article in the* Yemen Daily News
*Translated from the Arabic by tarjim.ajeeb.com*
*(Arabic Internet-based translation site).*

**Fish project is spawning new initiatives**

The piscatorial initiative of Sheikh Muhammad ibn Zaidi bani Tihama is reaching new levels today. Work has now started on the construction of artificial lakes in which salmon from UK will swim around until summer rains are coming. When the rains are coming, the salmon will leave the lakes and swim up the Wadi Aleyn.

Considerable sporting interest is already arousing amongst the peoples in the Wilayat Aleyn. Well known and famous local businessman, Ali Husseyn, is already importing through his extremely notorious and excellent business Global Import Export LLP, the finest fishing rods manufactured by his family interests in Mumbai, India.

Also interesting tourism possibilities are occurring, with the promised opening after Ramadan of two new guest bedrooms in the Aleyn Rest House, with inside washing room facilities in the European style.

Soon a team of top scientists and engineers is coming with

the sheikh to stay at his palace and make scientific observations and deductions, in order to have the best possibility for the future survival and sporting value of the introduced fish.

The *Yemen Daily News* is gladly announcing such initiative by Sheikh Muhammad, who is also a personal friend of the British Prime Minister Mr Vent.

# 19

## Correspondence between Captain Robert Matthews and Ms Harriet Chetwode-Talbot

Captain Robert Matthews
c/o BFPO Basra Palace
Basra
Iraq

1 November

Darling Robert

I keep writing to you and they keep returning my letters marked 'Addressee unknown'. I got my father to ring up one of his old friends in the regiment and they gave him the runaround and even the commandant general could find out nothing about where you are or what you are doing.

So now there's this new thing. I sit and look at this pile of letters returned to me, and I think of all the words I wanted to say to you – did say to you, in fact – and which you have never read. You will never read them either, when you come back – I would be far too embarrassed to show them to you. For now, I will keep them though. It's a bit of a one-sided conversation, like talking to someone as they lie asleep. But it's better than no conversation at all. When you come back, we'll talk of other things.

I keep looking on the MoD website where they list

fatalities for Operation Telic 2. That's what the MoD calls what you are all doing in Iraq, isn't it? Your name is never there, but every morning I log on and there's a moment of nausea as I scroll down and look at the new names. The list is growing.

How hypocritical people are. I don't go to church; I haven't done so since I left school except for friends' weddings and the funerals of my parents' friends. But now I find myself muttering prayers for you. I am praying to a God I don't believe exists, but I am praying to him all the same.

And both from God and from you there is a deafening silence. It all became too much a few days ago, and I did something I swore I never would do, because I know it will make you angry when you find out. I rang 41 Commando Royal Marines last week and asked if anyone could tell me where you were. I was passed from one man to another, and none of them seemed to have any idea at all. They were hardly prepared to acknowledge that you even existed. I kept ringing though, and eventually I must have got through the outer defences because a cheerful-sounding voice quite different to the other people I'd been talking to said, 'Good God, how did you get put through to me? Bob Matthews? Last I heard he was working around As Sulimaniyah. Bandit country. Close to the Iranian frontier.' But before I could get any real news out of him, somebody shut him up and then I got a different voice, a smooth purring voice on the line: 'I'm sorry, madam, we don't give out information of that sort for operational reasons.' I must have tried a dozen times since then, ringing up your regiment, ringing up the MoD. I even tried the Family Support Group, but they said they had not been given any information.

I've had your mother on the telephone once or twice. They have been very stiff upper lip about the whole thing. I know your father served in Northern Ireland, and probably other dangerous places too, so perhaps they are more used to the idea that people can be out of touch for weeks on end. Your mother keeps on saying, 'Don't worry, dear. He always turns up in the end. I expect he's a bit busy to write just at the moment.' I think she is worried though. I think I can hear worry in her voice. Robert, I'm getting on with my life. There's plenty to do. But I have to be honest with you even if you never read this. The worry is like an ache. Sometimes it is more like I imagine a malignant ulcer must feel like, deep within me. Sometimes, not often, the pain is fierce. Mostly it's just a remote but ever-present hurt.

There's any amount of work to keep my mind off things. The project, which is how we all refer to the sheikh's salmon fishing plan, is all-consuming. You probably don't remember what I am talking about – I can't remember how much I told you about all this before the letters started being returned. I do long to tell you all about it. The whole thing is so absurd: a mad scheme to introduce salmon fishing to a desert country. And yet it's happening.

Next week I am flying out to the Yemen. We will be there for several days as guests of the sheikh completing our field studies and doing the final checks before the project goes live. So, darling, I will be in the Middle East at the same time as you! I am going with Fred Jones, the fisheries scientist, and the sheikh himself, and we will inspect the construction work that has now started and have a look at the Wadi Aleyn, which one day the sheikh believes will have salmon running up it. Fred is getting really excited about the trip. He works as a consultant to Fitzharris & Price now.

NCFE fired him, for political reasons which neither he nor I understand. The sheikh understands though, I think. He is now Fred's employer. So we are travelling in his plane to Sana'a and then driving into the mountains, the mountains of Heraz. It sounds so mysterious, a name from the Old Testament.

How frustrating that you are only a few hundred miles away and yet you might be on the other side of the planet for all I know. Actually, I looked at a map and I know you are more than fifteen hundred miles away from where I'm going to be. I wish I knew exactly where it is that you are, just this moment, as I write these words.

I can't bear this.

Loads of love

*Harriet*

Captain Robert Matthews
c/o BFPO Basra Palace
Basra
Iraq

4 November

Darling Robert

I'm writing again so soon because we are off in three days' time, and I don't know how long it will be before I can write again. Something happened tonight that I have to tell you about.

Tomorrow we fly to the Yemen and spend a couple of days in Sana'a, the capital, before travelling to the sheikh's house at al-Shisr, close by the Wadi Aleyn. There's been so much work to do this week, I've hardly had a moment to think about anything except the preparations for the journey. Fred (that's Dr Jones) has been brilliant. When I first met him I thought he was very pompous. He told me the whole project was a joke and not worth him spending five minutes even thinking about. He's improved out of all recognition since then. He's a really nice man, rather old-fashioned, very strait-laced, I should think, and totally dedicated to his work. He's also going through a rather difficult patch in his marriage, but he hasn't let that affect his work in any way.

The sheikh inspires him. The  sheikh inspires all of us. Most of the time I am so wrapped up in the detail of the project that I haven't had time to think about what we are all doing. I think it's self-protection, really, because the whole concept behind the project is totally bizarre. If I ever did really try and think about what we are trying to do, I'd probably never be able to go on with it. I didn't need Fred to tell me (when he was still Dr Jones) that salmon needed cool, oxygen-rich water to swim in, and that conditions in the Yemen were less than ideal. I had worked that one out already.

But the sheikh believes he can do it. He believes that Allah wants him to do it, and therefore he must and will complete his task. He never contemplates failure. He never shows fear or doubt. And he manages to keeps us all believing, just as he believes. We concentrate on the detail of each step we have to take, and think 'If this can be made to work, then maybe we can take the next step. If we can get the salmon, alive and well, into the holding tanks in the mountains. If we can keep them reasonably cool in the holding tanks until the rains come. If the rains come and the flows in the wadi are good enough, we can release them through the gates into the wadi. If they turn upstream and run ... If, if, if ... But, as Fred keeps saying, we have the technology. The rest is up to the salmon.

I try to think of other insane projects where belief has overcome reason and judgement: the Pyramids, Stonehenge, The Great Wall of China – the Millennium Dome, come to that. We are not the first and will not be the last people to defy common sense, logic, nature. Perhaps it is an act of monumental folly. I am sure it is. I am sure people will laugh at us and scorn us for the rest of our lives. You won't be able to marry me because I will always be the girl who once worked on the Yemen salmon project.

Last night we sat late in our office together, going over equipment inventories, cash flows and project milestones. The sheikh maintains an iron grasp of the detail of his project. If we fail, it will not be because he has forgotten something. While I was clearing papers away and switching off computers he said, 'Harriet Chetwode-Talbot, I shall always be in your debt. You have worked for me diligently and well.' He nearly always calls me by my full name. I don't know why. Anyway, I blushed. He usually gives instructions, rarely praise. 'You think our project will fail.'

It was not a question. I stammered something in reply, but he brushed aside my words. 'Think of it in a different way. The same God who created me, created the salmon, and in his wisdom brought us together and gave me the happiest moments of my life. Now I want to repay God and bring the same happiness to my people. Even if only one hundred fish run, if only one fish is ever caught, think what we will have achieved. Some men in my position, with great wealth and the freedom to spend it as they like, have built mosques. Some have built hospitals or schools. I, too, have built hospitals and schools and mosques. What difference does one more mosque or one more hospital make? I can worship God outside my tent on the sands as well as in a mosque. I want to present God with the opportunity to perform a miracle, a miracle that he will perform if he so wills it. Not you, not Dr Alfred, not all the clever engineers and scientists we have employed. You and they have prepared the way, but whatever happens will be God's will. You will have been present at the delivery of the miracle and you will have been of great assistance to me, but the miracle is God's alone. When anyone sees a salmon swimming up the waters of the Wadi Aleyn, will they any longer be able to doubt the existence of God? That will be my testament, the shining fish running in the storm waters of a desert land.'

My poor attempt on paper, my inadequate recollections of the sheikh's words, full of error and omissions, can't capture the power of the man's personality. When he speaks like that I can imagine the effect on their listeners that the prophets of the Old Testament must have had. His words, his very thoughts, get inside my head and echo for a long time in my memory, and my dreams.

Now I come to something dark, something I wish had not happened. But I must tell you about it.

When I left the office with the sheikh, his car appeared from somewhere and pulled up beside him and, as he often does, he offered me a lift back to my flat. The chauffeur drops him off first at his house in Eaton Square and then takes me on home, and I usually accept the offer. But tonight I had a headache from looking too long at tiny figures on computer screens, so I said I'd rather walk for a bit, and then jump into a taxi.

I was walking up St James's Street in the direction of Piccadilly when a tall man in a long navy-blue overcoat fell into step beside me. I hadn't seen or heard him coming and it gave me one hell of a start. My natural instinct was to turn away from him and cross the street, but before I had a chance to move off, he spoke. 'Don't worry,' he said. 'I'm a friend of Bob Matthews.'

He stopped then and let me have a good look at him in the street light, and my heart rate slowed down to something like normal. It was so obvious to me that he was a soldier. When my father, and your father and you, and a good many other of one's friends and relations either are or have been in the forces, it doesn't take a lot to spot a soldier. He was tall, thin-faced, rather dark-complexioned, with slightly receding black hair and arched black eyebrows over a pair of brown eyes. I don't know if you will recognise him from that description. He didn't smile.

'Who are you? What's your name?' I asked him. I think my voice must have been trembling. He had startled me, appearing so suddenly and silently from nowhere.

He didn't tell me his name. He simply said he was a friend of yours and in the same regiment, and that he had something to tell me. Then he said, and his words chilled me, 'It's a lot better for both of us if you don't know my name. I want to tell you something, but not out here in the street. Do you trust me enough to let me buy you a drink? There's a place I know nearby.'

I wasn't so alarmed by then. Instead, I was overwhelmed by the need to know what it was he had to tell me. I knew he would no more harm me than his sister, if he had one. I nodded, still not sure I could trust myself to speak again without a quaver in my voice, and again he scared me by saying we had better not walk together, but that I should follow him after a moment. It made me feel something I never expected to feel, a sense of being watched, a sense of threat in the shadows beyond the light from the street lamps and shop windows. He turned and strode off up the street without waiting for my reply.

He crossed Piccadilly and went down Dover Street. I followed him into a side street where he turned into the doorway of a small pub. It was cramped and noisy and busy inside, but there was a quiet corner where I found your friend sitting at a table waiting for me. Before I could ask him any questions, he suggested we had a glass of wine. I nodded and mumbled something and in a very short time he was back at the table with two large glasses of white wine.

'I'm not supposed to speak to you,' he said, without any preliminaries. 'I'd probably be in a lot of trouble if it was found out I had given information about operational matters to a civilian. So please forget we ever met as soon as I leave here.'

I promised him I would. I looked at him, willing him to get on with it, say whatever dreadful things were as yet unsaid. I knew we would not be sitting there if he could tell me anything good, anything I would want to hear. I thought 'Oh God, I hope you're not dead.' I think he understood, for he reached across the table and patted my hand briefly. Then he told me he was the officer I had spoken to when I rang up the regiment. I didn't recognise his voice. A cheerful voice had spoken to me; this man was not speaking to me cheerfully.

I told him that everyone kept telling me your whereabouts

couldn't be made known for operational reasons, even though you told me when you went out to Iraq you were just doing a short tour in Basra province.

'You're being given the runaround.'

'What do you mean?' I said. He paused, then took a slow sip from his glass of wine. He raised his eyebrows and looked at my glass, and I knew he was telling me to have a drink before he spoke again. I drank some wine. It was not very cold or nice but I barely tasted it. The wine went inside me and the alcohol briefly warmed me.

'I mean that Bob's somewhere he shouldn't be. He's with a team inside Iran, and they're stuck. The bad news is, the IIGF know roughly where they are.'

'Who is the IIGF?'

'Their army. Western operational command. That's the bad news.' I didn't ask what the good news was. I didn't see how there could be any good news. I took a second gulp at my wine. I had to use both hands to get the glass to my mouth, I was trembling so much.

'The good news is the same. The IIGF know *roughly* where they are; they don't know exactly. There are a lot of places to hide in that part of the world so Bob may be okay for a while. A while.'

'So what will happen to Robert?'

'He and his team must be extracted by helicopter. Soon.' I asked why they just didn't extract you, if you were in such danger. 'We aren't allowed to overfly Iranian air space. We aren't allowed to admit that we have any teams in Iran, although of course we've had teams in and out of there for years. It's a black operation. If we sent helicopters in and they were spotted, the Iranians would raise hell about it. Then it would have to be admitted that we'd sent people into the area. Questions would be asked in Parliament. There'd be a hell of a row. Unfortunately, sending helicopters in is exactly what the IIGF expect us to do right now.'

I asked him who had sent you into Iran in the first place, if we weren't supposed to be there. 'We never know who dreams up these things, but of course it will go all the way back to Downing Street. Bob and his team were supposed to infiltrate, blow up something that somebody decided had to be blown up and then get out. Bob got in all right, but someone saw them coming.'

'What can we do?' I said. I must have spoken very loudly because your friend looked around the bar. I must have almost screamed. One or two heads turned briefly in our direction and then looked away from your friend's stare. I made an effort to calm down. 'So what can I do?' I repeated. 'Why are you telling me?'

He leaned across the table and spoke with great intensity. 'Someone needs to blow the whistle. Your father, General Chetwode-Talbot, is pretty well known and respected. Bob's father still has a few friends and admirers in the forces. You have to tell one or both of them. Get them to talk to their MPs. Get a question asked in Parliament and drag it out into the open. Then they'll have do something about Bob.'

'But what should I say?'

'Get your father to call his MP and say that he has received specific and detailed information that Captain Robert Matthews of 41 Commando and his unit are trapped inside Iran, having accidentally crossed the border in hot pursuit, following an operation against insurgents around Lake Qal al' Dizah in eastern Iraq. Write that down.' He gave me a moment to find a pen and a scrap of paper inside my handbag, and then spelled it out for me. 'Tell him Bob was in hot pursuit of an insurgent group, but now he and a six-man team are pinned down on the wrong side of the frontier, inside Iran.'

'But that's not what you told me before.'

'It doesn't matter if everyone thinks they were there by accident, it may be possible to cut a deal with the Iranians and get them out. Any other way is too risky now.' He paused, and finished the last of his wine. Then he added, 'The important point is you should say that you are acting on information received, that you are absolutely convinced it is genuine, and that the British government urgently needs to obtain safe conduct for these men from the Iranian government, to allow them to be extracted by helicopter and returned across the frontier into Iraq.'

'Will they do it?'

'If you can get your MP to ask a question in the House, they're going to have to do something. Put it another way: I don't like to say this so bluntly, but Bob's in a hell of a lot of trouble, and he'll be in a hell of a lot more if someone doesn't do something.'

He stood up. 'Don't go,' I begged him, grasping at the sleeve of his coat. 'There must be more you can tell me.'

'Nothing more,' he said, staring down at me. 'For your sake, for Bob's, do whatever you can, and do it tonight. Tomorrow at the latest.' Then he left.

And now I am at home, and I have rung my father, and he has rung my MP for me because by then I was in such a state that I could hardly string two words together. How pathetic I am whenever there is a real emergency.

I have written everything out as it happened. I won't post this letter to you because it will never reach you and the wrong people will read it, but there must be a record kept of what happened tonight. I can't believe they have done this to you, Robert. I just can't believe you could be betrayed like this. But we'll get you out. My father has friends who have friends that the government can't ignore or silence. If only you could hear me speaking out loud the words as I write them down, hear them wherever you are: *we will get you out*.

Love


*Harriet*

# 20

Intercepts of al-Qaeda email traffic (provided by the Pakistan Inter-Services Intelligence Agency)

From: Tariq Anwar
Date: 21 October
To: Essad
Folder: Outgoing mail to Yemen

I send you my greetings and messages from our brother Abu
Abdullah.
We hear the goatherd failed to get his goat. We hear some
hasty or ignorant people gave him the tribal robes to wear
that were not the tribal robes that should be worn in those
regions of Scotland. And so he was seen, and he was taken,
and now he is back in your country, talking to the authorities,
we do not doubt, as fast as his cursed tongue can shape the
words.
Abu Abdullah is aware that you will be very concerned to
make amends for this failure, or worse than failure, and asks
you to do three things for him.
First, find the goatherd. You know the building in Sana'a
where they will be keeping him. Gain access. You know
which of the guards in that building are enlightened and which
are not. Seek out the enlightened guards. Pay them whatever
is necessary to further their enlightenment. Gain access to the
goatherd and take him to join his goats. Take him out from

the place where he is and remove his head, and bury him on
the same hillside as his foul diseased animals.
Then, find his family. You know who they are. You know
how to find them. Find them, and remove their heads also.
Lay them down and bury them beside their son, their husband,
their brother. Then together they will be a testament to the
anger of Abu Abdullah, the righteous anger he feels against
those who fail him, my brother Essad.
Then, find the sheikh. We learn that tomorrow he comes to
the Yemen. Now he is in his own country and yours. There
need be no more mistakes concerning Scottish tribal dress.
You know his tribe. There are brothers who live amongst
them who know us and love us and are faithful to Abu
Abdullah. Find the sheikh, and do what was instructed, and
do it soon.
We ask God to lead you to the good of this life. We ask God
to lead you, and we hope it may not be sooner than was first
ordained, to the good of the afterlife.
Peace be upon you and God's mercy and blessings.
Tariq Anwar


From: Essad
Date: 28 October
To: Tariq Anwar
Folder: Incoming mail from Yemen


Dear Brother
Peace be upon you and the blessings of God be with you.
We have searched for the goatherd. He is gone and so is his
family. We think the sheikh has hidden them in the jebel.
We have started our operation against the sheikh. And we

have a man close to his household who loves us, and who loves and respects Abu Abdullah. He will find the goatherd for us, and he will help us to do what is necessary to the sheikh.

Ask Abu Abdullah to be patient. We must move without haste and yet without delay. We must make our move with great care. The sheikh is a dangerous foe, but not as dangerous, nor as powerful, nor as cunning, *nor as merciful* as Abu Abdullah.

We pray for your understanding and patience in this matter.
Essad


From: Tariq Anwar
Date: 28 October
To: Essad
Folder: Outgoing mail to Yemen

Essad
Describe your plan.
Tariq Anwar


From: Essad
Date: 28 October
To: Tariq Anwar
Folder: Incoming mail from Yemen


I send you my respectful greetings.

One of the sheikh's bodyguards was sent to Scotland to be taught how to fish for salmon. This he does not regard as suitable to his rank and family, having always believed that fishing was done by peasants who live in huts by the sea, and moreover he believes that fishing is not an occupation worthy of a family descended from the warriors who rode with Muhammad to Mecca nearly one and one half thousand years ago.

Furthermore he considers he has been deeply insulted by the Scottish bodyservant of the sheikh, the chief fishing teacher who is called Colin. Colin has told this man that we know of that he holds his fishing rod 'like a big girl'. This is an insult which may or may not be a killing matter in Scotland but it is certainly a killing matter here. So this man will kill the sheikh for us. Now we are discussing with him the *diyah* we must pay his family when he is dead. Please indicate what operational funds are available for the *diyah*.

More we will reveal in due course as the plan is developed. Peace be upon you, and the blessings of God.

Essad

# 21

## Extract from *Hansard*

*House of Commons*
*Thursday 10th November*
*(Mr Speaker in the Chair)*
*Oral or Written Questions for Answer*
*Written Answers*

**Mr Charles Capet (Rutland South) (Con):** To ask the Secretary of State for Defence for what reason he instructed that a six-man team, commanded by Captain R. Matthews of 41 Commando (RM), be sent into western Iran.

**The Secretary of State (Mr John Davidson)** [*holding answer*]: No elements of the battlegroup of which 41 Commando forms part are currently deployed anywhere except within the territorial boundaries of Iraq excluding those elements which have been rotated back to the UK for post-operational tour leave.

**Mr Charles Capet:** To ask the Secretary of State to confirm the specific whereabouts of Captain R. Matthews of 41 Commando (RM) at this date, if he is not in Iran. To ask if Captain Matthews is, in fact, in Iran, as information laid before us clearly indicates, what plans exist for extracting him and his team?

**The Secretary of State:** It has never been the policy of this government, or any other government, to comment on operational details of the deployment of units which might now, or in the future, compromise the security of those units. It is therefore the case that we cannot comment on the whereabouts now, or in the future, of the individual named. It is certainly the case that this government has a strict policy of non-interference in the affairs of sovereign states such as Iran, and therefore in no circumstances would a unit of 41 Commando (RM) have been deployed outside the territorial boundaries of Iraq where all armed forces units currently so deployed are operating with the sanction of appropriate UN resolutions. It follows, therefore, that the individual named could not be in Iran since there is no legal sanction for any units to be in Iran.

**Mr Charles Capet:** To ask the Secretary of State if it is possible that Captain Robert Matthews and his unit may have unintentionally strayed into Iranian territory whilst on legitimate duties inside Iraq close to the border, and in the region of Lake Qal al' Dizah? If this should be the case what procedures exist for ensuring the safe return of units in these circumstances?

**The Secretary of State** [*holding answer*]: We have not been advised of any accidental incursions but will continue to look into the matter as requested and will report to the House as and when any new information on this matter becomes available.

# 22

## Extracts from the diary of Dr Jones: he visits the Yemen

**Friday 18 November**
We are here in the Yemen at last.

The landscapes are breathtaking – towering cliffs that are ochre in the sunlight and purple in the shade, wadis slashed as if with a giant knife cutting thousands of feet between sheer rock walls, with an occasional thread of water at the bottom surrounded by date palm, gravel plains that are an endless expanse of dun, marked here and there by the white crust of the *sebkha*s where moisture beneath the sand leaches salt to the surface. These are dangerous places where a vehicle might sink if driven across them. On one trip we caught tantalising glimpses of a sea of sand: the beginning of the Empty Quarter, a quarter of a million square miles of uninhabited desert.

And the towns are as wonderful as the desert. From the desert, driving towards a town through the haze and dust, it is as if one is approaching Manhattan: many-storeyed tower houses white with gypsum that from a distance look like skyscrapers poke above the walls of ancient fortifications or seem to totter on the edge of brown cliffs. They are beautiful and unlike anything I have ever seen or heard of. Once one is in a town it is a din of shouting voices, a riot of colour, unimaginable smells of drains and spices, and then you turn the corner and there is a garden, hidden away behind the houses.

We spent the first few days here staying in one of the sheikh's houses outside Sana'a, or touring the country in a convoy of his huge air-conditioned Toyota Land Cruisers. He wants us to get to know his country a little before we travel into the mountains. In the Empty Quarter we saw the beginnings of the dunes, an endless landscape of sculpted sand, dunes like low hills, dunes like long fingers, which shift and change endlessly so that no track through them ever lasts for more than a few minutes before it is obliterated in the restless wind that stings one's skin with grains of sand.

We drove into the mountains along crumbling tracks of loose gravel, always with a precipitous slope on one side, lurching up steep winding roads along which it seemed impossible from below that any vehicle could travel. We found tiny villages, perched at the foot of great cliffs and in permanent shadow, where a few herdsmen lived tending their goats. We saw deep pools of water coloured an unearthly blue-green, oases where date palms fringed the water's edge, and where brown-skinned boys in their coloured *futah*s, a sort of skirt wrapped around like a sarong, jumped in and out of the water.

Once we were stopped as we approached a tented encampment of Beduin by armed tribesmen gesturing with their rifles. The driver of the lead vehicle of our convoy of three stopped some way from them and got out. He bent to pick up some sand, then stood and let it run through his fingers, and showed his empty hand, palm out, to the Beduin.

'He shows that he has no weapon,' remarked our driver to Harriet and me.

'But hasn't he a weapon?' I asked, thinking of the rifles I had seen lying on the floor of one of the vehicles.

'Yes, of course. Everyone has guns here. But he doesn't show his gun. He says he comes in peace.'

The Beduin let us approach their tents and Harriet and I breathed more easily. I remember we dismounted and drank cardamom-flavoured coffee with them from tiny cups, sitting on a carpet under the roof of a tent with three sides.

I am overwhelmed by this country. It is so beautiful, in a savage way, especially in the mountains of Heraz, where the sheikh lives most of the time when he is not in Glen Tulloch. The people are like the country, crowding around one in the souks or even just in the streets.

'Britani? You Engleesh? I speek little Engleesh? Manchester United? Good? Yes?' And one smiles and says something or other, like the phrase the sheikh taught us: '*Al-Yemen balad jameel*' (The Yemen is a beautiful country).

And they nod back and smile, delighted to hear any word of their own language spoken even if they do not understand what you are trying to say, as friendly as could be. At the same time there is a sense that the friendliness could turn in a heartbeat to violence if they thought you were an enemy.

I worry about Harriet. She is her usual calm, cheerful self for most of the time, then in a moment her face becomes pinched and white, and she is silent. She must be worrying about her soldier. Maybe something has happened. I should ask. I haven't asked.

We stayed in the sheikh's house outside Sana'a for ten days. It was a comfortable house with every modern convenience, large, airy and cool inside. It did not have much character. The sheikh explained to us that this was his 'official' residence, for when he came to Sana'a on rare visits for business and politics. During those days in Sana'a he was busy, and so we were given a glimpse of the country by his drivers.

Once Harriet and I borrowed a car and drove ourselves around for a while. We went into Sana'a and saw the old city, with its riot of grey and white houses with their curious arched windows and towered storeys. We visited the spice souk, where great bowls of saffron and cumin and frank-incense, and every other possible spice, were set out on display. We saw through the entrance to a *diwan*, where men reclined on cushions chewing khat, exchanging gossip or dreaming of Paradise. But we didn't have the courage to go into any of the local restaurants. I didn't know if Harriet was allowed to enter those places, which seemed populated only by men. In the end we went to one of the Western-style hotels on the ring road. Here the twenty-first-century world intruded itself, with piped music, beer being drunk in the bar by engineers back from the oilfields, and a few tourists. We had a late lunch – a plastic-tasting Caesar salad – and drank a glass of white wine each because we didn't know when we would get our next alcoholic drink. The sheikh might permit drink in Scotland and even have a glass of whisky himself when he was there, but there was no question of his doing so here.

I tried to take Harriet out of her mood of abstraction, and talked about the places and the people we had seen since we arrived here, but although she attempted to keep up the conversation I could see it was an effort.

Then we drove back to the sheikh's house. As we passed through the villages along the edge of town, the call for prayer sounded from a hundred minarets, the faithful lined up to wash themselves in the communal baths outside the mosques, and then, leaving their sandals and shoes outside, went in to prayer. There were mosques everywhere, their domes vivid blue or green, with the symbol of the crescent etched against the darkening blue sky. Everyone was at prayer, it seemed to me, a whole people five times a day praying as naturally as breathing.

In this country faith is absolute and universal. The choice, if there is a choice, is made at birth. Everyone believes. For these people, God is a near neighbour.

I thought of Sundays at home when I was a child, buttoned up in an uncomfortable tweed jacket and forced to go to Sunday communion. I remember mouthing the hymns without really singing, peering between my fingers at the rest of the congregation when I was supposed to be praying, twisting in my seat during the sermon, aching with impatience for the whole boring ritual to be over.

I can't remember when I last went to church. I must have been since Mary and I were married but I can't remember when.

I don't know anyone who does go to church now. It's extraordinary, isn't it? I know I live amongst scientists and civil servants, and Mary's friends are all bankers or economists, so perhaps we are not typical. You still see people coming out of church on Sunday morning, chatting on the steps, shaking hands with the vicar, as you drive past on your way to get the Sunday papers, relieved you are too old now to be told to go. But no one I know goes any more. We never talk about it. We never think about it. I cannot easily remember the words of the Lord's Prayer.

We have moved on from religion.

Instead of going to church, which would never occur to us, Mary and I go to Tesco together on Sundays. At least, that is what we did when she still lived in London. We never have time to shop during the week and Saturdays are too busy. But on Sunday our local Tesco is just quiet enough to get round without being hit in the ankles all the time by other people's shopping carts.

We take our time wheeling the shopping cart around the vast cavern, goggling at the flatscreen TVs we cannot afford, occasionally tossing some minor luxury into the trolley that we can afford but not justify.

I suppose shopping in Tesco on Sunday morning is in itself a sort of meditative experience: in some way a shared moment with the hundreds of other shoppers all wheeling their shopping carts, and a shared moment with Mary, come to that. Most of the people I see shopping on Sunday morning have that peaceful, dreamy expression on their faces that I know is on ours. That is our Sunday ritual.

Now, I am in a different country, with a different woman by my side. But I feel as if I am in more than just a different country; I am in another world, a world where faith and prayer are instinctive and universal, where not to pray, not to be able to pray, is an affliction worse than blindness, where disconnection from God is worse than losing a limb.

The sun set lower in the sky, and the dome of a mosque was dark against its glare.


**Saturday 19 November**
This country was not made for salmon.

Today we drove into the mountains of the Heraz, to the Wadi Aleyn.

The mountains of Heraz rise in huge ramparts above terraced slopes where farmers eke out a basic existence growing millet and maize. From below it looks impossible for anyone to penetrate the mountains on foot, let alone in a vehicle. But, as we had noticed before, cunning tracks made their way round the side of huge shoulders of hillside, snaking between boulders the size of churches, careering down loose and crumbling slopes and up the other side. Harriet had her eyes tight shut most of the time on the drive in, and I could hardly bear to look out of the window myself. An error of six inches by the driver would have had us off the edge of the track, bouncing down on the roof of the car into the valley below. But our driver, Ibrahim, a tall bearded man in a maroon turban, check shirt and jeans, drove one-handed while he smoked incessant cigarettes with the other, and the wheels of the Toyota scraped the edges of the track but never quite went over.

Suddenly we went from bright sun into thick mist, and drops of water covered the windows and windscreen. We could hardly see twenty yards in front, but then the mist began to clear. In front of us we caught glimpses of a fortified village standing on a prow of rock.

'Al-Shisr,' said our driver.

Al-Shisr is the sheikh's ancestral home.

We drove up the track to the village. Perhaps a hundred tower houses stood on top of a cliff, with another cliff above the village soaring up into the mist. It made me think of some forgotten, hidden world from a childhood story. We drove through a gate in the walls surrounding the village, and along narrow lanes of sand and gravel. It was as if we had travelled back in time hundreds of years. The streets were empty, but occasionally a child would peer at us from a darkened doorway. A few chickens scattered before the wheels of our Land Cruiser. We turned uphill up another lane and came to a set of beautiful carved wooden gates set in a high wall, which opened inwards as we approached.

Inside the whitewashed walls was a garden of paradise, cool and mysterious. Water rippled from a fountain and splashed over the edge of a basin, cascading into marble channels that formed a grid of running water going backwards and forwards across the garden. Palms and almond trees provided shade, and a spiky grass grew everywhere, with bougainvillea climbing the white walls, and oleander and euphorbia and other shrubs, the names of which I do not know, planted here and there alongside the channels of flowing water.

It is a magical place.

Beyond the garden an arched colonnade led to the interior of the house, and along it came white-robed men, to greet us and collect our luggage. Beyond the colonnade we entered a marble hall of infinite coolness and grace, clad in tiles of intricate geometrical designs, where the sheikh awaited us.

In the afternoon, when the midday heat had passed and the sun was sinking in the sky, I left Harriet behind at the sheikh's villa, and set off with Ibrahim down the hill from the village and into the Wadi Aleyn. There was another way into the wadi than the perilous tracks along which we had come. A graded track, the red sand scraped smooth by earth movers, ran alongside the wadi, and along it rumbled huge Tata lorries and dumper trucks, churning up clouds of dust which coated our vehicle in grit. Soon we could see the construction site where the holding pens for the salmon are being built. Gangs of Indian labourers were spread all over the site, where three large basins have been excavated in the side of the mountain and are being lined with concrete. Two tanks will hold freshwater. The third will hold saltwater.

From the first freshwater basin a spillway has already been built down to the edge of the wadi. When the summer rains come, the gates of the holding tank will open, and the salmon will swim down the spillway, and run the waters of the wadi. At least, that's the plan, anyway.

Ibrahim drove up to a line of Portakabins and stopped. I got out and was greeted by a large man wearing orange overalls and a hard hat. 'Hi,' he said, extending a hand and speaking with a Texan accent, 'Dr Jones? I'm Tom Roper, and I'm the project engineer here. You want a look around?'

We went into the Portakabin and Tom showed me a huge wallchart with the project plan mapped out on it. He went through the timetable. It looked to me as if we were on schedule.

'Sixteen weeks to completion of the holding tanks. Then four weeks to plumb them into the aquifer and start filling them with water, to test the integrity of the lining and the sluice gates and check our oxygenation kit is working. Then we wait for the salmon to arrive, and the summer rains to come.'

We went through everything in detail, and then I looked out of the window at the activity across the site. There must have been several hundred people spread about the hillside, digging, laying concrete onto wire mesh or unrolling huge coils of Alkathene pipe.

'The guys are working well,' said Tom. 'We haven't had any major problems on site. It's just a very hot and dusty job. I'm working a month on, a week off.'

'Where do you go on your week off?'

'If I can get up to Dubai, I go there, but the flight connections aren't great. Otherwise I just sit in the Sheraton in Sana'a, drink a few beers and lie around the pool. There's nothing to do here; there's nothing to see except rocks and sand.'

I thought of the beautiful village of Al-Shisr, the ancient mosques and even older pre-Islamic buildings and tombs we had seen on our drive through the mountains, and wondered at his lack of curiosity, but said nothing.

I told him I wanted to walk down to the bed of the wadi for a closer look at what the salmon would have to cope with. 'Yes, do that,' said Tom. He laughed and said, 'I guess those fish will just fry and die. You know that, don't you?'

'Well, maybe they will. We'll try and avoid that if possible.'

Tom Roper shook his head and laughed again. 'It's not my business what y'all do with your money. I'm a project engineer; l do what I'm paid to do. I've built stuff in oilfields. I've built dams. I've built airstrips. I tell ya, I've never built fish tanks in the desert before now. You might as well take a heap of dollar bills and burn them as build all this. Your fish will just fry and die. But, hey, I'll do what you pay me to do.'

I left Tom in the cabin. He might be an excellent engineer, but I am not especially interested in his views on salmon. I am the fisheries scientist, and it is my considered opinion that we will achieve something here. He should stick to digging holes and lining them with concrete.

I walked the few hundred yards downhill to the bed of the wadi. By the time I got there, even though it was dry heat and late afternoon, I was dripping with sweat.

The wadi bed was a mass of boulders, small and large. A trickle of water ran through it, and as I scrambled along I saw that in some places stone channels had been cut to ease the flow of water. There was just about enough flow in the wadi at the moment for a couple of minnows to swim along. Upstream, the wadi ran through a date palm plantation where I knew that the water would flow through irrigation gutters hewn out of the stone. Beyond the plantation I could see where the wadi came down from the hills. The gradient was not as steep as I had feared, and I could see no obvious obstacles to salmon running up when the wadi filled with water.

Turning the other way I could see a few blue pools lying under cliffs so steep and tall the water was in shade all day long. The permanent shadow prevented complete evaporation of the water coming down the wadi. There had been no rain here for twelve weeks, so this water was likely to be coming from the aquifer. It dried up altogether in the heat of spring and early summer, and then filled again in the heavy summer rains.

I leaned back against a boulder, closed my eyes, and tried to shut out the noise of lorries and bulldozers, and men's voices from the hillside above. I tried to imagine darkening skies and the rain falling. I tried to imagine the first heavy drops sputtering in the dust, leaving minute impact craters wherever they fell. I tried to imagine the rain falling faster, little rivulets forming, running down into the wadi. I tried to imagine streams of water running down the surrounding ravines, and the trickle in the wadi turning to a stream, then to a river, then to a brown and boiling torrent.

I could half picture this in my mind if I tried hard enough, and forgot about the sun that was now reddening my face and neck and burning my forearms. Even in November the heat here is more than I am used to.

Then I tried to imagine the gates of the holding tanks

opening, and a bow wave of water coming down the new concrete spillway a few hundred yards away, and waves slapping together where it met the water of the wadi. I tried to imagine the salmon slipping down the spillway, finding the waters of the stream and, following the instincts of tens of thousands of years, heading upstream to spawn.

I could not imagine it.

This evening I sat beside Harriet in the dining room in the sheikh's villa. My face and arms were smothered with Aftersun, but I could still feel the heat in my skin. I drank copious amounts of cold water, which a servant poured from a copper jug into copper goblets. We ate *selta*, a kind of vegetable broth with lamb, fresh-baked Arab bread and *hummus,* and a spicy mixture of garlic and tomatoes and other vegetables I could not identify. The sheikh was in a humorous mood. 'So, you have walked along the Wadi Aleyn, Dr Alfred. What do you think of our project now?'

I shook my head. 'It will be very difficult. I must confess, Sheikh, I am very daunted. It is one thing to plan this project thousands of miles away and another thing to see the rocks and sand of the wadi.'

'And another thing to feel the heat,' added Harriet, looking rather pointedly at my sunburned nose and cheeks. Under the sheikh's influence her mood has improved a little since we came here. She is more cheerful, although from time to time a sad, inward look still crosses her face.

'No one who has not seen the wet season can imagine it, what it is like, how the rains fall so swiftly; just as no one who has not been here in the dry season can imagine the heat and the dust that brings. You shall see. Yemen is not just desert. There are green pastures and fields in the Hadramawt, and at Ibb and Hudaydah. Have faith, Dr Alfred, have faith!'

And the sheikh smiled and shook his head, and laughed to himself as if amused by something a child had said.

Harriet and I have been put in a guest wing at the far end of the house, away from where the sheikh and his retinue sleep. There are half a dozen bedrooms here, all large and luxurious with big comfortable beds and marble floors, with prayer mats laid out and a green arrow set in mosaic tiles, pointing the way to Mecca. The bathrooms have huge sunken baths with (I think) gold fittings. Bowls of fruit and flowers are set out and iced water can be poured from a giant Thermos. Sometimes someone lights frankincense in a burner in the central courtyard, and its strange and exotic scent pervades the whole house, making me think of church again in a distant childhood.

As I made my way along the corridor to my room just now, I passed a half-open door and heard the sound of someone weeping.

I stopped. Of course it was Harriet. Gently, I pushed at the door. She was sitting on the edge of the bed. There was just enough moonlight coming in through the filmy curtains to see the glint of tears running down her cheek. I stood there tentatively, my hand still on the door, and said, 'Harriet? Is something the matter?'

Of course there was something the matter. What an idiotic question. She mumbled something in a choked-sounding voice. I could not make out the words. I stood there awkwardly a moment longer and then instinct took over, and I sat on the bed beside her and put my arm around her. She turned and buried her face in my neck and I could feel the moisture on her face against my skin.

'Harriet, what is it? Please tell me.'

She sobbed for a while longer and my shirt collar became damp. It was a curious feeling, holding her in my arms like that. It didn't feel wrong. It felt right.

She said, 'I'm sorry. I'm being pathetic.'

'No. Tell me what has upset you.'

'It's about Robert,' she said in a trembling voice. 'I keep thinking something dreadful has happened to him.'

Harriet had told me about her engagement to Robert Matthews, a captain in the Royal Marines. She never speaks much about him, and I never think much about him as a result, although if I do, it is with an odd, irrational twinge almost like jealousy.

'I haven't heard from him for weeks and weeks,' she said. 'I'm so worried. It's like an ache, all the time.'

'Perhaps he's somewhere where he can't answer letters,' I suggested. 'I imagine the communications in Iraq are difficult.'

'It's worse that that,' she said into my shoulder. 'Promise me you won't tell anyone, if I tell you.'

I promised. Who would I tell?

She told me how the letters she had been receiving from Robert had at first been almost obliterated by the censor and then had ceased to come altogether. What was worse was that she had been contacted by something called the Family Support Centre, and all the letters she had written to him had started being returned. Then she hinted that, in some way she did not make clear, she had received information that, wherever Robert was, he was in serious danger. I tried to think of words to comfort her, and she clung to me for a moment longer, but then she became calmer and sat up straight and I removed my arm.

'God,' she said, 'I must look a mess. Thank goodness it's

so dark. I'm sorry to have let you see me like this. I just lost it for a while.'

'It must be a huge worry for you,' I said. 'I completely understand. I have no idea how you've kept so calm all this time. You mustn't bottle it up. We must help each other. You should have said something about it before.'

'You have your own worries, I know,' she said. 'I had no right to bring my troubles to you.'

'Harriet, I know we started out on this project – that is, I know *I* started out on this project – on the wrong foot with you. Since then I've gained a great deal of respect for you, and I'm very fond of you. I want you to talk to me as you would to any other friend, whenever you want to.'

She looked at me and gave a sad smile. 'That's very sweet of you.' Suddenly, she leaned forward and kissed me briefly and coolly on the lips. Then she stood up and made for the bathroom, saying over her shoulder, 'I must clean my face up. Thank you, Fred. Goodnight, and sleep well.'

I came back to my room, and now as I sit here finishing this entry in my diary, I still feel the touch of her lips on mine.

### Sunday 20 November
Harriet and I went for a walk along the wadi this morning, before the sun got too hot. We left the sheikh's house very early, and Ibrahim drove us down the bed of the Wadi Aleyn and as far along it as he could get the Land Cruiser, which was a lot further than I could have managed. Then he went and sat on the ground on the shady side of the vehicle, his back propped against it, and let us get on with it.

I had thought there would be a constraint from last night,

and that Harriet would feel embarrassed by the fact I had found her in tears. But she said, as we set out along the wadi, 'Thank you for last night. It helped to talk about it all.'

I said I was glad if I had been of help.

As we walked up the path that ran alongside the wadi, I felt a feeling of contentment I had not known for a very long time. Sheer rock walls formed the sides of a canyon, and above their tops I could discern ridges of higher mountains yet. The sky was a dark blue, and buzzards screeched and wheeled far above – their eerie cries echoed between the rock walls. There was little vegetation here: a few thorn bushes, tufts of grass, the green fading to brown as the memory of the summer rains disappeared. Here the wadi became steeper, and I could envisage it as a series of rills and small waterfalls when it was full. The salmon could get up this far. We turned a corner in the canyon and to my delight the area widened out into a gravel plateau, dissected by the dry beds of smaller streams that formed the tributaries of the main wadi.

The sight of those gravel beds filled me with excitement. I said to Harriet, 'Spawning grounds. If the salmon ever get this far up, they will love this.' I bent down and scooped some of the gravel up and let it trickle through my fingers. 'The gravel is small enough here for the salmon to dig trenches with their fins and lay their eggs in them. I would never have imagined it! Perfect!'

Harriet smiled at me. 'You look like a little boy who's been given a toy car,' she said. Then her smile faded. We were looking at each other and there must have been an expression on my face that gave me away, that gave away the fact I had at that minute, and in that second, fallen in love with her. I didn't even know it until I saw the look on her face.

217

'Fred ...' she started to say, in an uncertain tone, but I had caught sight of movement behind her. Someone was coming.

Harriet turned round, and we both saw a girl walking towards us. She was dark-skinned and thin, not veiled but dressed in a *sitara,* a brightly coloured robe of greens and pinks, and she wore a headscarf of a deep rose colour. In that barren place the vividness of her dress was all the more striking. On her head she balanced a pitcher and in her hand she carried something. As we watched her approach, I saw that she had come from a small house, not much more than a cave, which had been built into the side of the mountain wall that formed the far boundary of the gravel plateau we were standing on. I now saw that the side of the mountain had been terraced in places and that there were a few rows of crops growing on the terraces. Small black and brown goats stepped up and down amongst the rocks with acrobatic grace, chewing the tops of the thorn bushes.

As the girl approached she gave a shy smile and said, '*Salaam alaikum,*' and we replied, '*Wa alaikum as salaam,*' as the sheikh had taught us. She took the pitcher from where it was balanced on her head, kneeled on the ground, and gestured to us to sit. She poured water from the pitcher into two small tin cups, and handed them to us. Then she reached into her robe and drew out a flat package of greaseproof paper from which she withdrew a thin, round piece of bread, almost like a large flat biscuit. She broke off two pieces, and handed one to each of us, and gestured to us to eat and drink. The water and the bread were both delicious. We smiled and mimed our thanks until I remembered the Arabic word, '*Shukran.*'

So we sat together for a while, strangers who could speak

no word of each other's languages, and I marvelled at her simple act. She had seen two people walking in the heat, and so she laid down whatever she had been doing and came to render us a service. Because it was the custom, because her faith told her it was right to do so, because her action was as natural to her as the water that she poured for us. When we declined any further refreshment after a second cup of water she rose to her feet, murmured some word of farewell, and turned and went back to the house she had come from.

Harriet and I looked at each other as the girl walked back to her house. 'That was so ... biblical,' said Harriet.

'Can you imagine that ever happening at home?' I asked. She shook her head. 'That was charity. Giving water to strangers in the desert, where water is so scarce. That was true charity, the charity of poor people giving to the rich.'

In Britain a stranger offering a drink to a thirsty man in a lonely place would be regarded with suspicion. If someone had approached us like that at home, we would probably have assumed they were a little touched or we were going to be asked for money. We might have protected ourselves by being stiff and unfriendly, evasive or even rude.

My thoughts turned back to the water we had just drunk. I asked Harriet, 'Did you notice how cold the water was?'

'Yes,' she replied, 'it was delicious.'

'That means there is a well somewhere near here, going deep into the aquifer. To be that cold it must be a long way from the surface. If we can get water at that temperature pumping into the wadi, my salmon will have a far better chance of survival.'

'Our salmon,' said Harriet.

We turned and walked back down the canyon to where Ibrahim was waiting.

This evening the sheikh noticed a difference in my mood and asked what we had found on our walk. I told him of the gravel plateau where I thought fish might spawn, and I told him of the girl who had poured out for us the cold water of the aquifer, and he heard the excitement and pleasure in my voice. He said, 'Now you are beginning to believe, Dr Alfred. You are beginning to believe it could happen. You are beginning to learn to have faith.'

I remembered the words he had spoken a few weeks before, or maybe they were words which had formed themselves in my head: 'Faith comes before hope, and hope before love.'

'We will live to see those salmon swim the Wadi Aleyn, Sheikh,' I told him.

He answered, 'The salmon will swim the wadi in due time, and if God spares me, I will see them.' I thought of the man who had come through the trees at Glen Tulloch and tried to shoot the sheikh, and I knew he was expecting another such to come.

Harriot went upstairs, and I sat for a while talking with the sheikh. He was in a communicative mood. We talked about the ancient land that was now the Yemen: the frank-incense trade routes across the desert, the arrival of Greeks, Sabaeans, Romans, all seeking the fabled riches of gold and spices from this remote tip of the Arabian peninsula. He told me about the arrival of Islam and the Imams of Zaidi ('to whom I am a distant relation,' added the sheikh with pride) over 1200 years ago.

'This house was first built in the year 942 according to your calendar, and in the year 320 according to ours, and my family have lived here ever since, here and in Sana'a. It always interests me when European people come here, that they have no idea how old our civilisation is. Do you not think we have learned how to live and conduct our lives according to God, in that time? That is why some of our people hate the West so much. They wonder what the West has to offer that is so compelling that it must be imposed upon us, replacing our religion of God with the religion of money, replacing our piety and our poverty with consumer goods that we do not need, forcing money upon us that we cannot spend or if we do, cannot repay, loosening the ties that hold together families and tribes, corroding our faith, corroding our morality.'

It was the first time I had ever heard him speak so openly, this usually guarded and private man. And I realise it must have been because he was beginning to trust me, because I myself am changing.

## Monday 21 November

I wrote my diary entry for yesterday before I went to bed. I took some time over it because I want to capture as faithfully as I can everything that happens on this journey. It is a journey, in more than one sense. One day I hope this diary will be a record of something momentous, but whether that momentous thing is the arrival of the salmon or some other event in my life, I am not sure.

Last night I had a dream. I fell fast asleep as soon as I climbed into bed, but then I dreamed that a sound awakened me, and that Harriet was in my room standing by the bed, naked. I dreamed that she climbed in beside me, and the rest of the dream I don't wish to write about even to myself, but it was the most wonderful, the most real dream I have ever had. When I awakened the memory of the dream came to me at once. My lips felt bruised. I wondered if perhaps it had been more than a dream. I tried to see if I could smell her perfume on the pillow, but somewhere they were burning frankincense again, and its rich, spicy smell was everywhere. It must have been a dream. I dreamed it because something has happened between myself and Harriet. I felt it on the mountain when we walked up the dry riverbed together. I felt it, and I don't know what Harriet feels or thinks, but my wish that she should feel for me what I now feel for her is so strong it must have invaded my subconscious and directed all my dreams last night.

It was pure wish-fulfilment, of course.

I am married to Mary and have been happily married to her for many years. I know we are having a difficult passage in our life at present, but it is unthinkable we could part, that there could ever be anyone else in my life. I am just not that sort of person.

Am I?

Harriet is engaged to her soldier and visibly pining for him, and therefore nothing could possibly happen between Harriet and me. Therefore it must have been a dream.

But if it wasn't! What then?

I cannot sit still. Something has happened to me, but what? The windows are open and a soft breeze off the mountains is moving the curtains. It is still early. A golden sunrise is infusing the edges of the soaring cliffs and ridges around us and above us. Through my window come faint scents – of flowers I have never smelled before, of unknown spices. The noise of the village waking comes with them: cocks crowing, the bray of a donkey, the clatter of tin water containers, and occasionally a burst of Arabic.

I have journeyed this far, to this strange place. The man

who started the journey months ago as a staid, respected scientist at the National Centre for Fisheries Excellence is not the same man now standing at a window looking out onto the wild mountains of the Yemen. How much farther will this journey go? Where will it end, and how will it end?

# 23

## Extract from *Hansard*

*House of Commons*
*Monday 28th November*
*(Mr Speaker in the Chair)*
*Oral or Written Questions for Answer*
*Written Answers*

**Mr Charles Capet** (**Rutland South**) (**Con**): To ask the Secretary of State for Defence if he will comment on a report in the *Daily Telegraph* concerning an explosion at a military installation in western Iran. Will he comment as to the possible involvement in this event of a team from 41 Commando (RM) to which I referred in a previous question laid before this House? Will he once again look into the whereabouts of Captain Robert Matthews, as I requested in a previous question to him? And will he comment as to what, if any, measures are being taken to ensure the safe return of Captain Matthews to his regiment?

**The Secretary of State** (**Mr John Davidson**) [*holding answer*]: We have looked into the alleged explosion at an alleged military installation in western Iran. We are informed by the Iranian authorities that there was an industrial accident at a factory producing dental floss which unfortunately led to the deaths of 127 employees. We are informed that no third parties were involved in this incident and, given that the products of that factory are reported by the Iranian government to be solely concerned with dental hygiene (and not the reprocessing of nuclear waste, as reported in the *Daily Telegraph*), we believe the event is not a concern for this government. Accordingly, we have conveyed the deepest sympathies of HMG to the government of Iran and have no further official interest in the matter. With respect to the whereabouts of Captain Robert Matthews, I refer the honourable gentleman to my previous answer to the previous question he raised.

**Mr Charles Capet:** To ask the Secretary of State if he is, indeed, the only man in the United Kingdom to believe the official Iranian explanation for the devastating explosion in western Iran? To ask if he continues to deny the involvement of British forces, which, it is widely believed, were involved in an operation in that area? To ask, once again, if he will not bring relief to the distressed friends and relations of Captain Robert Matthews by stating whether he believes Captain Matthews to be alive or dead, and if he is alive, to state his whereabouts?

**The Secretary of State:** If the honourable gentleman will look at the website of the MoD on the page 'Operation Telic 2' tomorrow, he will find, regrettably, that Captain Matthews is now posted, or will be posted, as 'Missing in Action'.

# 24

## Correspondence between Ms Chetwode-Talbot and herself

Captain Robert Matthews
c/o BFPO Basra Palace
Basra
Iraq

21 November

Darling Robert

This is the last letter I will write to you, until you come home, when there will be no more need for letters. I shall not post it because there is no way I can post it from here that I know of and because of course you would never get it anyway. But I had to put these words on paper, to try and understand the feelings I have. First, I will tell you about what we are doing here. If I write about the everyday things, perhaps I will get my balance back.

I am writing this in a place called al-Shisr, in the mountains of Heraz, in the western highlands of the Yemen. It is a wilderness of mountains and fortified hill villages, connected by tracks that even you might hesitate to drive along (I have to keep my eyes closed most of the time). Although they have a satphone and computers down at the construction site in the Wadi Aleyn, up here in this mountain village there are no computers and no phones. My mobile long ago ceased to find a signal. This is the sheikh's ancestral home and he likes to keep everything just as it was in the ninth century, when it was built. Of course we have air conditioning and running hot water and a fantastic chef in the kitchen, but everything else about this place could be from any century except the present one.

Down in the Wadi Aleyn, there is a huge amount of activity: masses of trucks and earth-moving equipment, hundreds of Indian construction workers, more stuff being driven in every day. It is fascinating to see the concrete basins taking shape. They are doing a terrific job. The basins will be filled with water when they are ready and then, after we have done a few tests, we will be ready to fly the salmon out from Fort William down to London, and from there to the Yemen.

Fred and I have walked nearly every yard of the Wadi Aleyn, and he and the project engineer have prepared a profile of the wadi bed, showing where we need some additional engineering to help the salmon get over natural obstacles. It will just be a question of putting in some concrete steps or slipways here and there, to help the fish get past what will be waterfalls when the wadi is flowing. We have spent a fair amount of time with the engineers working these extras into the construction plans.

Fred says that, for the first time, he really believes we might achieve something. The topography of the wadi pleases him. The quality of the water coming from the aquifer pleases him. Even the size of the gravel pleases him. He thinks his fish – our fish – will survive here, even if only for a while. But something will happen; something will be achieved. The sheikh has infected us all with his own sense of belief. In this

Old Testament land it is difficult not to believe in myths and magic and miracles.

I have another week here before I can go back, but Fred is going to stay longer, to wait for the construction of the holding basins to be completed and for the engineers to sign off on the job, so that he can satisfy himself that the basin doesn't leak, the oxygen bubblers work and the sluice gates open, and so on. Then he is flying back to start planning the last phase of the project, the transport of the salmon.

My job is nearly over now. I still have to manage the administration and accounting of the project but the hard part – the design and engineering, the feasibility studies, the planning and construction – is nearly over. Now all we have to do is finish this stage and wait for next summer's rains, which will fill up the holding basins. When the rainy season is close, then we will start the crucial job of transporting live salmon from Scotland to the mountains of the Yemen. For Fred, that next stage is the vital moment, the culmination of all of our work. I expect he will be in and out of the Yemen over the next few months and I will see a lot less of him. Sorry, I seem to be going on about Fred a bit. He has become a good friend.

Now I must write about myself. I have been worried absolutely sick; there has been no news of you, only rumours. Some of the rumours I heard, a few weeks ago, have made it worse. How is it possible that so much time can go by, so many questions be asked about where you are and what you are doing, and yet still there are no answers? How can people be so cruel as to keep me in ignorance? I dread writing these words, but even if the news about you was the worst possible, the news that I have feared I would receive almost hourly since you went away, would not that be better than this endless not knowing?

I've lost weight. No bad thing, you might say. But I look at myself in the mirror and some of me has gone. I have been evaporating with worry. Now I come to the thing I have to set down in writing, even if you never read it. Today, for the first time, I feel a profound sense of relief. Or is it a sense of release? Whatever the right word is, I have a strange certainty that you are out of danger now. I don't know where you are, but I feel sure you have reached somewhere where no one can harm you. I hope it's true. I believe it's true. I feel sure now that when I return to the UK in a few days' time there will be some news of you after these weeks and months of silence.

I dreamed about you last night. I dreamed you were staying with us here, in the sheikh's villa, that somehow you had got leave from your regiment and found out where I was, and had flown down south to be with me. It was all mixed up as to how you got here. Dreams never make sense. But it was a wonderful dream, and we were together. We were as together as any two people could be, more together than I have ever been before with you, or with anyone. When I awoke I burst into tears. The dream was so wonderful, I wanted to be back in it; I wanted it to go on and on. I tried to smell you on me. I smelled my own skin to see if, somehow, magically, it had been real. It felt real. But they were burning frankincense and the smell of it was everywhere. It was a dream, of course, how could it have been otherwise? But its reality was so strong that for a while the waking world was quite unreal to me.

But what if it had not been a dream? How could you possibly have been with me?

Now a brilliant sunrise is climbing over the ridges high above us. I can smell spices, flowers and coffee when I stand at the window and inhale the mountain air. How strange it is that I am here, and yet, how calm and how natural everything feels now. The despair I have sometimes felt over the last few weeks has, for the moment, quite gone from me.

Down in the village, the muezzin calls the faithful to prayer.

I'll stop now and put this letter away. I won't read it again until you have come back to me, and then I'll look at it once and throw it on the fire.

Love

*Harriet*

# 25

## Extract from Peter Maxwell's unpublished autobiography, *A Helmsman at the Ship of State*

The image of the ship of state was, my researcher tells me, first created by Tenniel or another of the Victorian illustrators in a cartoon for *Punch* magazine. It was a metaphor for government: the captain of the ship was, naturally, the prime minister of the day. His concern was to keep the passengers happy, and to keep control of the crew. The analogies are too obvious to labour, but it is the figure of the helmsman that so often commands our attention.

In my long association with Prime Minister Jay Vent – as employee, colleague but above all friend – I believe I was, for him, the helmsman. In the Victorian illustration we see the figure of a man, clad in oilskins, on the foredeck of the ship, lashed to the helm to prevent him from being swept overboard. Drenched by the spray from towering waves, pitched in every direction by the motion of the sea, he keeps his eye on the firmament. Above him through the wrack of cloud is the gleam of the North Star. Without thought for his own safety, he concentrates his whole being on keeping the ship on course, guided by the light from above. He is focused, selfless; for him, the only task is to bring his captain and all the complement of the ship safe to harbour.

Of course, I would never overstate my role in Jay Vent's administration: I was one of many cogs in the machinery of government. But I was the cog that so often laid his hands upon the wheel and, by a touch this way, a tug the other way, helped shape our course.

That winter, at the invitation of the government of Iraq, we sent troops back to deal with local instabilities which were once again threatening the reconstruction of the oilfields. There were, unfortunately, other issues to deal with around that time. Apart from our renewed operations in Iraq, there was the unfortunate explosion in a dental floss factory in Iran which everyone seemed to assume was something much more sinister, the result of a covert operation by our forces. We were also asked by the US government to make a contribution to the Saudi Aramco Defence Force, which had been deployed to prevent further terrorist attacks on oilfields in the kingdom.

On top of everything, we had a cold winter. Understandably, our own administration and previous governments have not been quick to restart the building of nuclear power stations in this country. I have often said it is the right direction to take, but not before we have had the opportunity for measured debate and a review of the relevant town and country planning acts. Meanwhile, the temporary deficit in our energy supplies has been kindly met by the government of the Ukraine, which has agreed to increase the supply of natural gas to the UK. Unfortunately, as a result of some over-lengthy discussions about pricing which were perhaps not best handled by our then minister for energy despite the advice I gave him, the supplies were turned off for most of December and January. Regrettably, a few old age pensioners died when the gas was shut off, so there was a lot of difficult press to deal with, and it is no secret that the fate of the government was very much in my hands. Unless we could clearly explain why we had managed to both cancel the power station building programme and fall out with our main supplier of natural gas, there would be some difficult days ahead in the House of Commons.

There was a lot of pressure on me from the boss, as I used to call my friend Jay. I was working fourteen hours a day, seven days a week, for most of that autumn and winter. And a lot of it was like pushing water uphill. Whenever we managed to get a positive story into the press or launch a new policy or rush some new piece of legislation through Parliament, a wheel came off somewhere else. That picture on the front page of the *Independent* during the energy crisis of the old lady's corpse with her hand frozen to a cold radiator and icicles on the end of her nose was not good press for us. The public thought Jay was a nice guy, and the public was right. Jay Vent was a wonderful prime minister, and his greatest skill was picking the right people to support and guide him through difficult times like these. But, under pressure, Jay became very demanding of his closest lieutenants. In particular he looked to me, 'Mr Good News', as he sometimes liked to call me. And the record shows that Jay could be very tough on people who didn't deliver.

My job was to ensure that the news was as good as possible as much of the time as possible. I was paid to do it, and paid well. I have no right to complain. The result was, I was a little stressed that winter. There were one or two issues in my personal life as well. When you are working as hard as I was, it can take a toll. My health suffered, and some of my colleagues felt I was overdoing it. Some quite senior Cabinet members urged me to take a long holiday, in woeful ignorance of how much they needed me to watch their backs.

Mostly, I react well to stress. A lot of my best ideas come bubbling to the surface when the pressure is on. Readers will remember the prime minister playing in a cricket match at the St Helen's Orphanage for Partially Sighted Children. That was after a particularly difficult patch during which legislation to enable a newly trained corps of health and safety inspectors to provide logistical support for operations in Iraq and elsewhere in the Middle East was struggling to get through the House of Lords. The Opposition and, I am afraid, some of the less well informed public had no conception of the overstretch of our armed forces at that time, otherwise we would never have faced such time-wasting arguments. We needed a distraction and that cricket match at the orphanage was it. That was one of my ideas: thought up in five minutes and put into action ten minutes later. I can still feel a prickling of excitement when I think how good that was.

So now I started to think about ways in which we could take the pressure off the government agenda. I thought about initiatives in the National Health Service, in education, in crime, but when I looked into it the last three governments had all taken so many initiatives in those areas, there simply wasn't room for another one. So I turned my attention to policy initiatives abroad. It's always easier to do things abroad; you don't need planning permission or public enquiries or White Papers. You just go abroad – either on a fact-finding tour, a goodwill tour (which means taking a chequebook) or you invade. Those are generally the choices available. Unfortunately, we were already using all three methods in a number of different regions.

But Jay Vent had not employed me to tell him that something was impossible. My job was to find the solution. No matter how radical, there was always a way forward, and

Jay recognised that. He called me his pathfinder, although I prefer, as I have said, the image of the helmsman. I started to look for other choices. I asked myself the question: what if there are other options in the Middle East? To be absolutely candid, the Middle East has been something of a graveyard for the reputation of a number of governments, and Opposition parties too. I found myself wondering if there was anything that we could do about that.

I decided to do what I often do when I'm in this situation; it's one of the reasons I was so good at the job. I have a great ability to put myself in the place of the average voter, sitting watching television, just as I did, every day. What images would he see? Which of them would he select as representative of what was happening in the world? Which would remain in his mind and form the basis of his opinions?

One of the consequences of some of the things going on in the Middle East was that there was an increasing divide developing between those who wanted to keep theocratic government, sharia legal systems, and women in the home and not behind the steering wheel of a car or in a restaurant; and those who wanted democratic government, votes for women, a judiciary separate from church and state and so on. These, of course, are fundamental arguments which have been going on for decades. It could be said that the Middle East has polarised around these choices. I saw a shot of Damascus on the television the other day: a city of endless tower blocks, each apartment with a satellite TV dish on the balcony, and, among the tenements, the spires and domes of a thousand mosques. It seemed to me to sum up the conflict, the choices, at the heart of modern Islam. As I said in an earlier chapter, I watched a lot of TV in my job. I had a big flatscreen TV on all the time in my office tuned to CNN, another one tuned to BBC 24, and another with Sky News.

Mostly I watched the TV with the sound turned off – when it looked like there was breaking news, I hit the remote for sound. Most of the time I was just watching images. They washed over the surface of my mind and then they were gone, but every now and then an image would stick. I would remember it. It would shape my thought.

I would watch the images on the screen and think about what they meant. I saw young Kazakhs and Ossetians in baseball caps and tracksuits throwing stones at riot police trying to keep them off the streets at night, trying to stop them using mobile phones and wearing Western clothes. I saw those who had failed to dodge the bullets lying in dark pools in the street. I saw other images, of men young and old, in the traditional dress of their people, rioting against Westerners. And I saw that this was a society at a tipping point. Fourteen hundred years ago Islam began in the Arabian desert and within a century controlled an area which extended from Spain to central Asia. The same thing might be about to happen now. Or it could go the other way.

Images of people in the Middle East dressing like Westerners, spending like Westerners, that is what the voters watching TV here at home want to see. That is a visible sign that we really are winning the war of ideas – the struggle between consumption and economic growth, and religious tradition and economic stagnation.

I thought, why are those children coming onto the streets more and more often? It's not anything we have done, is it? It's not any speeches we have made, or countries we have invaded, or new constitutions we have written, or sweets we have handed out to children, or football matches between soldiers and the locals. It's because they, too, watch TV.

They watch TV and see how we live here in the West.

They see children their own age driving sports cars. They see teenagers like them, instead of living in monastic frustration until someone arranges their marriages, going out with lots of different girls, or boys. They see them in bed with lots of different girls and boys. They watch them in noisy bars, bottles of lager upended over their mouths, getting happy, enjoying the privilege of getting drunk. They watch them roaring out support or abuse at football matches. They see them getting on and off planes, flying from here to there without restriction and without fear, going on endless holidays, shopping, lying in the sun. Especially, they see them shopping: buying clothes and PlayStations, buying iPods, video phones, laptops, watches, digital cameras, shoes, trainers, baseball caps. Spending money, of which there is always an unlimited supply, in bars and restaurants, hotels and cinemas. These children of the West are always spending. They are always restless, happy and with unlimited access to cash.

I realised, with a flash of insight, that this was what was bringing these Middle Eastern children out on the streets. I realised that they just wanted to be like us. Those children don't want to have to go to the mosque five times a day when they could be hanging out with their friends by a bus shelter, by a phone booth or in a bar. They don't want their families to tell them who they can and can't marry. They might very well not want to marry at all and just have a series of partners. I mean, that's what a lot of people do. It is no secret, after that serial in the *Daily Mail*, that that is what I do. I don't necessarily need the commitment. Why should they not have the same choices as me? They want the freedom to fly off for their holidays on easyJet. I know some will say that what a lot of them want is just one square meal a day or the chance of a drink of clean water, but on the whole the poor aren't the ones on the street and would not be my target audience. They aren't going to change anything, otherwise why are they so poor? The ones who come out on the streets are the ones who have TVs. They've seen how we live, and they want to spend.

And so I had my inspiration.

All of a sudden I knew there was a better way to spend the taxpayer's money. I didn't know the latest Treasury estimates of our various military operations but they were enormous and growing all the time. At the time of writing we were operating in fifteen different countries, five of them officially. Because the reasons for our overseas interventions are sometimes complex and politically quite sophisticated, the sad fact is that sometimes the general public does not always appreciate the value of these operations. Who can blame them? Some of our involvements overseas have been going on an awfully long time.

But, I reflected, there are other institutions which we also traditionally spend money on without making much effort to understand the value of the investment. For example, there is the BBC World Service. What's that for? It's protected by charter and much as I would like to have taken an axe to it during the earlier years of our government, I knew I could not touch it. I also had to admit that a lot of people listened to it and, I speculated, does that not demonstrate an enormous thirst for information about the European and in particular the British way of life? I have never listened to the World Service myself. I imagined from looking at some of the programme lists that it was mostly repeats of *Farming Today* or recent speeches in the European Parliament or magazine programmes about tribal rituals in the Congo, and this made me realise that there were audiences in the Arab world and beyond who really must be desperate for a glimpse of a world beyond their own. So, what would they do if they had access to a really zippy British-owned and -controlled TV channel?

The idea I developed that winter was to set up a TV station called, let's say for argument's sake, Voice of Britain. From the outset I was enthralled by the possibilities and I determined to produce a pilot of a show, in order to take it to the boss. We scripted the show with Noel Edmonds in mind as presenter, but his agent wasn't keen on the idea. In the end we used a lookalike presenter from *al-Jazeera* for the pilot. The other problem was that the contestants spoke either Farsi, Pashto, Arabic or Urdu and we needed to put the show out in English, so simultaneous translators were needed. But on the whole I think it worked extremely well.

# 26

Script of TV pilot for *Prizes for the People*

| Episode One (Duration 30 minutes) | *Prizes for the People* |
|---|---|
| **Title sequence**<br>*00.30*<br>*Theme music* | |
| Presenter welcome and introduction<br>*00.30*<br><br>Presenter is standing in the ruins of a village. | <u>Muhammad Jaballah (in vision)</u><br>'Good evening. I'm Muhammad Jaballah, and I'm standing here in the middle of the village of Dugan in the Northern Frontier District of Pakistan. The villagers of Dugan have been going through a tough time recently, as their government battles for the control of the area with the Taliban and al-Qaeda. But now things are about to change for them. They are going to join me in my new show, a show that will test the wits of contestants from all over the Middle East and Asia. And, if they get the right answers, their lives will undergo the most incredible transformation. They will win prizes beyond their wildest dreams. Welcome to our great new show, |

| | |
|---|---|
| *Theme music* <br><br> Still photograph of a Pakistani male in his early twenties. | *Prizes for the People.'* <br> Male voice/over <br> 'Farrukh from Dugan will be our first contestant. But for now let's learn more about Dugan, the wonderful village which Farrukh comes from.' |
| **Presenter location link** <br> *00.60* <br> Dugan, Northern Frontier District, Pakistan <br> Presenter walks through the ruins of drystone-walled houses, surrounded by the remains of an almond grove in blossom. Blackened stumps indicate a recent fire. Presenter stops in front of the remains of one house distinguished by a bomb crater in front of it. | Muhammad Jaballah (in vision) <br> 'This is Dugan, once a thriving village in the north of Pakistan, set amidst beautiful almond groves with snowcapped mountains behind. A lovely place, and in a moment we'll meet the lovely people who live here. <br> Sadly, as you can see, a Tomahawk cruise missile landed here a few months ago and did some damage. The house behind me was Farrukh's and unfortunately the explosion knocked down most of the building, and some of Farrukh's family were fatalities. <br> But, hey, that's why we're here – to try and bring a smile back onto the faces of Farrukh and his friends.' |
| **Presenter studio** <br> *00.40* <br> Muhammad Jaballah is now seen on set, in the studio. <br> He is wearing black robes edged with gold. In the background are cutout images of sand dunes. An inflated plastic camel pokes its head up above the dunes while Muhammad speaks. | Muhammad Jaballah (in vision) <br> 'Tonight Farrukh and his friends from his village, Imran and Hassan, will compete in the very first show of *Prizes for the People*. I am thrilled to have this opportunity to change their lives. This is more than just a quiz show – |

| | |
|---|---|
| The camera pans across to two chairs facing each other centre stage at the front of the set.<br>*Theme music*<br>The first contestant, Farrukh, enters from stage left and walks across to sit opposite Muhammad.<br>*Applause* | we're going to do good.'<br><br>Male v/o<br>'And now, a big welcome for …<br>Farrukh from Dugan!' |
| **Presenter studio**<br>*1.00* | Muhammad Jaballah<br>'Tell us about yourself, Farrukh. Where do you come from?'<br><br>Contestant (camera pans across)<br>'I come from Dugan, in the Tribal Areas.'<br><br>Muhammad Jaballah (in vision)<br>'Farrukh, in a few moments we are going to ask you a question. Not very hard, but you have to get it right. But first tell us about Dugan.'<br><br>Contestant (in shot with presenter)<br>'Dugan is a very beautiful village but it has been a little bit exploded. The generator is blown up and the well is filled with sand and stone, and some of the houses have fallen down.'<br><br>Muhammad Jaballah (in vision)<br>'Farrukh, that's very sad, and I hope that today you will be able to win some prizes. So now let's see if you can answer the first question?' |
| *Theme music* | Fade to black, then back in vision |

| | |
|---|---|
| **Presenter studio**<br>*1.20*<br><br><br>*Dramatic background music* | <u>Muhammad Jaballah (in shot with contestant)</u><br>'Okay, Farrukh, here's the first question:<br>what animal can cross the desert for ten days without any food or water?'<br><br><u>Contestant (close up)</u><br>'It sounds like a . . .'<br><br><u>Muhammad Jaballah (close up)</u><br>'Don't guess now, Farrukh. Don't say the first thing that comes into your head, otherwise you'll be on your way back to Dugan with nothing, and we wouldn't like that now, would we?'<br><br><u>Contestant (in shot with presenter)</u><br>'It is a . . .'<br><br><u>Muhammad Jaballah (close up)</u><br>'Before you answer, Farrukh, have a look at these choices and tell me which of these three possible answers is the correct one.' |
| *Audience shots of 'No!' and 'Way to go, Farrukh!'* | |
| **Multiple-choice question**<br>*00.30* | <u>Male v/o</u><br>'Okay, Farrukh, if you can answer correctly which of these three animals can cross the desert for ten days without food or water, then you will win the first of tonight's major prizes: |

| Graphics | A. Elephant<br>B. Ox<br>C. Camel<br>Find out what Farrukh thinks the right answer is after the break.' |
|---|---|
| **COMMERCIAL BREAK** | |
| **Presenter studio** | <u>Muhammad Jaballah (in vision)</u><br>'Farrukh, is the answer A, B, or C? Take your time now.'<br><br><u>Contestant (in close up)</u><br>'Is a . . .' |
| *Dramatic music* | <u>Muhammad Jaballah (in close up)</u><br>'Take your time, Farrukh – you don't want to get this first question wrong. But, give me the right answer and the first of tonight's fabulous prizes will be yours.' |
| *Audience applause* | <u>Contestant (close up)</u><br>'. . . is a camel, no?' |
| *Audience laughter* | <u>Muhammad Jaballah (in close up)</u><br>'Well done, Farrukh. It's the right answer! It is a camel!' |
| *Inflatable camel jogs up and down the dunes*<br><br>*Audience applause* | <u>Muhammad Jaballah (in vision)</u><br>'And here's the first big prize tonight, Farrukh, and it's yours to take home with you to Dugan after the show tonight!' |

| | |
|---|---|
| **Onscreen picture of a dishwasher** | <u>Contestant (in shot with presenter, shaking hands)</u><br>'Thank you very much, Mr Muhammad, what is this machine?'<br><br><u>Male v/o</u><br>'Farrukh, tonight you have won a dishwasher with fourteen place settings, a six-wash programme, three wash temperatures, a high-grade stainless steel interior, a double waterproof system and a child safety lock. You can load it with porcelain, crystal glasses, bone-handled cutlery and it won't do the slightest damage. And – there's a three-year parts and labour warranty.' |
| *Studio applause* | <u>Muhammad Jaballah (in vision)</u><br>'A big hand for Farrukh. And now let's welcome our next contestant!' |

# 27

## Extract from Peter Maxwell's unpublished autobiography

After I had come up with that idea for the TV quiz show, I knew I had been granted an absolutely brilliant insight into how to win the war of hearts and minds in the Middle East. So I took it to the Cabinet. When I say the Cabinet, I mean the three or four of them who would come over and sit in the Terracotta Room at Number 10 on Friday nights unless they got stuck for some reason in the House.

They would sit around with Jay, crack a few bottles of Chardonnay and decide how to run the country. The usual ones were there: Reginald Brown, who was home secretary; Davidson, who ran defence at that time; and the foreign secretary, as he was then, before he became prime minister. Usually James Burden, the chancellor of the exchequer, would also be there.

I had told Jay earlier that I was developing quite an exciting idea which could get us back on the front foot. I wanted to run it past him, and them, and get some feedback before I worked it up into a detailed plan. Jay asked me to join the next Friday evening session. At eight o'clock I knew they would all have arrived and would have had at least one drink, but would still be capable of addressing any subject I brought to them, as I sometimes did. It was the best moment to capture their attention. I went upstairs and knocked on the door, and Jay called to come through.

The five of them were sprawled in armchairs and on sofas, a couple of bottles of white wine half empty on a low table between them. Jay offered me a glass, which I accepted but did not touch. I would have a drink afterwards, when they were patting me on the shoulder and congratulating me on my idea.

'Gentlemen,' I said, 'I'm going to tell you how to win the hearts and minds of the everyday working people of the Middle East without firing another shot.'

I had not given Jay any advance warning of what I was going to say. He trusted me. He knew if I had something to tell them, it would be worth listening to. I often sat in on those sessions anyway, but Jay liked to make it clear I was there by his invitation. Anyway, there they sat around the table, coats off, ties loosened, faces a little flushed from the wine. As I came in they were talking about the Middle East anyway, so it seemed my timing was just about right.

Tell them what you're going to tell them, tell them, and then tell them what you've told them. That's what my system has always been, and it never fails. So I told them in outline what I was going to tell them, then I gave them a summary of my proposal for a new Voice of Britain channel and went into some of the ideas I had started to develop on programme content. I also told them about an idea for a new easy-to-use credit card for general issue in the Middle East – instant credit approval for anyone who could actually sign their name on a form, backed by all the major British clearing banks and underwritten by the Treasury using money no longer needed for defence. I saw the chancellor and the secretary of state for defence both look up at this, and I knew my message was getting through.

I told them about the low-cost TV sets that would be distributed in the countries we most wanted to extend our influence in, TV sets that would only tune into one channel, Voice of Britain, and the network of transmitters that would beam in the new programmes twenty-four hours a day, seven days a week, not forgetting the sabbath. Then I told them about my quiz show, the flagship programme for the channel.

I did my presentation without a laptop or digital projector, without PowerPoint, without charts or notes. People have often said to me that I am at my very best when I speak unaided, straight from the heart. It was one of my better efforts. At the end I said, 'The total funding requirement for a campaign of this type needs to be properly costed, and of course that has not been done yet. But I am convinced that it would cost just a fraction of what we are spending right now on military operations. And it would deliver ten times, a hundred times, more in terms of getting our messages and values across.'

There was quite a long silence when I had finished. Jay picked up a pencil and looked at its point, then put it down again. The foreign secretary stretched back in his chair and studied the ceiling. The chancellor fiddled with his Blackberry. Then Davidson said, 'Peter, you need to get out more.'

I stared at him. I couldn't believe anyone in his position could make such an infantile remark, although my knowledge of Davidson should perhaps have prepared me for such a possibility. It was as if the last fifteen minutes had counted for nothing all.

I was about to say something I might have regretted when Jay looked up and said kindly, 'Peter, this is visionary stuff.

Just like you. But it needs thinking through a bit more carefully. There are some religious and political issues here that need sensitive handling. And you've got a lot on your plate just now. You've been working very hard. You need to ease up a bit. Maybe take a short break. And then we'll come back to this, perhaps. Maybe kick it around a bit more. The secretary of state for culture, media and sport ought to be involved in the debate. Maybe education as well. I'll ask them both to give it some thought. But for now, great as it is, I think we have to park your idea. We're pretty much committed to going down a particular road in the Middle East and it would be difficult to change that very much without people beginning to ask why we'd started down it in the first place.'

For some reason, as Jay finished speaking my eyes filled with tears. I stood up and went to the alcove where the bottles were kept and poured myself a glass of water with my back to the table, then wiped my eyes with the back of my hand while nobody could see my face. I felt rejected. I felt my vision had been so clear, so perfect, so lateral. Why could nobody else see that this was the way to go? The foreign secretary was speaking.

'Nevertheless, boss,' he said, 'Peter's got a point. We may have an excellent set of policies in the Middle East, and as you well know I have always endorsed and supported them to the hilt. Moreover, we know that in the long run we will succeed. We know militant Islam is being rolled back and that democratic consumer societies are springing up to replace the old theocracies. House prices are rising again in Fallujah. And in Gaza. That is tremendously exciting stuff and endorses some of what Peter has been saying.'

I smiled gratefully at him. A tear ran down my cheek. Nobody seemed to notice.

'But we must acknowledge that there is a perception amongst some of our voters that we are not succeeding quickly enough. Those images of the helicopter crash in Dhahran last week ... The arson attacks in the Bull Ring in Birmingham. The recent explosion in Iran, which everyone seems to know was us—'

'The leaks didn't come from my department,' said Davidson.

'Nevertheless. There have been a lot of negative stories out there. Then those American Baptist missionaries in Basra, trying to convert the locals by offering them a hundred dollars a head. That didn't play well back here, and if they hadn't been kidnapped and executed I don't know how much public relations damage they could have done. We do need a different angle. Not instead of what we are doing, but as well as what we are doing. We need to change the growing perception amongst our own public that we are treating the Muslim world with contempt and indifference.'

The boss looked thoughtful. There was silence while we all waited for him to speak. Then he looked at me and said, 'Peter. What about that salmon project thing? In the Yemen?'

I nodded. I still didn't trust myself to speak. Then I swallowed and said, 'We stepped back a bit from that one, if you remember.'

'Well,' said the boss, 'you need to reassess that decision. I'm not sure you made the right call there, Peter. I was keen on that project and I'd like to see it succeed.'

It was no use reminding him that only a few weeks previously, in this very room, he had ticked me off in front of more or less the same audience for having dinner with the sheikh and getting too close to the project. The boss was right then, and he was right now. That is why he was the boss.

'Yes, boss,' I told him. 'I'll get right on it. I'll get us back in there.'

# 28

Evidence of a marital crisis between Dr and Mrs Jones

From: Fred.jones@fitzharris.com
Date: 12 December
To: Mary.jones@interfinance.org
Subject: Absence

My dearest Mary
How are you? I am sorry I have been out of touch but I have
been in a remote part of the Yemen for several weeks and
access to the Internet has not been possible for much of that
time.
Since I returned I have been very busy catching up. Also
something rather dreadful happened to a colleague, which
has been distracting, to say the very least. So I know you will
understand why you haven't heard from me for a while.
I trust you are well and in good spirits and that the job is
going well.
Do get in touch and let me know how you are.
Love
Fred

From: Mary.jones@interfinance.org
Date: 12 December
To: Fred.jones@fitzharris.com
Subject: Re: Absence

Well! I thought you had forgotten about me.

Don't tell me that even in the Yemen you can't wander into an Internet cafe and send a quick email. I just don't believe you can go anywhere these days and be that cut off.

Since you ask, I am fine. I have lost a little weight as I tend to forget to eat, living on my own as I do. Do you find that? Or perhaps you are with Ms Chetwode-Talbot and your friend the sheikh all the time. I imagine you must be leading a grand sort of life in such eminent company and eating restaurant food twice a day?

My job is going very well, thank you for remembering to ask about it. My contribution to the Geneva office is being recognised, and the hard work I have put in over the last few months is paying off. It is gratifying to see both the result and the recognition one has received for one's efforts. I shall be coming to London in the fairly near future for a review meeting at the European head office there, and possible promotion is in the air. I trust my visit will give us an opportunity to meet and spend some time together. I feel it is important that we have some fairly serious discussions about our life together and our future.

I will let you know my plans as soon as I have some firm dates for this visit.

Mary

PS You don't say anything at all about how the salmon project is getting on. Have you finally realised just how irrational the whole idea is? I always wondered how you could

let yourself be taken in by the idea in the first place. I would
have supposed your scientific training would have made it
impossible for you to allow yourself to become involved in
something like that. One is constantly surprised by the
elasticity of people's standards, but I am surprised you have
been so quick to compromise. As for when people ask me
what you do, which they sometimes do as I am still relatively
new here, I don't know what to tell them. I did once admit
to someone (thankfully not in this office) that you were being
paid to introduce salmon into the Yemen and she screamed
with laughter for about five minutes and wouldn't believe I
wasn't joking.

As you know, I find jokes and facetiousness childish and don't
tend to indulge myself in that way, so if colleagues ask what
you do, or if I have to supply the information to human
resources, I just say you are a fisheries scientist and leave it
at that. But then, how do I explain why you are working for
an estate agent?

From: Fred.jones@fitzharris.com
Date: 13 December
To: Mary.jones@interfinance.org
Subject: Salmon project

Mary
Thank you for asking about my work in the Yemen, even if
I found some of your remarks somewhat negative. You
almost appeared to be questioning my scientific integrity,
although I am sure you did not intend to.

Anyway, since you ask, allow me to reassure you that the
Yemen salmon project is going to work. We may not live to

see Yemeni anglers catching salmon on the fly as they run up
the Wadi Aleyn, although even that is far from impossible,
but we will see salmon run up the Wadi Aleyn. Of that I am
confident. And I think there is every chance that the fish will
run all the way up the wadi, and some of them will manage
to spawn in the headwaters before the waters recede. What
will happen after that we cannot say.

Will any salmon fry actually be produced in the gravel beds
at the head of the wadi, and will any of them survive long
enough to head downstream before the waters evaporate?
Probably not. Will we succeed in catching some of the hen
fish in order to strip their eggs and rear salmon fry in the
more controllable conditions in the little experimental
hatchery we have built alongside Holding Basin No. 1? Yes,
I think we may succeed in that. Will we be able to catch
enough live salmon running back down the wadi to restock
Holding Basin No. 2 (which is now going to be doped with
salt to mimic the salinity of seawater)? Time alone will
tell.

If we can trick the salmon into wanting to run upstream to
follow the smell of freshwater, if we can trick the salmon
returning downstream to smell the saltwater in Holding Basin
No. 2 and swim into the salmon trap — then we will have
achieved a scientific miracle. And I use the word miracle
because that is what the sheikh believes it will be: a scientific
achievement which has come about through divine inspiration
and intervention. I am not sure, when it finally happens, that
I will want to disagree with him.

I look forward to telling you more about it all when we meet,
and I am delighted that you may be finding some time in
your busy schedule to come and see your husband. Please
give me as much advance notice as possible as I have a heavy

travel schedule myself at present between London, Scotland and the Yemen.

Fred

PS Your remarks about my supposedly extravagant lifestyle provoke me to comment that the sheikh lives simply, but well. He and I and Harriet Chetwode-Talbot dined together every night at his house, and we dined well but on the kind of healthy Arabic food that does not tend to fatten one up. In the daytime Harriet and I made do with copious amounts of water and fruit, to keep us going through our busy schedule.

From: Mary.jones@interfinance.org
Date: 14 December
To: Fred.jones@fitzharris.com
Subject: (no subject)

Fred
Are you having an affair with Harriet Chetwode-Talbot? I would be interested to know where I stand.
Mary

From: Fred.jones@fitzharris.com
Date: 14 December
To: Mary.jones@interfinance.org
Subject: Harriet

Mary
If you knew the full situation, then you would not ask such an insensitive question. Harriet Chetwode-Talbot is, or was, engaged to a soldier called Robert Matthews. You may or

may not have seen stories about him in the press.

To cut a long story short, Harriet came back from the mountains of Heraz (where she, like me, had no access to the Internet for most of the time, or any other form of communication with the UK) to find some dreadful news waiting for her. When she arrived in Sana'a, the capital of the Yemen, she found a stack of messages which had not been forwarded to al-Shisr, the village we have been staying in for the last few weeks. The dreadful news that she received was that her fiancé was Missing in Action, and is presumed dead. Of course she flew straight back to the UK to see Robert's parents, and from there went to her own family home, and there she remains at present. I gather the poor girl is prostrate with grief and hardly able to speak, let alone do anything else.

Does that answer your question?

From: Mary.jones@interfinance.org
Date: 14 December
To: Fred.jones@fitzharris.com
Subject: Re: Harriet

No.

From: Fred.jones@fitzharris.com
Date: 14 December
To: Harriet.ct@fitzharris.com
Subject: Condolences

Harriet

I just want to say again how dreadfully, dreadfully sorry I was for you when you heard the news about Robert. I know you had been worried sick, and then you told me just before you left me at al-Shisr and drove back to Sana'a that somehow you felt Robert was out of danger.

What a bitter blow for you then to receive the news that you did. It is almost worse that he is missing and you do not know for certain what has happened to him. But, as you said, it is almost certain that the worst has happened and I expect the MoD or his regiment will confirm that all too soon. When that happens, you must be brave. And you must not hesitate to turn to your friends for whatever comfort and succour they can give.

I hope you are picking up your emails at home, and I hope the week's rest and being with your parents are giving you some comfort and new strength. All I wanted you to know is that if there is anything I can do to help, now or in the future, you have only to ask. Harriet, I think a great deal of you. You are not only a valued colleague but now a dear friend. More than a friend, someone very special to me. I think of you always.

My fondest wishes
Fred

From: Harriet.ct@fitzharris.com
Date: 16 December
To: Fred.jones@fitzharris.com
Subject: Re: Condolences

Fred

Thank you for your sweet email. It helps so much to hear
from my friends, but nothing can bring back Robert. I always
thought that having your heart broken was something that
only people in novels experienced, that it was a form of
words. But that is exactly what this feels like – a pain, in my
heart, with me day and night.

I can't sleep. I can't eat. I cry all the time. I know I am being
pathetic but I can't help myself. I know thousands of others
are going through, or have gone through, what I am now
experiencing. It doesn't make much difference to my own
loss.

You remembered me saying how I felt Robert was out of
danger, how I felt that sensation of relief, or release, that day
after we had walked up the Wadi Aleyn together for the first
time. Robert was out of danger that day, forever out of
danger, forever safe. He died that day.

The MoD got in touch yesterday. They confirmed the time of
his death, and just said it occurred during 'anti-insurgent
operations in eastern Iraq, in the line of duty, killed by enemy
fire together with the rest of his unit'. But that was it: that is
all I will ever know about the circumstances of Robert's death.
Twenty-odd words represent the full extent of the MoD's
comment on Robert's life, his ten years' service with the
marines and his death.

I'm going to pull myself together and come back to work next
week. That's the best chance I have of getting through this.

Although at the moment I'm not sure this is something I ever will get through. But I know you and all my friends will help me try.
Love
Harriet


From: Harriet.ct@fitzharris.com
Date: 14 December
To: Familysupportgroup.gov.uk
Subject: Captain Robert Matthews

Please could someone tell me how I can get more information from the MoD? I was engaged to Captain Robert Matthews who was reported as Missing in Action in Operation Telic 2, and this was posted on the website on 21 November.
The MoD has refused to give me any further information. I would like to know more about the circumstances of his death – where he died and the mission he was engaged on. I do not believe I am being told the full truth about any of this, and I think I and Robert's family have a right to know.
Harriet Chetwode-Talbot


From: Familysupportgroup.gov.uk
Date: 21 December
To: Harriet.ct@fitzharris.com
Subject: Re: Captain Robert Matthews

Dear Ms Chetwode-Talbot
We are unable to help you with any of your queries, as we are dependent on the MoD to supply us with any information

of the kind you are seeking. As Captain Matthews was on
operational duties in an area with maximum threat level
rating, the MoD has reserved the right to make a judgement
about what information can, or cannot, be released on the
basis of security considerations. We cannot assist you further.
However, we recognise the stress this must cause, and suggest
that you contact a new unit which has recently been set up
by the MoD to supplement our own services, which is located
in Grimsby. The contact details are: Bereavement Management
Centre on 0800 400 8000 or at Bereave@Grimsby.com.


From: Harriet.ct@fitzharris.com
Date: 21 December
To: Bereave@Grimsby.com
Subject: Captain Robert Matthews

My name is Harriet Chetwode-Talbot and I was engaged to
a serving officer, Captain Robert Matthews, who was recently
(21 November) posted as Missing in Action on the Operation
Telic 2 website. Please can you help me. I desperately need
to know:
- how he died
- where he died
- why he died
Please can someone contact me as soon as possible?

From: Bereave@Grimsby.com
Date: 3 January
To: Harriet.ct@fitzharris.com
Subject: Re: Captain Robert Matthews

Owing to the volume of enquiries and current MoD budgetary constraints, this operation has recently been offshored to Hyderabad, India. Please call us on 0800 400 8000 and you will be answered by one of our highly trained staff. All of our staff have taken the UK NVQ in bereavement counselling or a local equivalent of the same qualification. As this operation has only recently been transferred, you may experience some linguistic difficulties with some of our newer staff. Please be patient, they are seeking to do their best to help you.
All calls will be monitored for training and quality purposes. The counselling service is entirely free, but calls cost 50p per minute.

# 29

## Interview with Dr Alfred Jones: dinner at the Ritz

**Interrogator:** When did you last meet the sheikh in the UK?

**Dr Alfred Jones:** I met him in a hotel in London, in early July. We had dinner together, and Harriet joined us.

**I:** What was the purpose of the dinner? Was Mr Peter Maxwell present?

**AJ:** No, Peter Maxwell was not present then, although I met him that same day. It was a few days before I went out again to the Yemen for the final project launch. The sheikh had asked Harriet to dine with him at the Ritz. I had never been to the Ritz before. It was a beautiful, elegant room, with large round tables well apart from each other. I arrived first, of course; I am always too early for trains, planes and dinners. I spent ten minutes gazing at the expensively suited, smartly dressed inhabitants of the other tables. Have you ever dined at the Ritz?

**I:** No, I have not dined at the Ritz.

**AJ:** If you ever do, you'll understand that I felt, even in my best dark suit, rather shabby, and I was glad when I saw the sheikh arriving, clad as usual in his white robes and followed by a respectful maître d'hôtel.

'Good evening, Dr Alfred,' said the sheikh as I rose from my seat to greet him. 'You are early. You must be hungry. Good.' He sat in the chair the maître d'hôtel had drawn out for him and ordered a whisky and soda for himself and a glass of champagne for me. I remember the sheikh turned to me and told me how good the food was there. I said I felt sure it was, and the sheikh nodded and said, 'I know it is. The chef who now works here in the hotel used to work for me at my houses in London and Glen Tulloch, but I think he became bored with just cooking for me, and of course many weeks he was on his own when I was in the Yemen or elsewhere. So I understood when he accepted the offer of a job here, and of course I can still come and sample his cooking. I often do.'

The drinks arrived and, with them, Harriet. I had not seen her for weeks. She had gone back to work at Fitz-harris & Price but then had experienced something that I think must have been close to a nervous breakdown. Now she spent most of her time living at home with her parents, working from a laptop in her father's study. My first impression was how pale and thin she was. Then she smiled at us, and her smile brought a lump to my throat. She still looked very pretty, despite her worn out air. I felt a great wave of pity mixed with desire sweep across me. I remember thinking, Desire? I am fifteen years her senior, for God's sake.

'You are off to a good start,' she said, looking at my glass. 'Yes, please, the same for me, if it is what I think it is.'

'The Krug '85,' murmured the wine waiter who had handed us our drinks and was waiting for further orders. 'His Excellency orders no other champagne.'

'I didn't know there was any other kind,' said the sheikh. He smiled at us, and then there was the business of menus being handed round. Once this was done and orders had been taken, the sheikh raised his glass and said, 'A toast!

To my friends, Dr Alfred and Harriet Chetwode-Talbot, who have worked without pause, who have set aside every difficulty both small and great – some difficulties, Harriet Chetwode-Talbot, have been very great for you, very great indeed – and have succeeded against all odds in bringing my project to this point.'

He raised his glass and drank to us. I saw the people at the next table gazing at the unusual, but in that place perhaps not unknown, spectacle of a sheikh drinking from a large tumbler of whisky and soda. He may have been aware of such glances, but they meant nothing to him.

I, in turn, raised my glass and said, 'To the project, Sheikh Muhammad, to its successful launch and its great future, and to the vision that inspired it!'

Harriet and I drank to the sheikh and he inclined his head in acknowledgement and smiled again. 'To the project!' he repeated.

This was our celebration dinner. The sheikh had suggested it a few days ago, after a project review meeting at Harriet's office. Everything was now ready. I had been out on a final tour of inspection in June. The holding tanks had been built, as had the channels that led from them into the Wadi Aleyn. Water had been pumped from the aquifer into the holding tanks, and they had been leak tested. The sluice gates had been tested. The oxygenation equipment, which would keep the salmon alive when the temperature rose, also worked. The heat exchangers, designed to cool the water in the holding basins when the sunlight reached them, were fine. All the equipment had been checked and rechecked. We had run, and rerun, our computer models a hundred times. Nothing had been left to chance, except the great chance of the project itself.

And the wadi had been re-engineered too. There were ramps for the fish to swim up where before large boulders might have obstructed their passage. There was a graded track running alongside the wadi to allow safe access for spectators and anglers, when it was full. Concrete casting platforms had been built at fifty-yard intervals, to allow fishermen who did not want to wade the ability to cover the river with their flies.

Cases of equipment had been flown out to al-Shisr. Stacked in a room at the sheikh's palace were dozens of fishing rods: fifteen-foot rods, twelve-foot rods, nine-foot rods. There were reels of floating line, sinking line; sink tips and leaders of all types. There were boxes and boxes of flies, of every different mixture of colour, size and shape. The selection had been made from flies which were known to catch fish on every imaginable salmon river, from the Spey to the Vistula, from the Oykel to the Ponoi, because no one really knew what fly a salmon in the Yemen would take, and what fly it would not take. The sheikh, I know, was looking forward to hours of experimentation.

The sheikh's honour guard, who had received training in the arts of fly fishing from Colin McPherson, were all back in the Yemen, and would be kitted out with rods and tackle, and encouraged to keep their hand in until the great day. They had been ordered to find a flat bit of desert, and practise Spey casting for an hour every day. The guard to a man were competing to become the first man to catch a salmon in the Wadi Aleyn (and indeed in the whole Islamic world) and the sheikh had already made it known that the first man to catch a fish would receive privileges and riches beyond his dreams, sufficient for the rest of his days, and all the days of his children, and all the days of his children's children.

The previous week we had received a final sign-off from the project engineering team that we were 'good to go'. Now I was counting the days off on the calendar until the great moment came. I was flying back out to the Yemen two days after this dinner, to make the final, final checks and await the arrival of the sheikh and, after him, the prime minister and his party.

I: Tell us about the involvement of the prime minister?

AJ: I've told you before how my memory operates. Let me tell it as it happened. I'm trying to cooperate. If you did not keep interrupting, it would make it easier for both of us.

*Pause while the witness refused to talk for a few minutes. Then he resumed.*

I was no longer in any doubt about the success of this project. I believed it would work. I believed it would be a transforming moment in the history of fisheries science, in the history of the species *Salmo salar,* and in the history of the Yemen. But above all I believed it would be a transforming moment in my own life.

Already I was a quite different person to the Alfred Jones who had started work on this project over a year ago. That man had counted his greatest achievement an article he had written on caddis fly larvae which he had hoped would be published in *Trout & Salmon.* So far, it had not been. That man had lived trapped in a loveless marriage, for so I now realised it had been, accepting his fate meekly and without question. Then, I had not known the nature of love. Now I knew that I might not know much more about love, but at least I understood I had never known what it was before.

And other things were changing in me.

The first course arrived, and as we ate I asked the sheikh how he had come to learn about fishing in the first place. For some reason there had never been a moment to ask him this question before.

'Many years ago,' he said, 'I was asked by my friend Sheikh Makhtoum, the ruler of Dubai, to go and shoot with him in the north of England. He has a very big estate there, with very many grouse, and I have shot sand grouse at home in the Yemen. I may say, I am a very good shot, or at least I thought I was. But when I got there I found that instead of walking after the grouse or pursuing them from vehicles, one was expected to stand still and wait for them to come to the guns. It was very different. We waited and we waited, and then, just as I had given up hope of ever seeing a grouse, clouds of them started flying past us. And the little brown birds, they flew so fast that I could not hit them for a long time. And I was very ashamed, for in the Yemen I am accounted a good shot.

'Then Makhtoun said to me, "If you think that is so difficult, then you must try salmon fishing, and then you will have tried all these strange British sports, and you will agree with me that they are wonderful!" So the next day, when we were not shooting, I went with a man to a river not far away, and he showed me where the salmon lay in the water, and he taught me a little bit how to cast, and then I fished. I did not catch anything that day, but by the end of the day, when I was tired and wet and cold, I knew that there was no other sport for me any more. This was what I wanted to do, with every spare minute that God granted me.

'When I left at the end of my visit, that man came with me. I offered him much money to come, but in the end he came because he could see my love for the fish was as great as his. And the name of that man was Colin McPherson.

'I have not been asked back to shoot grouse by my friend Makhtoum, but I hope he has forgiven me for taking his man.'

Harriet and I laughed. The plates were cleared away and wine was poured for Harriet and me. The sheikh, as usual, drank water with his food.

'Now you must return the compliment,' he said, 'and tell me, Dr Alfred, where you first learned to fish and who was your teacher. In my pride I also now think I am a good fisherman, may God forgive me, but when I see you cast, I think I see a better fisherman than I am.'

I blushed and muttered a denial.

'No, no, do not be embarrassed,' said the sheikh. 'We are both of us true salmon fishermen and all comparisons apart from that are unimportant. But tell me, and Harriet Chetwode-Talbot shall learn as well, how it was you became a fisherman.'

So I told him about my father, who was a schoolmaster in the Midlands. There was not a salmon within a hundred miles of us, at least not in those days, and he used to take me to Scotland every summer. My mother died when I was young, and my father was too busy to spend much time with me during term time. My aunt took care of me most of the time. But in the summer holidays we would go up and fish on little spate rivers in the north of Scotland, in the Flow Country or on the west coast. In those days it did not cost too much to buy a bit of fishing for a couple of rods for a week. Sometimes we went onto the estuaries of larger rivers where you could buy a ticket and fish for the day. And we used to rent a little bothy and sleep in that, and my father and I would gather up wood and light a campfire, and if we caught a fish he'd show me how to gut it and cook it, and the whole experience just got into my blood. I remember those long summer evenings in the far north, when there was just enough wind to keep the midges away, as the happiest moments of my life.

I stopped for a moment, feeling I was talking too much, but both the sheikh and Harriet were looking at me raptly. I could tell that they too could see what was in my mind's eye, as nearly as one person can ever see what is in the mind of another. A small boy of twelve or thirteen, standing on the shingle of a wide stream turning silver and gold in the evening light, the bothy behind him, where smoke curls up from a wood fire. He takes his rod up to the vertical and the line flies back over his head. A pause, then a snap of the wrist and the rod whips the line back out, so that it lands light as a feather on shadowed water under the far bank. I remembered the low hills in the distance and the cries of curlews and oystercatchers which had flown in from the nearby estuary, and I remembered the stillness and fulfilment in my heart as I saw the fly come round perfectly, and saw the swirl of the fish following it.

The next course arrived and broke the spell.

'And your father taught you?' asked Harriet.

'Oh yes,' I said. 'He had fished for sea trout in Wales, as a boy. He knew all about it. He was a true expert, a better fisherman than I will ever be And he taught me the "Fisherman's Rhyme".'

'What is the "Fisherman's Rhyme"?' asked the sheikh. 'I have never heard of this.'

'It,' I explained, 'is the rhyme that every fisherman chants to himself before he leaves the house, to make quite sure he does not forget anything essential. Do you want to hear it?'

'Of course,' said the sheikh. 'I insist we hear it.'

I glanced apologetically at Harriet and then said, 'Rod, reel,/Flask, creel,/Net, fly book/And lunch.'

They both laughed out loud, and the sheikh had to have the rhyme repeated to him. Then Harriet said, 'What happened at your meeting with the odious Peter Maxwell? You haven't said. Sorry, Sheikh, but he *is* odious even though I know you are too polite ever to admit it.'

I: Please tell us now about your meeting with Peter Maxwell.

AJ: As I told you before, it was earlier the same day. Some time at the beginning of July but I can't remember the date. I went to Downing Street and was shown into his office after only the briefest of waits, which was unusual with him. To my surprise, instead of the usual dark blue suit he was wearing a safari jacket, an open-necked shirt, chinos and desert boots. He stood up, shook my hand and greeted me like an old friend.

'This is my desert outfit,' he told me, indicating the safari jacket. 'What do you think?'

'Perfect,' I assured him.

'Do you know,' said Peter Maxwell, as he showed me to my seat, 'there are four million anglers in this country? Four million!'

'No,' I said, sitting down and accepting the cup of coffee he handed me, 'I didn't know, but the number doesn't particularly surprise me. It sounds about right.'

'Do you know how many paid-up members there are of our party in the country?' He held up his hand to forestall my guess. I'm not political anyway; I wouldn't have known. 'Less than half a million,' he informed me. 'More than ten anglers out there for every committed party member. I mean, it puts a whole new spin on the project, doesn't it? *Doesn't it?*'

'I don't know,' I confessed. 'I'm a bit slow at grasping these political ideas.'

Maxwell seemed very excited. '*You've* been slow? Not you. *I've been slow.* You, Fred, have been doing a great job. No one would have given odds on the Yemen salmon project succeeding a few months ago. Thanks to you, I don't think many people would bet against it now. That is why I am so excited by what is happening. You know, if you don't get a knighthood at the end of this, then I'd like to know what the honours system is all about. And the chairman of the Patronage Committee is an old, old friend of mine. No, the only person who hasn't been doing his job as well as he should have is me. Me, Peter Maxwell, who was supposed to see every political angle in every story. How could I have missed this until now? How could I?' And he struck his brow, rather dramatically, with the heel of his hand.

'Thank God, it's not too late,' he said. 'There I was thinking that the real spin-off for the project was all those guys out there who don't agree with our various military interventions. You've seen the placards on demonstrations: "Troops out of Iraq", "Troops out of Saudi Arabia", "Troops out of Kazakhstan". I mean, it's becoming like a bad geography lesson. The original idea was we were going to provide a distraction to all these protest groups by doing something a bit different in the Yemen – fish, not guns. You understood that, didn't you, Fred?'

'Yes,' I said, 'I got the general idea. I'm afraid I've been concentrating on the technical side of the project and haven't given enough thought to the other aspects, but yes, I think I had grasped the basis of your interest. Is that no longer the case?'

'Oh, it is still the case. Very much the case We still want the media coverage and the "fish, not war" story. We still want to go ahead with the PM's visit, and we still want the goodwill we think we will bank from that. But there's so much more. Don't you see?'

'I'm still not sure I do,' I said, feeling stupid and slow.

Maxwell stood up again and began pacing up and down the carpet in front of three vast, silent, flickering TV screens. 'Well, here's the maths,' he said. 'We think there might still be a hard core of half a million people out there who are troubled by our various Middle Eastern wars, especially the ones in Iraq. Half of them are probably our natural voters but now they might not vote for us at the next election. So, when we launch the project, we win some of them back. Maybe half of them, so that's – are you following me – just over one hundred thousand votes which could swing our way. Plus a lot of advantages if we could get the media off our case for a few days.

'Now, let's look at the angling community. There are four million of them, and we don't have the research that tells us how they vote. It's not in our database. Isn't that incredible! We analyse our voters by socio-economic class, by geography, by whether they own their own home or not, by whether they had a university education or not, by

273

age, by income group, by whether they drink wine or beer, by what their skin colour and sexual preference is, and by what their religion is. They're so analysed it isn't true. But we don't know whether they fish or not. The biggest popular sport in the country, and we don't know how many of them are, or could be, our voters.'

I was beginning to see the point.

'But I tell you this, Fred,' said Maxwell, stopping in mid-pace, wheeling round and pointing a finger at me, 'by the time I'm finished we'll know everything we need to know about them. They'll be the best-analysed voter group of the lot. And I'll tell you the other thing about them: they will see and read stories, starting with this project, of just what a keen angler the PM is. He said so last year in the House. We'll build on that statement. We'll repeat it in all the papers and on TV. And then we'll show the people that we are the government for anglers. There'll be more money for fisheries. There'll be angling academies. There'll be a fishing rod for every child over the age of ten. I haven't worked it all out yet, Fred, but by God if less than three million of those anglers don't vote for us at the next election, then I will have lost my touch.'

I nodded my head and said, 'Well, we will do the best we can with our part of it.'

Peter Maxwell sat down behind his desk again. 'I know you will, Fred; I have great faith that you will deliver on the project. But, just one thing' – here the finger pointed at me again – 'the boss has got to catch a fish. And our schedule still says he has only twenty minutes to do it in. But it is crucial that we have that photo opportunity. Fred, you, and you alone, have to guarantee he gets that salmon. Can you do it?'

I had been preparing for this question and I knew the answer. 'Yes,' I said, 'I can make the sure the prime minister has a fish on the end of his line by the time he has to leave.'

Peter Maxwell looked relieved, and impressed. I think he was expecting to have to fight a battle with me over this.

'How will you do it?' he asked curiously. 'I'm told it's not that easy to catch these things.'

'You don't want to know,' I told him.

The rest of the conversation was all about the prime minister's schedule, his private meetings in Sana'a and the press arrangements, and I didn't repeat any of it to Harriet and the sheikh because they had helped arrange all that part of it anyway.

I: This has nothing to do with anything except my personal curiosity, but how *would* you get a fish on the end of someone's line?

AJ: That's exactly what Harriet asked me at dinner that night: 'How on earth can you guarantee that the prime minister catches a fish?'

I smiled. The sheikh leaned forward, his face full of interest.

'When I was a boy my father played a trick on me once. He put a fly several sizes too large on the end of my line. He knew that the fly would sink too fast into the water and that I was bound to snag the fly on a stone. And he knew that, because I was so inexperienced, I would think the stone I had caught was a fish. It takes a while before you know the difference.'

'It is true,' said the sheikh. 'I made the same mistake myself once or twice, when I started fishing.'

'So then he went out with the net and pretended he was having difficulty landing the fish. But actually what he did was stand with his back to me, get a salmon he'd caught earlier out of the poaching pocket in his jacket, take it out of the newspaper he had wrapped it in, pull my fly from under the stone where it was caught, hook it into the salmon's mouth, and jerk the line and splash about to give the impression there was a bit of a fight and there was the fish in the net.'

The sheikh and Harriet laughed.

'But did he tell you?' asked Harriet.

'Oh yes, he told me. I'd caught a couple of fish by then and the point of the joke was to teach me the difference between the pull of a fish on the line, and the pull of the weight of water on the line, when the fly is simply stuck on a rock or in a bit of weed.'

'Your prime minister must never know,' said the sheikh seriously. 'I do not want to give offence or distress to a guest, no matter what happens.'

'He won't know,' I promised him.

Dinner was over, and the sheikh said he would sit in the foyer to wait for his car. Harriet and I agreed we would like a walk before finding taxis to take us to our homes. It was a beautiful evening, and the sky was still light. We walked slowly along Piccadilly together.

'What a good evening,' said Harriet. 'I do love the sheikh. I will miss him.'

'Won't you see him next time he comes to Glen Tulloch?'

'He won't be coming back for a long while. He wants to stay and attend to the future success of the salmon project, and he knows the launch is just the beginning and there will be many, many problems and crises to deal with after that. And you, I hope, will go there and help whenever he needs it.'

'Of course I will,' I agreed, 'but won't you?'

'I don't know,' said Harriet. 'Maybe it's time for me to move on. I've put a lot of myself into the project, and really there isn't that much more for me to do. And Robert's death, as you know better than most people, has been a very heavy blow. I just need to take stock. I need a break.'

'Of course you need a break, Harriet,' I told her. 'No one deserves it more than you.' We had stopped by the railings that ran alongside Green Park, absorbed in our conversation. The evening traffic was still busy. The park gates were still open, so we stepped inside for a moment to get away from the noise of traffic.

'But you'll come to the Yemen for the great day?' I asked.

'No, Fred, I won't,' said Harriet. 'I will be there for you in spirit, but not in the flesh. The truth is I couldn't bear it if something went wrong. I couldn't bear another disaster. I'd rather be here, and then if I don't want to see what's happening I can just switch off the television until it is over.'

'But there won't be a disaster,' I said.

'I know there won't,' she said. 'I know you've done everything you can to make this work, and I know that if anyone can pull this off, it's you. But. . . my head tells me all of that, and my heart tells me something else.'

I stared at her. She stood close to me, her face white in the faint street light, still beautiful to me despite the lines of strain.

'But, Harriet . . .'

277

'I'm going away,' she said, 'the day after the project is launched in the Yemen. I've got leave of absence from Fitzharris for six months, and they'll keep my job open in case I want it back. At the moment, I don't think I will.'

'But, Harriet . . .' I said again, hopelessly.

Tears began to roll down her cheeks. It was too much. I took her in my arms and kissed her. At first she let me hold her and responded briefly to my kiss, but then she went limp. I let her go and she stepped away.

'Don't, Fred,' she said.

'But when will I see you again?' I asked. 'You know how I feel about you. I can't help it, and I'm so sorry to have done what I just did, so soon after Robert, but I can wait. I'll always wait for you, if you just say that one day there could be some hope for me.'

'There isn't any hope,' she said in a dull voice, 'not for you, not for me.'

'But, Harriet,' I said again, 'you know what happened at al-Shisr. Didn't that mean anything to you? It meant everything to me. It changed my life.'

'I can't see you again, Fred,' Harriet told me, her voice still not quite steady, 'and whatever happened, or didn't happen, at al-Shisr was just a dream you had. I only remember a dream. And now we're in waking life and the reality is you are married to Mary. You are fifteen or twenty years older than me, and we come from completely different worlds. I am still grieving for Robert, and I have to rebuild my life without him. And I have to do it without you or anyone else. It just isn't possible there could ever be more between us. We've been friends – you've been the best friend I could have ever wanted – but I can't give you any hope that there would ever be anything more.'

I turned away from her for a moment. The lamps in the park had just come on and must have dazzled my eyes, for they were watering. With my back to her I said, 'I understand, Harriet. You're right.'

She came up to me and put a hand on my shoulder. 'I know I'm right. I hate myself for it, but it's the truth. Come on, Fred, help me find a taxi.'

*The interview resumed the following morning.*

I: Describe the events that took place in the Wadi Aleyn.

AJ: The thing to realise about the Wadi Aleyn in August was that it was hot. It was hot beyond the imagination of anyone who has never been in the desert. The sun in the Wadi Aleyn was hotter than a dozen English suns. It burned down out of a milky sky, and the rocks were hot to the touch. The thought of a salmon surviving unprotected in that heat, in that incandescent light, was beyond belief. And yet they had to.

I had been a dozen times around the holding basins, which were slowly filling with water from the aquifer. The oxygen bubblers were working rhythmically at the sides. Water temperatures were being held stable at around 21 degrees Celsius and we thought we could drop that three degrees when the rains came. I had checked everything, and rechecked, and I knew I was driving the project teams, and myself, mad with my constant questioning. In the end I took myself off up the wadi. I wore a hat and covered myself with sun cream, but still I felt as if I was in a furnace.

This was the time before the rains came. Out in the desert sandstorms would build themselves on giant thermals. In the towns and villages people and animals moved about as little as possible in the heat of the day, found shade wherever they could and waited for the sun to go lower in the sky.

In the wadi the heat and airlessness were almost too much for me. There was a sense of something building, like a distant storm. When the rains came, we would make a call to the UK. Within twenty-four hours of that call, the fish at McSalmon Aqua Farms would be taken from their cages and placed in the flying aquariums, which is what everyone called the stainless-steel pods in which they would be flown out to the Middle East. In another twenty-four hours they would be ready for delivery into the holding basins. And then we would wait. We would wait for the waters of the Wadi Aleyn to flow, and as the flow grew from a trickle to a stream, from a stream to a river, we would open the sluice gates. And then we would see.

I found I was breathing hard and feeling a little dizzy. The heat was getting to me. There was no one within a mile of me, at least no one I could see. I found a flat stone in the shade of overhanging cliffs that was not too hot, and sat on it, trying to recover myself. I took a Thermos of cold water from my backpack and took a pull on it. After a moment I felt a little better.

The silence around me was absolute. Even the buzzards were quiet. Rock walls stretched above me. There was not a single sign of vegetation. What did the goats live on now, the goats belonging to the girl further up the wadi who had once brought us water?

I tried not to think about Harriet, but she kept intruding into my thoughts, as real as if she was standing in front of me. I could almost see her, like a ghost, now gaining substance, now fading again, her voice, thin and insubstantial, saying, 'There isn't any hope, not for me, not for you.'

I thought about the sheikh saying, although I could not remember his exact words, 'Without faith, there is no hope. Without faith, there is no love.'

Then in a moment, in that vast space of rocks and sky and scorching sun, I understood that he had not meant religious faith, not exactly. He was not urging me to become a Muslim or to believe in one interpretation of God rather than another. He knew me for what I was, an old, cold, cautious scientist. That was what I was then. And he was simply pointing out to me the first step to take. The word he had used was faith, but what he meant was belief. The first step was simple: it was to believe in belief itself. I had just taken that step. At long last I understood.

I had belief. I did not know, or for the moment care, what exactly it was I had to believe in. I only knew that belief in something was the first step away from believing in nothing, the first step away from a world which only recognised what it could count, measure, sell or buy. The people here still had that innocent power of belief: not the angry denial of other people's belief of religious fanatics, but a quiet affirmation. That was what I sensed here, in this land and in this place, which made it so different from home. It was not the clothes, not the language, not the customs, not the sense of being in another century. It was none of these. It was the pervading presence of belief.

I believed in belief. I didn't exactly feel as if I was on

the road to Damascus, and I was aware I could not think straight because of the power of the sun, but now I knew what the Yemen salmon project was all about. It had already worked its transformation on me. It would do the same for others.

# 30

## Dr Jones fails to find a date in his diary to meet Mrs Jones

From: Mary.jones@interfinance.org
Date: 15 July
To: Fred.jones@fitzharris.com
Subject: Visit

Fred

I am coming back to London for a review meeting in the first week in August. I know this is slightly later than I originally suggested, but I had to get a date in the diary of our CEO western hemisphere, and that is never easy.

I trust you will be able to accommodate this change in your own plans as I think it is most important we meet. I am concerned that you have allowed my extended absence in Geneva (which I think we agreed at the time was an essential career step for me, and one I think that, in the light of the insecurity of your present position, I was wise to take) to lead you into a state of complacency about our marriage. While I am working every hour in the day every weekday and most weekends in order to provide for our future financial security, you appear to be leading a life progressively more and more disconnected from reality. Of course you tell me very little, but from what I can gather, you have spent the spring fishing in Scotland with your sheikh and his lady friend or sunning yourself in the Yemen with the same lady, while our flat is neglected, and I am neglected too. It is very difficult for me to say it, but I am neglected.

So please be sure to be available when I arrive in London. We need to talk.

Mary


From: Fred.jones@fitzharris.com
Date: 16 July
To: Mary.jones@interfinance.org
Subject: Re: Visit

Mary

While you are at the mercy of the InterFinance CEO western hemisphere and his timetable, my own schedule is now decided by the office of the prime minister. They have decreed I must be in the Yemen on the dates you say you will be in London, and I am afraid there is nothing I can do about that. I have to be there.

I am terribly sorry. I agree we need to meet. I will be back in mid-August, if all goes well, and I suggest either I fly to Geneva or you fly to London one weekend.

Love

Fred

From: Mary.jones@interfinance.org
Date: 16 July
To: Fred.jones@fitzharris.com
Subject: Re: Re: Visit

Fred
I cannot for a moment imagine that the prime minister
couldn't do without you for a day or two in the Yemen. He
has a whole government at his beck and call, surely he could
do without one fisheries scientist for a couple of days? I can
only assume you are deliberately avoiding me.
You can fly to Geneva if you like. I cannot guarantee my
availability that far ahead. I have a lot of travel commitments
coming up.
Mary

From: Fred.jones@fitzharris.com
Date: 18 July
To: Mary.jones@interfinance.org
Subject: Yemen trip

Mary
OK.
I know you don't believe that the PM wants me in the Yemen
but I think this trip and these dates have been in his diary
for some weeks now, which was why I was careful to let you
know about them. I can't help it if your boss changes his
plans around.
I was trying to be accommodating but if that's the way it is,
that's the way it is. See you some time – I shall always be

glad to see you – but it takes two to arrange a meeting.
Love
Fred


From: Mary.jones@interfinance.org
Date: 18 July
To: Fred.jones@fitzharris.com
Subject: Re: Yemen trip

Fred
Please come back to me.
Mary

# 31

## Extract from Peter Maxwell's unpublished autobiography

Now I come to one of the most difficult chapters in a political life that has never been without its challenges. I must speak of events which transcended political life. No Aristotle, no Shakespeare, no writer that I can think of has had to describe events such as I will now write of. I do not aspire to their talents. I am simply a modest journalist who has found himself drawn into the centre of events which have changed this country, perhaps the world, for ever. I must do the best I can, with my limited powers, to help my readers understand what happened.

It all started so well.

The boss was in holiday mood. It had been a bad week in the House of Commons, and when he finally got to the plane he was almost behaving like a small boy who has been let out of school early. On the flight out to Sana'a it was, nevertheless, mostly work. We had to prep for a private meeting with the Yemeni president, and there were one or two other tasks to be dealt with, but four hours into the flight Jay loosened his tie, stretched his arms and said, 'Peter, is there some of that Oyster Bay Sauvignon in the fridge?'

I went and opened a bottle and brought back a couple of glasses.

I *loved* it when it was just the boss and me on a trip. It

didn't happen often. There was usually some irritating third person, like the Cabinet secretary or some other civil servant, and the boss wouldn't be able to unwind. He never trusted those people. They were always resigning and writing their memoirs, and anything careless he said in front of them would end up in print. When he and I were alone like this, I think a lot of the real business of government was mapped out. We used to noodle around the big ideas: what to do with the National Health Service; where we stand on China; why should ASBOs have a lower age limit at all? It was creative stuff. I loved it, and the boss had many of his big ideas after these sessions with me.

On this trip it was just the two of us again. I don't mean that literally. In the back of the plane was a carefully selected group of media people to cover the launch of the Yemen salmon project; there were the security people; there were communications people. But there were only two real players on the plane on that trip – the boss and me. We sat up at the front, in a private part of the cabin.

The boss sipped at the cool wine when I handed him the glass and said, 'You know, Peter, I give you a lot of marks for spotting those angling votes. No one else saw that. Not the party chairman, not the campaign coordinator, none of them. And it's so obvious.'

'Well, boss, it took *me* long enough to get the point,' I said.

'It certainly underlines the importance of this trip. It was important beforehand, but now it is crucial. We can gain so much from this if everything goes right. Who are the media people on the plane?'

I looked at my list. 'Well, we've got the usual BBC and ITV people. You said no Channel Four.'

'Not after the coverage of my visit to Kazakhstan.'

'They'll have a reporter on site anyway; it can't be helped. At least they'll have to pay their own air fares.'

'Who else?'

I looked down at the sheet of paper again. '*Daily Telegraph, Daily Mail, Times, Independent, Mirror* and *Sun*. We didn't ask the *Guardian*. Their whole line on this project has been bloody patronising and actually we're on non-speaks at the moment. And we have some new faces.'

'Oh,' said the boss. 'Who?'

'*Angling Times, Trout & Salmon, Atlantic Salmon Journal, Coarse Fisherman, Fishing News* and *Sustainable Development International*. All the broadsheet and tabloid boys are having gin and tonics in the back, but this new lot are huddled together away from the regular journos, drinking tea out of Thermos flasks. They've even brought their own sandwiches.'

The boss seemed pleased. 'I must make a special effort with the fishing press. I want that photo of me with a fish on the front cover of every angling magazine in the country next month.'

'It'll be there,' I said. 'I guarantee it.'

The boss stretched again and poured himself another glass of wine. 'How long have we got until landing?' he asked.

'Another three hours.'

'I might have a kip before we get in. You know, Peter, I've been having some private tuition in fly-fishing for the last week or two. I want the photos to look right.'

'I'm sure they will, boss,' I said loyally. 'You pick up that sort of thing really fast.'

'Yes, I do, luckily. But I tell you what, I think fishing might be quite fun. I really do. I wouldn't mind trying it again when

I have more leisure. I mean, I suppose I'll only have time ... How long have we got at Wadi Aleyn?'

'Thirty, forty minutes, then back to Sana'a and on to Muscat for your speech to the Gulf Coordinating Council.'

'Yes, I'll only have time to catch one salmon, perhaps two at the most. But I'd like to have another go, on another occasion, when we get back to the UK. Do you think you could arrange it?'

'I know exactly the place where you could catch loads of fish, boss,' I said, thinking of McSalmon Aqua Farms.

'Good,' he said, stifling a yawn. 'Let's make a plan. And now I think I'll go next door and have a rest before we land.'

When we landed at Sana'a it was early evening and dark. But the heat radiating from the tarmac hit us in the face as soon as we stepped out of the door of the plane, and with the heat came strange scents which could not be drowned out by the normal airport smells of aviation spirit and diesel. They were unsettling scents, hinting of a strange and unfamiliar world somewhere beyond the city lights. Then we were tripping down the steps and shaking hands and climbing into the air-conditioned limo.

The evening in Sana'a was long, polite and tedious. I don't think we expected to achieve anything, and I don't think we did, except that by dining with our host we implicitly received his sanction for our 'private' visit to the Wadi Aleyn. He seemed bemused by the whole thing and at one point over dinner asked me, in a low voice that the boss could not have overheard, 'Why is your prime minister interested in this salmon project? Everyone here thinks it is quite mad.'

'It has captured his imagination, President,' I replied.

'Ah,' he said, leaning back in his chair and looking baffled.

I could see he had decided not to ask me any more questions on the subject, as I was clearly not going to tell him anything of use. The conversation became general again, and we spent the rest of the evening discussing how to put the Kazakhstan peace process back on the rails.

The next day we got up at dawn and had an early breakfast at the embassy. I can still feel the sense of almost childish optimism with which the boss and I boarded the helicopter. It was such fun to be going off to fish for our country! That was how we both felt. The boss was all smiles, shaking hands with the journalists, who were following on in a second Chinook, shaking hands with the ambassador, who had come to see us off, shaking hands with the pilot and co-pilot. He only just remembered in time not to shake my hand as well. Then we were in the helicopter, and the ground was slipping away sideways below us.

As we took off, the smallest knot of tension began to form itself in the base of my stomach. I'm used to helicopters, so that wasn't it. I remembered, in a brief flash of something I imagined was déjà vu, a dream I had once had about the boss and me standing in a wadi. The dry heat was running like flames across our skin. He had pointed upstream and said something. I couldn't remember what he had said to me or whether I had really ever had such a dream. It was probably jet lag. I shook my head and concentrated on the immediate situation.

We sat there talking, laughing and joking with the security people in the back, and pointing out the grey and white tower houses and mosques of Sana'a, as they receded into the distance. Then we were approaching the mountains, and everyone fell silent as we approached the enormous walls of rock. We flew over mountain ridges, above great canyons a thousand feet deep, through cloud and mist that caught upon the peaks. The sky was grey, and cloud was boiling up in the south. It was pretty boring scenery, but the weather looked right.

'Look at all those clouds,' I said to the boss. 'The water in the wadis will be rising with all this rain coming in.'

The water in the wadis will be rising – hadn't those words been in my dream?

I was right. When we looked below us, we could see the occasional thread of white where water was running through the wadis; and where the flat gravel plains met the foothills of the mountains, pools of lying water had formed here and there.

I was so excited. This was so different to a normal trip. There were no men in grey suits waiting at the end of it, no tough negotiations, no speeches to be made. Instead of men in suits, there would be the sheikh and those great-looking guys who had made a guard of honour for me when I visited Glen Tulloch. It would just be an hour or two of fun, pure and simple. Jay would press a button to open the sluice gates and let the salmon run down the channels that lead into the wadi. Then he would go and stand in the river with his fishing rod and cast away for the benefit of the photographers. Fred had promised me the boss would catch a fish, and that would be it. There would be a short speech, followed by pictures of Jay standing in the river in his waders, with his fishing rod in one hand and a salmon in the other. I could picture how it would look on the front pages the next day. Mission accomplished. A great trip, a day in the desert, and well on the way to swinging several million voters across to our side.

Then we started to lose height, and the helicopter dropped down between the rock walls of the wadi towards a flat patch of ground and what looked like a giant construction site.

As the blades stopped turning we ducked out of the helicopter and walked through the swirling dust to a wooden platform. I could make out the sheikh, Fred Jones and a group of men in hard hats, presumably the site engineers. Beyond them stood a couple of dozen or so of the sheikh's people in white robes and emerald-green turbans, some armed with rifles, others empty-handed.

Behind the platform, curving out from the side of the mountain, were the walls of three huge concrete basins: the holding tanks. For a moment I was truly awestruck by the enormity of this construction project. Listening to Fred's presentations back in Downing Street I had thought, it's like building another primary school or another supermarket. I simply hadn't grasped what an enormous undertaking it was. This was more like the Aswan Dam, or the Pyramids. I hoped the photographers would capture the drama of the site.

In the centre of each basin wall was a pair of iron doors connected by a concrete channel to the wadi bed. Looking across to the wadi, I saw a wide, shallow river running down it. The sun had emerged for a moment from behind white towers of cloud and the sunlight glistened on many streams winding around islands of gravel or cascading over boulders. The fronds of green palms waved in a rising wind on the far bank. Behind us mountains rose, familiar as something once seen in a dream, of a staggering savagery and beauty, into an overcast sky.

I said to the boss, 'Look at that! The river looks perfect. This is going to work!'

The boss looked at me in surprise. Of course it was going to work, the look said; you wouldn't have dragged me 6000 miles for something that didn't work, would you, Peter? Not if you wanted to stay in the job you like so much for another day. Before I could explain, we were at the platform, shaking hands again, smiling, joking, talking. Behind us I heard the second Chinook, with the press on board, coming in to land.

Of course the boss expected it to work. He had no conception of how much work had gone into the project, how much effort I had put into making sure it happened against all obstacles, how I had supported Fred Jones and the sheikh. I looked around me while the boss and the sheikh started shaking hands all over again for the benefit of the journos and the TV cameras, and I heard Fred at my side say, 'Impressive, isn't it?'

'It's fantastic,' I said, with real enthusiasm. 'I had no idea of the scale of all of this.' I gestured to the concrete walls of the holding basins and the channels waiting for the gates to be opened and the salmon to come tumbling and leaping out. 'Our project is going to be a huge success, Fred.' I saw he was holding a landing net.

'We hope so,' he said, and gave me a smile of real friendliness. For a moment I found myself liking the guy. I'd never given him much thought before, not as a person, I mean. 'Come and look at the salmon,' he said. The boss and the sheikh, the boss's security people and some of the press were making their way up a ramp to the edge of a holding basin. The sheikh's men mostly held back. I noticed again that a few of them held rifles and remembered where we were – in the heart of the Yemen, not visiting a new hospital in Dulwich. But, I thought, the Yemen must be safe now, mustn't it? The security people would never have let the boss come if it hadn't been. I mean, there had been that strange story about al-Qaeda attempting to murder the sheikh in Scotland, but we had all discounted that as a piece invented by some Scottish newspaper.

We stood at the top of the ramp and looked over the edge of the wall. The basin was full of silver salmon, darting here and there or else lying motionless in the shaded parts of the water. At intervals around the edge of the basin were machines that looked a bit like huge outboard motors, churning and aerating the water.

'How are they doing?' I asked Fred.

'We've had a few deaths from stress, but whether that was from the heat or the journey I'm not really sure. Anyway, the number of deaths is well within our projections, and the temperature of the water in here is quite stable.'

I stared at the fish, quite fascinated. Then I looked around me at the towering mountains, the slopes of sand and gravel below us, the palm trees and the Yemeni tribesmen standing guard on the top of rocks and on the nearer ridges.

'It's unbelievable,' I said. 'If I wasn't seeing it with my own eyes ...'

'You see,' said Fred, 'the sheikh was right. He has made us all believe. And now we are ready to open the sluice gates, and the miracle will begin.'

'Will it?' I asked him. I could see Fred was tense, but I think it was anticipation and not doubt.

'There's every chance. The air temperature has dropped steadily for the last few days. It's only about 25 degrees Celsius now, and we are coming up to the hottest part of the day. The water temperature in the wadi is perfect and ...' He glanced up at the sky, where fluffy grey and white cumulus now obscured the sun. 'I think we can expect some more rain soon.'

We trooped back down the ramp and walked past the platform to a row of Portakabins. Jay and the sheikh went inside to change into their fishing kit and Colin McPherson, whom I hadn't seen in the crowd before, started unloading rods from the back of a pickup, and then assembling them and making up the cast and flies. A crowd of excited tribesmen gathered around him shouting and gesticulating. Not all of them, though; I could still see a watchful ring of guards further away, staying aloof from the proceedings and scanning the hills around us. One in particular, it struck me, would make a particularly dramatic photo: he stood higher up than the others, on a rocky promontory overlooking the river, his robes fluttering in the strengthening breeze, his rifle resting on his shoulder, the muzzle pointing uphill. I thought of asking a friendly cameraman to take a picture for me, but then there was a roar of applause as Jay and the sheikh both appeared from the Portakabin, wearing chest waders and tartan shirts. They walked towards the pickup, where McPherson was handing out rods to a select few of the tribesmen. When Jay and the sheikh drew near, he picked out two rods he had reserved for them and handed them over. There was another roar of applause, and some of the tribesmen started ululating. Even the journos were entering into the spirit of the moment. I saw old McLeish from the *Telegraph*, a hardened cynic if ever there was one, brush something from his eye. I like to think it was a tear but it may only have been a piece of grit.

Jay and the sheikh walked back to the wooden platform beside the first holding basin. As they did so, I felt something hit the back of my neck, and I looked up in surprise. It was beginning to rain: just a few drops, big, surprisingly cold drops, which made little craters in the dust where they fell. Somebody handed Jay a portable transmitter, and everyone started going, 'Sssh! Ssssh!' Gradually the silence spread, until the only sound was the busy murmuring of the water a few hundred yards downhill. Into that silence, the boss spoke. 'What a tremendous honour it is,' he said, 'to be asked to be here today.'

More cheers and ululations, but the boss held up his hand, and dead silence fell again. He turned to the sheikh. 'Thank you, Sheikh Muhammad, for inviting me, and from the bottom of my heart I say this: yours is the vision, yours is the imagination, yours is the boundless financial generosity without which this project would never have been realised. And we are proud, proud that you have chosen to work with British scientists, British engineers, and indeed engineers of many nations, to realise this project and bring it to fruition. Who would ever have dreamed that one day salmon would swim in the rivers of the Yemen?'

He paused again. The silence was again absolute.

'You dreamed it, Sheikh Muhammad. You had that courage and that determination, and now today, at last, the moment has come. Let us go together, you and I, and fish for salmon in the Wadi Aleyn!'

Tremendous cheering started, faded away and then started again as the boss held the transmitter up in the air, so that we could all see what was happening, and then pointed it, like a TV remote, at the sluice gates. He pressed a button. Slowly, the gates began to open. They did not open fully, but enough for a steady flow of water to emerge, enough for the fish to swim in. In the water spouting from the foot of the sluice gates and in the concrete channel I could see glistening shapes tumbling and wriggling as they were swept down to the river.

At once the crowd started moving towards the river. It was beginning to rain quite steadily now, and it was getting darker. We all bunched up together near where the concrete channel debouched into the wadi itself.

'Make way for Dr Alfred,' cried the sheikh in a clear voice, and the crowd fell back to allow Fred to come forward. He was not wearing waders, but nevertheless he strode in his boots into the stream and peered down into the water. We were all going to get wet soon enough anyway, I thought. It was raining harder and the sky far above us at the head of the wadi was almost black.

Even from where I stood I could see the fins of the salmon cutting through the shallow waters of the Wadi Aleyn. Some of them leaped from the water, almost dancing on its surface. And they were turning upstream! A few were going the wrong way, downriver, but most of the salmon were going upstream. The salmon were running the waters of the Wadi Aleyn, in the heart of the mountains of Heraz!

Jay and the sheikh waded into the river holding their fishing rods, and picked their way carefully over boulders until they were each standing in the centre of the wadi about thirty yards apart. The press cameras and TV videocams were now all pointing at the two of them. We had live feed to Sky TV, BBC24, ITV, CNN and al-Jazeera. Amidst all the press crouching or standing on the riverbank, I saw Colin keeping an eye on his master. I saw our security people take up positions on the bank opposite Jay, their eyes watchful, their hands never far from the concealed holsters they wore, scanning the rocks and ridges on either side of the river. A dozen Yemenis carrying their fishing rods and landing nets strode past, along the new track that ran along the wadi, heading for the casting platforms that had been built further upstream.

Then the sheikh cast out his line, and a moment or two later so did the boss. I had to hand it to the boss; he looked like he'd been doing it all his life. The line went straight out and didn't make much of a splash when it hit the water. It was typical of the man: everything came easily to him. If he'd been told he had to ski the next week or play in a water polo match, he'd have done it, and looked good doing it, as well.

Then I heard Fred shout, 'Be careful! The water is rising! Keep an eye on it!'

The boss either didn't hear, or didn't want to hear. He had let his fly come round and was making his next cast. The rain was coming down like stair rods now, and the river looked as if it was almost boiling under the weight of water coming down out of the sky.

'I think you should come out now!' shouted Fred. 'There's a hell of a lot of water coming down!'

Even I could see that the water in the wadi was rising. I found I had unconsciously stepped back a couple of yards, higher up the bank. At the same moment Colin began to wade into the river, I suppose to help the sheikh out. I saw our security men looking at each other, wondering what to do.

There was a flash of lightning, or perhaps it was not lightning, but it made me turn my head and I saw the tribesman I had noticed earlier on the promontory, with his rifle raised to his shoulder. He had either just fired a shot, or was about to fire one. Had I heard a shot? The water coming down the river was beginning to roar now. One of the security people pulled a gun from under his jacket in a single fluid move, and I think he shot the tribesman. At any rate the man fell backwards off the rocky crag and disappeared from my sight. I don't know who he had been intending to shoot. I think it must have been the sheikh, but I can't be sure.

There was uproar and several more shots were fired by the Yemenis, I don't know what at. I don't think they had yet grasped what was going on. The crowd broke up, people scrambling up the bank to get away from the river and from the shooting. I found that I was several yards higher up the bank again, my heart thumping in my chest, staring down at the boss.

He had turned to look at the noise, but he wasn't moving. I think he was smiling. I don't think he had seen the tribesman either shooting or being shot, although he knew something had happened, because he had turned to look downstream.

I saw him look at the sheikh, who was bent over, supported by Colin, who was now at his side and struggling to keep his balance against the weight of water. Maybe the sheikh had been shot. I don't know.

Behind the boss I saw a wall of white and brown water come round the corner of the canyon and surge down the wadi towards him. I could see, rather than hear, Fred still screaming to him to get out. Then Fred, too, turned and started to scramble towards safety, up the bank.

The boss was still smiling, I think. I was some distance away by then, but you can tell sometimes from a person's posture that they are smiling. He was facing away from the wall of water coming towards him. He must have heard it. I don't know. Maybe he didn't. They say you can get very absorbed fishing. At any rate, I like to think – I am as sure as I can be – that as he lifted his rod to make another cast, he was very happy. He was far away from politics, far away from wars, from journalists, from MPs, from generals, from civil servants. He was in a river and there were salmon running past his feet, and with the next cast I am sure he believed he would catch a fish.

Then the surge hit him. A boiling torrent of brown water, mud, rocks, palm fronds raced down the wadi with a noise like a train, and in a moment Colin, the sheikh and the boss instantly vanished without trace. The wave then powered on and disappeared round the next corner into the canyons far below.

One second the boss was standing there; the next he was gone. And I never saw him again. Or the sheikh. Or Colin McPherson. They never found their bodies.

That was what happened when we launched the Yemen salmon project, and the salmon ran in the Wadi Aleyn.

# 32

# Dr Jones's testimony of events which occurred at the launch of the Yemen salmon project

**Dr Alfred Jones:** From a scientific perspective, the Yemen salmon project was a complete success.

I knew it was a success from the minute I looked down and saw the salmon entering the water flowing down the wadi. A few days ago they had been thrashing about in a huge cage in a sea loch on the west coast of Scotland, now they were wriggling down a concrete chute from a concrete basin high in the mountains of the Yemen.

It did not matter to them. The salmon came wriggling down into the wadi, and a few simply went with the current and disappeared downstream. But most of them turned upstream, heading against the flow, not knowing where they might be going, only knowing that they had to head upriver until they found a place to spawn. Their instincts told them what to do, just as I had hoped they would.

Most of the fish were silver, but a few were already coloured, an indication that the hen fish were ready to spawn the thousands of eggs they carried, and the cock fish ready to inject their milt and so fertilise the eggs. My eyes filled with tears as I thought of it all: here, at the tip of the Arabian peninsula, though thousands of miles from their home waters, the salmon were ready to do their duty.

As I watched their fins cutting through the water, I

felt a sense of elation. And I remembered the sheikh's words, that we would see a miracle, and I knew that was what I had just witnessed. I remembered Harriet telling me the sheikh would think the project had been a success if one single fish ran up the wadi. Now there were hundreds. One fresh fish was already netted and killed, inside my jacket. I had to somehow insert it onto the end of the prime minister's line, to make sure he caught his fish.

Then I noticed the colour of the water changing, the sound of the river beginning to grow, the noise of the waters cascading down from the peaks far above becoming angrier and more threatening. The sky was darkening to a deep, inky black.

It was a plug. I should have anticipated it. Such things are not unknown on spate rivers, and that is essentially what the Wadi Aleyn is: a river that goes from almost dry to flash flood and back again in a few hours. Salmon running spate rivers learn to wait for the water. They smell the rain, they know a flood is coming, and then they surge upriver, meeting the torrent with impossible strength and courage, leaping the waves or hanging in the water at the sides of the river when the speed of the flow becomes too great even for them.

And in spate rivers sometimes you get a plug. The rain is too heavy to soak away into the ground. It runs straight off, and the run-off carries with it mud, dead trees, rocks, and if the debris should come to some constriction in the riverbed, then a temporary dam is formed. The water builds up behind the obstruction until the force is so great that the plug is breached, and then a wall of water goes surging through the breach and on down the river. You don't want to be standing in the water when that happens.

And the rain was heavy. The summer rains in the Yemen are really just the tip of a vast system of monsoon rains which miss the rest of Arabia but brush the southern coast of Oman and the Yemen for a few weeks. In those few weeks the rain can fall with the force of a tropical storm, causing flash floods of just the sort we experienced that day in the Wadi Aleyn. I suppose I should have known, but I'm a fisheries scientist not a hydrologist, nor a meteorologist. Nevertheless, I still blame myself for not foreseeing it. Not one of our computer models predicted what happened.

I remember shouting at the top of my voice to the sheikh and the prime minister to get out, but the growing noise of the river and the hiss as the rain struck the surface of the water drowned out the sound of my voice. Colin saw the change in the river, saw the colour go from clear to brown and heard the menacing change in its song. He knew exactly what was happening but he still waded out into the river to try and save his master. It was calculated heroism. Someone should give him a medal. But too much happened that day, and Colin's gallantry has been forgotten by most. But not by me.

I turned and shouted at Peter Maxwell to do something, but Peter's face was white and strained with fear, and I don't think he heard me. He started scrambling up the bank to get away from the river. The security men all knew that something was wrong, but they hadn't worked out where the danger was. They thought it would come from the ridges above; they thought in terms of a human enemy, not a natural one. They were looking the wrong way.

Then there was a flash, and a shot was fired from somewhere. That distracted the security people even further. I heard afterwards that one of the sheikh's bodyguards had been shot, but I never found out why. I didn't see it. I was looking upriver and screaming at the prime minister to get out of the water.

Then I saw the wave come round the corner, about 300 metres away, and I thought we would all die. It was a surge about ten feet high, brown and white, coming towards us at the speed of an express train and making much the same sort of noise. In that moment I remember thinking, I hope the salmon don't all get swept downstream, and then my own instincts took over and the next thing I remember was hanging on to a boulder at the top of the bank while the water tugged at my feet.

When the waters receded and most of the security people and the sheikh's bodyguard had headed off downstream to see if they could find the bodies, I stood by the mouth of the channel feeding salmon into the wadi. I watched fish after fish enter the flow, turn as it smelt the water, and head upstream. I stood there without moving for a long time, and my heart was too full to speak. At first a few journalists and TV people came down and tried to get me to comment on what had just happened, but they weren't interested in my salmon. They only wanted to talk about the accident and the prime minister. They weren't interested either in what had happened to Colin or to the sheikh. I had nothing to say to them. After a while they went away, and an hour or two later I heard one of the Chinooks lift off, taking them all back to Sana'a to file their stories.

When the last salmon had left Holding Basin No. 1,

I sat on a flat rock by the water's edge. The rain had stopped, and between ragged clouds the sun sank lower in the sky. From time to time I glanced over at the construction site, to see what was going on. I saw Peter Maxwell, a hundred yards or so away, talking endlessly into a mobile phone. I wondered what was so important until I remembered about the prime minister. I sat on the stone, and I thought about the project and the part I had played in it. No matter what happened to me now, they could not take this away from me. This was the greatest achievement of my life. It was not mine alone, but I knew that without me it could not have happened. I found myself wishing that Harriet could have been there, missing her dreadfully, because it was her achievement too, and this would have been her day too. But of course then she would have seen the sheikh being swept away. She had been right when she spoke of her foreboding. And I wished the sheikh could have been there so that I could have shared this achievement with him.

There was a shout from far upstream, and I saw one of the Yemenis who had gone further upstream to fish come running at top speed down the track. It was Ibrahim, our driver, one of the sheikh's men. He saw me and screamed, 'Dr Alfred! Dr Alfred!'

He ran towards me and I saw that he was carrying a dead salmon in his arms, nursing it like a baby. He must have abandoned his rod when he landed the fish. When he came near I saw that he didn't yet know what had happened. He might even have been fishing above the plug. At any rate, he had caught a salmon. It was bright silver and weighed, I would guess, about ten pounds. A good fish, an excellent fish. Ibrahim's face wore a huge smile, and he cried, 'Dr Alfred! I have one fish!'

We embraced and slapped each other on the back, and the tears of happiness ran down our cheeks. The fish had fallen into the dust and Ibrahim bent to pick it up, still laughing at his luck. It was the first and, for all I know, the last salmon ever to be caught on the fly in the Yemen. At any rate, I have never heard of any other being caught or even seen swimming in the wadi since that marvellous, terrible day.

Then I had to tell Ibrahim about the sheikh.

Later on, as dusk was falling and the rock walls around us turning violet, the search parties trudged back up the canyon. In the endless wilderness of rock and stone, of vertical cliffs and holes through the riverbed into chasms below that formed the lower sections of the wadi, they never found the bodies. I think they were probably swept down a sinkhole into the aquifer itself, and there, in a sunless sea, rest the bodies of Jay Vent, politician, Colin McPherson, matchless gillie, and the Sheikh Muhammad ibn Zaidi bani Tihama, the almost holy man who created the Yemen salmon project.

Peter Maxwell came over to me. His face was still white, his eyes red, and his mouth set in a bitter, miserable twist. He said, 'I hope you're happy now.'

'Yes,' I said, 'in many ways it has been an enormous success, though I wish with all my heart we could have avoided loss of life. But, if we are objective about this, Peter, we have achieved everything we set out to achieve from a scientific point of view. The big question is what will happen to the project now the sheikh is dead. You must help me find out who is in charge here now.'

Peter Maxwell stared at me for along time without speaking. Behind him I saw the security team climbing into the second Chinook.

'I'll tell you what will happen,' he said. 'Your project is finished. You are finished. And I'm finished. You should have known this would happen. You should have known ...'

He began to sob, and I touched his arm to comfort him, but he shrugged me off violently. 'You've killed the best man in the world, one of the greatest men who ever lived, and you've ruined my life at the same time. And all you can think of are your bloody fish.'

He turned away and stumbled towards the helicopter. A moment later, it took off, and I never saw Peter Maxwell again.

**Interrogator:** Did Peter Maxwell or any other representative of the prime minister's office contact you after your return to the UK? Has there been any attempt to influence your evidence to us in any way?

**AJ:** When I got back to the UK I had become a non-person. When I turned up at Fitzharris & Price to discuss the ongoing management of the project I found that my job there was over. The sheikh's heirs, whoever they were, did not share his enthusiasm for the project. The funding had been terminated before I even reached the UK. One of the partners in Fitzharris & Price met me in reception when I arrived in St James's Street to pick up the threads and start work again. He handed me a letter from the firm of accountants who had been managing the finances of the project. The letter thanked me for my efforts in not many more words than those and enclosed a cheque for the next three months' salary.

I read the letter then looked at Harriet's colleague.

'Is that it?' I asked him. He shrugged his shoulders and said, 'The rest of us never knew much about it. Grateful while it lasted of course, but we knew it couldn't go on for ever. It was always Harriet's baby, and she seems to have resigned her partnership.'

I never went back to St James's Street and, as far as I am aware, neither did Harriet.

I spoke to her once or twice by telephone. She was staying with friends in south-west France and vague about her plans.

'I'm so glad the project succeeded, if only for a day. You must never let anyone take that away from you, Fred. You must treasure that. But I'm sorry we had to pay so very high a price. I miss the sheikh terribly. It's another death in the family, in a way.'

'When are you coming back to the UK?' I asked.

'I haven't any particular plans. I'm not spending much money out here, and my friends seem happy for me to stay as long as I want. I've got my own flat in one corner of their house and my own front door, and I can come and go without disturbing them. You know, the sun shines most of the time in this part of the world, and no one bothers me. It's what I need. I know I'll run short of money sooner or later, and then I'll have to think about getting a job. But for now I just want to be quiet.'

'Will I see you when you come back?' I asked. I hadn't meant to ask any such thing. I had no right to.

'I don't know, Fred. I don't know. We'll have to see what happens.'

I heard some weeks later that she'd managed to get a

job in France, finding properties for English people looking for second homes.

I: Please confirm what contact you have had with Peter Maxwell or his office since your return to England.

AJ: Oh, I forgot you asked me that. Yes, I did pick up a voicemail from Peter Maxwell saying 'I'll make sure you never work again in this country' or something along those lines, but then I heard him burst into tears just before he hung up so I didn't take it very seriously. But maybe he did try and stop me being re-employed for some curious reason of his own. I do know that when I applied for my old job at the NCFE I received a very short letter from David Sugden complaining about cutbacks in their budget and regretting that my old position was not going to be filled as a result. I don't know that I could have gone back there anyway. Then I rang some old friends in the Environment Agency and in the end I did find another job. It's not a desk job. It's outdoor work, and the pay is what you might call minimal compared with my old salary. So Mary was right. The good times didn't last very long, after all.

I'm working in a new hatchery which has been built on the headwaters of the Coquet in Northumberland. Our job is to rear salmon fry from the egg in rows of stainless steel tanks in a small hut up on the moors. The idea is to ensure there will always be juvenile salmon available to be introduced into the river, even in years when natural production fails because of drought or some other disaster. I like the work. It's very interesting and often hard labour, but I have plenty of time to think. Thinking is what I do most these days.

I never talk to anyone about the Yemen salmon project,

although I am teased now and again about it by the people I work with.

The project acquired a degree of notoriety in the press after the deaths of the prime minister and the sheikh. It was written off as some kind of bizarre political adventure. There has been little appreciation in the scientific community at home of what we achieved. In the Yemen they remain very proud of it. The sheikh is remembered in prayer every day at the Ministry of Fish Wealth, which has taken over responsibility for the project. The holding basins have been drained, and all the machinery has been mothballed. In that dry climate it will take no harm for a few years. They say that one day salmon will be held in those tanks again and released into the Wadi Aleyn, but it hasn't happened yet.

The people of al-Shisr netted all the remaining salmon in Holding Basin No. 2 for several weeks after the sheikh's death. There were nightly barbecues on the wadi bed, and the smell of grilled salmon rose every evening into the sky.

The deputy minister for fish wealth has written to me that the next five-year strategic fishery plan is currently being formulated, and when they come to discussing the role of a salmon fishery in the future development of the Yemen's natural resources, I will be consulted. That was some while ago, and they have not been in touch since. I don't know whether to hope that I will hear from them or not.

Looking back to that day the sheikh died, I know now that I was in shock, and his death had not really hit me. There was just too much happening. I couldn't take it all in at the time. Since then I have grieved for him, and now, as I wade through the headwaters of the Coquet, emptying buckets of salmon fry into the river, I have conversations with him which are more than imaginary.

I hear him say to me, from somewhere behind my left shoulder, 'Yes, Dr Alfred, we did it in the end. We believed in it, and so we did it.'

'You were right, Sheikh. We believed. You taught me to believe.'

I hear the smile in his voice, although I cannot see it. 'I taught you to take the first step: to learn to believe in belief. And one day you will take the second step and find what it is you believe in.'

I empty the bucket of juvenile fish into the shallow, gravelly stream, and say, 'How will I know?'

And, fainter than the murmur of the rills of water trickling over the stones, comes the reply: 'You will know.'

So, I work at the hatchery, and at night I sit in my rented two-roomed cottage near Uswayford under the green and brown bulk of the Cheviot Hills. I sit and I think. I don't really know what it is I think about although I still think sometimes about Harriet. I try not to do that too often. That awakens memories I would rather not have.

Sometimes I think about Mary. I speak to her on the phone most weeks. I have given up email unless it is absolutely necessary. It is part of another life now. I speak to Mary on the phone but I reverse the charges because I really can't afford the phone bills. She is working in Düsseldorf now. I'm not sure if it was the promotion she was expecting. I think it has been more of a sideways move. We all have our disappointments in life.

We have sold the flat in London and bought a smaller one as neither of us is there very often. We travel to London once every other month. We meet and have dinner together, and try and make some sense of our lives. I'm not sure we will succeed. We've agreed we will remain married. Neither of us can think of anything else to do with our lives. We both have our work. I've told Mary I don't want her to feel financially responsible for me. She agrees, but I think she wants to look after me, really, if only I would let her. But I'm happy, here in these hills, raising juvenile fish and putting them into the river. These little salmon fry have more chance here than they would in the Yemen. This is their natural habitat, and this is my natural habitat, too.

In the evenings I read a lot. I can't get a television signal where I live, and I can't afford to pay for satellite TV. I don't miss it. I never watched it much, anyway. So I read. I read anything and everything, and at weekends, if I'm not in London, I browse the shelves of the second-hand bookshops in Alnwick and Morpeth, my nearest towns. I can't run to new books, but it seems to me so many good books have already been written I don't need to get new ones. I buy handfuls of old novels and biographies for a few pounds, or sometimes I just trade in the ones I have read. They let me do that. I'm a good customer. I buy the classics – Dickens, Thackeray, Fielding. Lately I've started on books of essays – Hazlitt, Browne, and so on. In one of them I read something I rather liked, and I've got it here. I keep it with me. I'll read it to you, if you like.

'And we recall that Tertullian, the son of a centurion that lived in Carthage, who wrote many sacred texts discoursing on the gospels, and on the nature of faith, once wrote "*Certum, impossibile est*." It is certain that this thing is impossible. Others aver that what Tertullian wrote was not "*Certum, impossibile est*" but "*Credo, quia impossibile est*." I believe in it, because it is impossible.'

I like that. Don't you?

I believe in it, because it is impossible.

# 33

## Conclusions of the House of Commons Foreign Affairs Select Committee

**The decision to introduce salmon into the Yemen**

*Conclusions and recommendations*

1. We conclude that it appears likely given the body of evidence that the decision to introduce salmon into the Yemen was not taken by any minister, but was the initiative of a private Yemeni citizen, the late Sheikh Muhammad ibn Zaidi bani Tihama.

2. We conclude that the home secretary was, as he stated in the House of Commons, unaware of the alleged attempt at an assassination of the Sheikh Muhammad at his residence in Scotland by an alleged member of al-Qaeda. As this event was never proven to have occurred by a UK court, we cannot criticise the home secretary or the security services for failing to predict another such attempt, which is alleged to have taken place in the Wadi Aleyn shortly before the hydrological event which unfortunately terminated the life of the prime minister.

3. In relation to the matter that was brought up during evidence of the death of Captain Robert Matthews, we conclude that the secretary of state for defence was genuinely unaware that Captain Matthews was on a mission in Iran, without the knowledge of ministers, and no blame

can be attached to anyone for the unfortunate series of events which led to Captain Matthews being posted as Missing in Action.

4. We conclude that the director of communications, Mr Peter Maxwell, was acting on his own initiative in advising the late Mr Jay Vent PM to take notice of the Yemen salmon project, and that Mr Peter Maxwell had concluded that some electoral advantage could be gained from Mr Vent's presence at the launch of the Yemen salmon project, and that was his basis for recommending Mr Vent's involvement with the project.

5. We recommend that future directors of communications have their job descriptions phrased so as to make clear their role is to communicate, and not to take future prime ministers into harm's way, regardless of electoral considerations. We recommend that Peter Maxwell should not be reinstated in his former role.

6. We conclude that insufficient attention was given to risk assessment by the project engineers and managers, not-withstanding that such assessments are not required in Yemeni law as they would be under the UK Health & Safety at Work Act. Had such an assessment been carried out, the hydrological event which led to the death of the prime minister and others might have been predicted and appropriate precautions taken. Notwithstanding this conclusion, we are unable to say that any one individual was culpable in this matter.

7. We conclude that the National Centre for Fisheries Excellence exceeded its mandate in agreeing to act as the primary technical resource for the Yemen salmon project, and we recommend that the centre be disbanded and merged with the Environment Agency.

8. We conclude that, in policy terms, we cannot endorse the view of the prime minister's office that an initiative involving the introduction of salmon into the Yemen would sit alongside its other policies in the region, which are mainly focused on military intervention in protection of regional oil resources and associated attempts at introducing the democratic process. We believe the government should choose between salmon and democracy in its regional initiatives. The combination of the two sends a confusing signal to regional players.

9. Nevertheless we have detected a benign outcome from the tragic death of the late James Vent PM. The perception in the region that UK policy can also focus on non-military, non-oil-related subjects, such as fly-fishing, has not been entirely negative. On the contrary, we understand that a statue of the late prime minister and Sheikh Muhammad ibn Zaidi bani Tihama is being subscribed for, showing both of them in chest waders and carrying fishing rods, as they were when last seen alive. This will be erected in the centre of Sana'a, if planning permission can be obtained.

# Glossary of terms used in the extracts

Readers may find the following helpful.

**alevin:** the earliest stage of the salmon after hatch, a translucent creature with an umbilical sac

*Allahu akhbar:* God is great

**anadromous:** able to tolerate both freshwater and saline environments

*Bedu:* nomadic desert tribesman inhabiting the Arabian peninsula

**broodstock:** hen fish from which eggs are stripped for rearing in a hatchery

**caddis fly:** invertebrate insect resident of freshwater streams *(Limnephilus genus)*

**DEFRA:** Department for Environment, Food and Rural Affairs

**dissolved oxygen:** The level of dissolved oxygen in a river is an indicator of how well migratory fish are likely to survive in it. The lower the level, the more they are at risk.

*diwan:* room set aside for the use of gentlemen wishing to chew khat (see below)

*diyah:* blood money

**Environment Agency:** department of DEFRA with responsibility for the management of rivers, the rural environment, flood management, and the enforcement of anti-pollution legislation

*falaj*: ancient system of irrigation used in arid regious consisting of stone tunnels or conduits taking water from aquifers in the mountains to farmers and others in more low-lying areas

FCO: Foreign & Commonwealth Office

fry: Once the baby alevin has absorbed the contents of its yolk sac it becomes a fry.

genetic integrity: idea, dear to fisheries scientists, that the genetic purity of salmon from a particular river should be preserved and not diluted by the presence of fish from other rivers – illegal when applied to humans

gillie: man or boy employed on many Scottish salmon rivers to stand at your elbow and explain why you are unlikely to catch a fish with your present technique

glide: when the current in a river is enough to turn a salmon fly but not fast enough to be a riffle (see below)

*Hansard*: official record of proceedings of the British Houses of Parliament

*imam*: someone who leads prayers in a mosque, a person of authority in the community

invertebrate: creature with no spine

*jambia*: curved dagger much favoured by Yemenis

*jazr*: Yemeni term for worker in an unclean trade, such as a butcher

*jebel*: general Arabic word for mountains

*jihadi*: person who devotes his or her life to the religious struggle, sometimes inaccurately conflated with a suicide bomber or assassin

*khat*: mildly narcotic leaf which is chewed

NCFE: National Centre for Fisheries Excellence, one of a

number of scientific organisations researching into fishery management, now abolished

**parr:** next stage of development of a salmon after a fry, similar in appearance to a baby brown trout, about the size of a finger with brown markings

**riffle:** when the surface of the river water is slightly broken, and the current is moving faster than a glide (see above)

*Salaam alaikum*: traditional Arab greeting (May God be with you)

**salmonid:** migratory fish including salmon and sea trout

*sayyid*: ruling class in the Yemen, a title given to tribal or religious leaders who claim descent from the Prophet Muhammad

*sebkha*: white encrustation of salt on the surface of the desert usually indicating the presence of moisture, a sign of quicksand

*selta*: vegetable broth very popular in the highlands of the Yemen

*sharia*: law as practised and observed by the Prophet Muhammad in his lifetime, in force in certain countries in the Muslim world

*sitara*: colourful shawl worn by women in the highlands of the Yemen

**smolt:** The juvenile salmon, at some point between sixteen months and two years after achieving parr form, starts to change physiologically. It develops salt-excreting cells, and it takes on a silvery appearance. Once fully silvered it becomes known as a smolt, a fish about six inches long. In this form it makes its way downriver to the saltwater estuary. From there, by degrees, it makes it way in the company of other smolts and salmon to the feeding grounds in the North Atlantic where it may remain from one to four years.

**Spey cast:** an elaborate double-looped cast much beloved by Highland gillies which has the merit that the fisherman never gets his line tangled up in the bank or the trees behind (as in an overhead cast) because the loop of the Spey cast is always in front

*thobe*: a robe worn in the highlands of the Yemen and in Saudi Arabia

*wadi*: a riverbed dry except in the rainy season (when it is a river)

Many of those who enjoy salmon fishing will at some stage have benefited from reading Hugh Falkus's definitive work, *Salmon Fishing* (published H.F. & G. Witherby Ltd) and its great store of knowledge about the life cycle of the salmon. I am no exception and gratefully acknowledge all that I have learned from reading his book.

# READING GROUP NOTES

## *In Brief*

Dr Alfred Jones is a man whose world is small. Indeed, the publication of his paper 'Effects of increased water acidity on the caddis fly larva' is the height of his ambition. Not that this is a bad thing, just that concentrating on the micro world hasn't really prepared him for Sheikh Muhammad and his world. For the sheikh has a vision. He sees salmon leaping in the wadis of his homeland, and all the disparate tribes of his country brought together by a love of fly fishing. Casting away the troubles of their lives, so to speak. And the sheikh needs Dr Alfred to turn his vision into reality. The only trouble is that the sheikh's homeland is the Yemen – not really known for its northern European climate – so salmon could never survive there, could they?

## In Detail

Through a collection of emails, diary entries, letters and reports, we learn of the plan to introduce salmon fishing into the Yemen, and the characters who try to implement the plan, those who are violently opposed to the project, and those who just think it's a bit daft.

Dr Alfred Jones is contacted by the representatives of Sheikh Muhammad, who want him to give them scientific advice about how best to introduce salmon into the Yemen. Dr Jones is understandably rather reluctant to pursue the matter, and attempts to fob them off. It then becomes clear that there is some interest in this project from 'high up' and pressure is brought to bear. Indeed, the interest goes right up to the Prime Minister, who really likes the idea of a 'fishing in a wadi' photo opportunity!

Dr Jones is, however, not a happy fisheries scientist. He wants to get on with his caddis fly larva paper, and what with the pressure from his boss, and the chilly emails from his wife, it's a good job he has his diary as an outlet for his understandable grievances.

Despite his grave reservations, Dr Jones finds himself forced into the eccentric plans of a Middle Eastern sheikh, whose sole basis for believing that his madcap scheme will work is the will of God! Dr Jones knows that it will take more than that to achieve the impossible. But the more he thinks it through, with the combination of his knowledge and the not inconsiderable funds available, maybe, just maybe, *something* could be achieved.

So Dr Jones finds himself flying to Scotland – with a most engaging companion – and meeting a man who will, quite simply, change his life. For as he becomes more and more involved in the sheikh's dream, he begins to see that there is more to life than facts and figures. Sometimes belief, combined with some good science of course, just might be enough.

And as the plan moves into its final stages, and all the players take their places, a conclusion of a sort no one predicted begins to unfold: a photo opportunity for the PM that he certainly didn't envisage.

## About the Author

Paul Torday read English Literature at Pembroke College Oxford before embarking on a very successful career in engineering. His work took him all over the world, from the Americas to China, and most places in between, including the Middle East. More recently he has been able to take a step back from business, and has had time to write. He has also travelled extensively in Oman, exploring the desert and back country in company with his wife.

He lives in Northumberland and has been a keen salmon fisherman for fifteen years.

## *For Discussion*

- What did you think when you first picked up the novel? Did you enjoy the construction (as a collection of documents), or did it put you off? Did you change your opinion as you read? How would you have told the story?

- The sheikh thinks that we have in this country 'a great deal of snobbery' about class. Do you agree that this is still the case?

- Sheikh Muhammad believes that bringing salmon fishing to his country will create the 'patience and tolerance' in his people he sees in fisherman in this country. Is there any merit in his vision? Would it work? Or do people who are patient and tolerant by nature simply choose to fish?

- The book has at its heart the contrast between the secular world of the west and faith-based societies of the Middle East. Which world comes out with most credit do you think?

- Did you notice the change in Dr Jones's diary entries as he becomes more involved in the world of Sheikh Muhammad? How does his style of writing evolve?

- Dr Jones has 'moved on from religion'. Instead of going to church on a Sunday, he goes to Tesco. Has he lost or gained?

- 'In this Old Testament land it is difficult not to believe in myths and magic and miracles.' Do our surroundings in the west make it harder to believe?

- In the west, we live in 'a world which only recognised what it could count, measure, sell or buy'. Dr Jones finds a land that still has the 'innocent power of belief', and he learns to believe in belief. Is the power of belief 'innocent', or is there a reason why the west has 'moved on'?

- How well do you believe the novel worked as a satire of our bureaucratic and spin-doctored political system?

- How happy were you with the end of the novel? Its structure meant we couldn't know too much of the future of the protagonists. Would you have liked to know more?

## Suggested Further Reading

*A Short History of Tractors in Ukrainian*
by Marina Lewycka

*Catch-22* by Joseph Heller

*Life of Pi* by Yann Martel

*Vernon God Little* by DBC Pierre

*Erewhon* by Samuel Butler

*The Unbearable Lightness of Being*
by Milan Kundera